MISTRESS OF TORMENT

Alex Jordaine

Published by Accent Press Ltd – 2009

ISBN 9781906373825

Printed and bound in the UK

Cover Design by Red Dot Design

To Mistress G, the love of my life

I envied King Gunther whom the mighty Brunhilde
fettered on the bridal night.'
– *Leopold von Sacher-Masoch, 'Venus in Furs'*

Chapter One

THE MAN, WHO HAS been blindfolded with a black leather blindfold and gagged with a ball gag of the same colour, lies on his front on the bed in the empty room. He is naked apart from wrist and ankle cuffs, which are also of black leather. The man's wrist cuffs have been attached together above his head and then tied to the central post of the bed head by a length of black bondage rope. His ankle cuffs, which are attached together too, have been tied to the central post at the end of the bed by another length of bondage rope. Rope has also been used to encircle the man's thighs and calves. It has been drawn so tightly that it indents the flesh.

The man's heart is thudding against his rib-cage fit to burst and he is trembling within his bonds with both fear and sexual excitement. He sees himself as he truly is: naked and helpless, unable to make out even a sliver of light because of his blindfold or to do anything more than utter incoherent noises from beneath his ball gag. Escape is impossible and he knows it. His captor can do whatever she likes to him. He is utterly powerless to resist her because of the restrictive bondage into which she has placed him. The door creaks open, startling the dense silence of the room, and making his erection throb. The man knows that she has come for him, that she is going to make him her slave.

His captor is a glacially beautiful brunette who is as sadistic as she looks. Her dark eyes are big but by no means soft. They are hard and cold. Her lips are sensuous and full but are as cruel as a harsh winter. She is naked like the man but could not be less helpless, more unfettered. She brandishes a heavy leather flogger in her hand as she advances purposefully towards him, her unbound breasts jiggling and swaying as she moves. The woman has a lush, sensual body and there is a sheen to her alabaster skin. She positively glows – with malice.

The man struggles futilely against his bonds, terrified and

panic-stricken but also incredibly sexually aroused. The woman smiles sadistically and then lets out a hard little laugh. She enjoys the sight of the man's struggling body as he strains against his restraints. It makes her bring the flogger down on his muscular backside all the more harshly. The bound man emits a muffled cry of pain from beneath his gag and a series of angry red welts appear on his naked flesh.

The next harsh blow lands, bringing another muffled cry from him, more angry welts. Then the flogger lands again. And again and again and again. The man starts to writhe and struggle under the severe lashings that the woman is inflicting on his body with such sadistic glee. He shrieks into his gag as the beating becomes ever more ferocious.

Mercifully, the woman stops whipping the bound man for a while in order to masturbate. She does this with great vigour, the sounds urgent and liquid. But when she returns to beating the man she does so with even more savagery. Agonizing pain is coursing through him now. And it is *exquisite*. He wallows in the pain, luxuriates in it, the sensation so intense that he knows he cannot hold out much longer, that he is close to climaxing ...

Paul Cooper awoke with a start, breathing heavily, his heart pumping wildly away in his chest. He was covered in sweat and his dark hair was damp against his brow. Paul was having bizarre masochistic dreams like that one all the time nowadays. They were usually variations on the same theme: a beautiful dominant woman was holding him as her captive, and he was helplessly bound. She was sexually torturing him, which he found both agonizingly painful and ecstatically pleasurable.

One thing was certain, though. Paul had never had such an experience or anything like it in real life. No woman had ever held him captive, needless to say. Nothing remotely like that had ever happened to him. But neither had any woman ever blindfolded or gagged him or tied him up, or beaten him. Paul wanted one to do those things to him though. Oh God, how he wanted that to happen. He wanted it to happen to him over and over again, day after day, week after week, month after month...

As Paul lay where he was, flat on his stomach in bed, he was aware of the stiffness of his cock pressing against the rumpled sheet beneath him. His erection felt like it had when he'd woken from the dream. It was so engorged that it seemed likely to erupt at any moment with the strength of his sexual excitement.

Paul was aware of something else as well. He was naked apart from the leather wrist cuffs that were attached together in front of him and the ankle cuffs that were also attached together. He was blindfolded with a leather blindfold and gagged with a ball gag too. No bondage rope held him to the head and base of the bed, though, or tightly encircled his legs. The bondage rope and the beautiful nude dominatrix and the vicious beating she'd administered to his naked body had been figments of his fevered imagination, courtesy of the highly erotic masochistic dream from which he'd just awoken.

That dream had left Paul extremely aroused – that dream he had deliberately precipitated by going to bed in self-administered bondage. It was such a crazy thing to have done, part of him realised that. But it was hardly the first time he'd done it, far from it. He was certainly in no hurry to free himself either – apart, that is, from rolling onto his back, throwing aside the duvet, and unclipping with one of his thumbs the metal snap trigger attaching his leather wrist cuffs together. He carried out this last action, which he knew from previous experience could be tricky when blindfolded, with a well practised manoeuvre.

Paul allowed his right hand, now that it was free, to stray to his erection. He uttered a low groan from under his gag as he began to masturbate, pushing his fist up and down on himself. As he stroked and pulled his throbbing shaft, he tried to recapture the dream, tried to transform into reality the sadomasochistic fantasy his subconscious had conjured up so realistically. But he didn't have much time because he was already close to orgasm, had been ever since he'd woken from the dream.

Paul felt waves of pleasure engulf him as he got ever closer to his climax. And the closer he got, his hand moving rhythmically over his hard cock, the more intensely he fantasized that it was the sadistic woman in the dream, his Mistress of Torment, who was making him feel this way. She it was who was holding him captive, holding him in bondage, subjecting him to incredible torment. She was showing him no mercy as she sexually tortured him, making him writhe helplessly in his bonds with pleasure and pain … and pleasure-pain. Then the pulse came and he began to shudder and shake without control as his orgasm took him. And as he climaxed – his cries of pleasure muffled by the ball gag – semen shot out of his aching cock in spurts, warm and silky.

Not long afterwards Paul, who remained blindfolded, gagged and with his ankles cuffed together, re-clipped his wrist cuffs one to the other in front of him with another well practised manoeuvre. He started to doze off almost immediately, to sleep, perchance to dream … a very particular kind of dream, all over again.

Chapter Two

PAUL WAS WOKEN UP by the shrill, insistent sound of his alarm clock going off. It was time to get up and go to work after a night in bondage that had been anything but restful and which had run to a definite pattern: sleeping, dreaming, waking, wanking, sleeping, dreaming, waking, wanking, sleeping ... With one final well-rehearsed manoeuvre he unclipped the metal trigger attaching his wrist cuffs together and gropingly switched off the noisy alarm clock. Then he took off his blindfold and gag, removed his wrist cuffs, and unclipped and removed his ankle cuffs. He cleaned the gag and put it and the other items back in what he thought of as his 'Fetish wardrobe', the one that held his steadily growing supply of BDSM accoutrements.

Wearing just his towelling bathrobe, Paul had breakfast and digested for a while, flicking absently through an old magazine. He then carried out his ablutions and after that went back to his Fetish wardrobe from which he selected two items. The first was a black silicone butt-plug and the second a chastity device constructed of lightweight aluminium, which had a key closure and a drainage hole. After he had lubricated the head of the butt-plug Paul eased it into his anus – a brief and, to him, satisfyingly painful experience. He then locked himself into the chastity device. It felt good to have his anus filled and his genitals imprisoned like this.

But it didn't feel right, not really. Paul wished for the umpteenth time since he'd got into self-bondage that a dominant woman was doing these things to him ... and more, much more. But no such woman had ever come into his life. Instead he had to be content with the elaborate masturbatory alternatives he'd devised for himself.

And that was OK when all was said and done, Paul told himself reassuringly. It was more than OK. He felt a tremor of sexual pleasure at the feel of the butt-plug deep inside him and the grip of the chastity device that tightly encased his genitals. Paul put the key to that device on top of his bedside table, got dressed for the outside world and set off for work. He groaned to himself at the dismal weather as he walked out on to the street. It was an overcast day, rain hanging in the air, and there was a sharp little breeze.

Paul would have been the first to admit that he was an underachiever at work, that he was a long way from being some kind of thrusting young entrepreneur. What he was was a very small cog in a great big wheel. He was one of a legion of copy-editors who worked for UK publishing giant, Palmerton's Publishing, which had its head offices in the heart of London. Because of modern technology Paul was able to work most days from his home, which was a small ground floor flat in Islington. This meant that he could sit at his old but serviceable home computer, working on one manuscript or another. It also meant that he could do this nude and in bondage of some sort, which was a big advantage as far as he was concerned. Today was one of those fairly infrequent days when Paul had to actually go into the office. But that didn't mean he couldn't put himself into appropriate restraints. So that was what he'd done. After all, who was to know? What the eye doesn't see …

Wait a moment though. Wasn't this all more than a little excessive? – Bondage throughout the night, bondage during the day, whether at home or in the office. This was obsessive behaviour by any standards. And Paul was indeed a man thoroughly obsessed, there was no getting away from that. In fact he was an obsessive person by nature. Frequently images would get stuck in Paul's head and go round and round in a loop like some insistent sequence of film. But the masochistic images that now spooled through his mind were something else again. They were constant, never ending, all-consuming.

But what had triggered this major obsession on Paul's part? Had he experienced some trauma during his childhood that had returned to haunt him in this extreme way in adulthood? No, it hadn't been anything like that at all. It had been an old book, of all things, that had acted as that all-important trigger – a trigger to something that had in fact always been innate to his being, deeply hard-wired there, had he but known it before.

One day Paul had been browsing around an antiquarian book shop in a gentrified corner of Bethnal Green in the East End of London. He had found in the shop what looked to his unpractised eye like an early edition of the erotic classic, *Venus in Furs*. It had been on sale for next to nothing. Paul had bought the musty old book for no other reason than that he'd thought the bookseller could conceivably have missed a trick, that such an old copy might have been worth something. But when he'd got home and started reading it he'd soon forgotten about any additional monetary value it might or might not have had.

The story had held Paul completely in its thrall. He'd found that he identified entirely with the male protagonist. The idea of being held in bondage, both actual and metaphorical, to a cruel Mistress had an instant appeal for him. From the day he read *Venus in Furs* a fundamental transition began for Paul Cooper.

The book had a profound effect on him, bringing to the forefront of his mind previously unformed masochistic fantasies and desires. It also made him anxious to know more about sexual masochism and he used the internet to research this major new obsession of his. Paul discovered that there were numerous websites catering for those with sadomasochistic desires. There was one that caught his attention early on. It was the website for a Portsmouth-based company called AQL Limited.

The initials stood for Affordable Quality Leather and that, Paul discovered when he started ordering items from them, was exactly what they supplied. And not just leather but metal too and rope and chain and pretty much anything related to BDSM. With a few notable exceptions their products were genuinely affordable as well, which was of particular importance to Paul since he did not earn a great deal. Also AQL's products did what they were intended to do. Paul discovered that fact by trying them on himself by means of self-bondage, an activity he soon found thoroughly addictive.

But what they didn't do was provide him with the partner he so desperately wanted to find who would use them on him. What Paul needed was a woman he could trust who would dominate him sadistically: tie him up and gag him, and beat him black and blue, constantly. But that was easier said than done. *Much* easier said than done.

Paul looked on the internet again and found a number of Fetish websites with contact sections. Among the *women looking for men* category for the London area there were various females, several undeniably sincere if one took at face value what they'd put on their profiles, who stated that they were looking for males to dominate and discipline. But Paul didn't think he could put himself in the hands of a complete stranger. What if, despite all appearances to the contrary and her sincere-sounding profile, the woman turned out to be some psycho bunny boiler? The time to find out was not when he was tied up and at the woman's complete mercy.

What other alternatives were there? Paul wondered. Find himself a nice girlfriend with a dominant personality and casually work into the conversation when the time was right (and when would *that* be exactly?) that what he wanted out of their sex life was for her to regularly tie him up and beat the shit out of him. Yeah, sure. Dream on.

So Paul continued with his copy-editing job, work that, while it kept him fairly busy, was well within his comfort zone and not at all well paid. It brought him in sufficient funds to pay the rent on his modest flat, though, and to meet the cost of utilities, groceries and the like. It also brought in enough money to enable him to keep his small second-hand Fiat on the road. There was just enough left over from Paul's meagre income after that to allow him to add steadily to his collection of bondage equipment like the butt-plug and the chastity device he had in place today. Both of these items were recent purchases from AQL, the chastity device having been his more than usually generous birthday present to himself.

Paul could dream and fantasize as graphically as he liked about being put into bondage by a dominant woman and cruelly used by her. And that's what he did all the time obsessively, night and day. But it wasn't enough, not nearly enough. He felt fundamentally unfulfilled, felt an ever-stronger need to find someone to do those deliciously perverted things to him for real, over and over again. But how could he make that happen?

Paul went back to looking at the contact sections of the Fetish sites on the internet. Perhaps he could post his details on one or more of these, saying precisely what he was looking for from a woman. But no. It was the same thorny issue. He'd end up having to trust himself to a complete stranger when he was entirely helpless. It was simply too risky, too risky by half.

What about visiting a professional dominatrix, Paul asked himself. She would have to be a good one of course, to avoid disappointment. The problem there was that for *good* read *expensive* – he'd seen the sort of prices quoted on pro-domme websites. If Paul visited such a dominatrix, he knew exactly what would happen. Given his obsessive nature combined with his deep craving for what such a woman had to offer, correction *sell*, he knew he wouldn't be able to leave it at just one visit, or two or three or four … He'd end up hopelessly addicted to his visits. And homeless. He could afford to pay his rent. He could afford to visit a professional dominatrix on a regular basis. He couldn't afford to do both. It was as simple as that.

That, therefore, was the position in which Paul Cooper found himself as he ventured off to work on that wet and windy morning – as far away from a solution to his problem as he'd ever been.

Chapter Three

PAUL CURSED THE DAMP, blustery weather as he set off for the office that day. But he couldn't help feeling grateful for small mercies. It wasn't raining as hard as it had been, just drizzling, and he didn't have to walk far at either end of his train journey – good news given what he had jammed up his backside! He raised the collar of his coat against the drizzling rain and walked around the corner and up the road to the station. It was rush hour and throngs of people were disappearing from sight into the underground as if being sucked into a quagmire. Paul joined them.

The tube train was crammed with people looking tired and depressed. Paul knew that the majority of them were, like him, on their way to work only because they had to earn a living. Paul was grateful for another small mercy, though. He'd managed with a small stroke of luck to grab a recently vacated seat.

Even so, he really didn't want to be on that crowded train full of disconsolate commuters. Who in his right mind would? He was thankful that most days he worked from home and therefore didn't have to do this disagreeable journey often.

Paul let his imagination take him away from the packed and heaving train carriage as he fantasized about being the captive of a predatory dominatrix. How would this sadistic Femme run him down? How would she snare him? What would she do to him once she'd got him into her lair? But did he need to ask that last question, Paul said to himself excitedly. He could see all too clearly in his mind's eye what she would do to him, could see himself bound and heaving, rock hard, sobbing, as his Mistress of Torment did her very worst with the heavy-duty whip she was using so savagely to belabour his already severely punished body.

The butt-plug inside Paul's anus and the tight chastity device encasing his genitals shifted rhythmically with the movement of the train. It felt nice and it felt nasty; it felt *nice and nasty*. He squirmed slightly in his seat so as to emphasize the sensations and carried on with his erotic fantasy, utterly absorbed by his lurid imaginings to the extent that he almost missed his station.

Paul got off the tube train at Oxford Circus in the nick of time, left the busy underground station and walked the short distance to the huge grey tower block that housed Pemberton's Publishing. He took the lift to the twelfth floor and walked over to his work station, with a nodded hello to a couple of nearby colleagues. He removed his coat and settled himself into his seat.

Paul was aware once again of the butt-plug shifting inside him and the tightness of the chastity device. All that fantasizing during the train journey had left him erotically aroused. If he hadn't been wearing the chastity device, he'd have gone off to the Men's room, entered a cubicle and masturbated to climax, no question. That option wasn't open to him; he was *locked* into the chastity device. Best think of something else, Paul reasoned. Hey, here's a novel idea, he smiled to himself. How about doing some work! And he did, he worked very diligently. When he next glanced at his watch it was coming up to one twenty. He was feeling quite hungry and more than ready for a well-earned break.

Paul took the lift down to the ground floor, left that monolith of an office block and went in search of a bite to eat. The day remained unprepossessing. The sky was the colour of a dirty dishcloth and the air still felt damp. However it had stopped raining altogether – wasn't even drizzling – and the wind had gone right down.

Just off Oxford Street Paul entered a café he'd frequented before where he knew the food was pretty good and the prices reasonable. He sat on his own at a table for two at the window, ate his light lunch and then sipped at the remains of his glass of water. Paul shifted in his seat a little, which caused his butt-plug to also shift and his cock to pulse within the constraining embrace of the chastity device. He allowed his mind to drift off ...

What would his Mistress of Torment do to him once she'd got him well and truly in her clutches, well and truly *enslaved*? He knew what she'd do all right, he knew ...She would bind his wrists behind him and get him grovelling down onto his knees. Then she'd press on his back so that he bent right forward with only his curved rear in the air for her to feel and to spank. She would spank him really hard, so hard (*Spank! Spank! Spank!*

11

Spank! Spank!) that his backside would turn as red as an angry sunset.

She'd then put on a strap-on dildo and push into his anus that would be *so* tight around the painful intruder. Then she'd start thrusting into him with ever increasing fervour. She would grip him by the hair as she pounded into his anal hole, entering and re-entering faster and faster. She'd pound into his anus so hard that it would make him shake all over and whimper with lust mixed with mind-fuck shame mixed with …

Suddenly someone tapped Paul on the shoulder, startling him out of his feverish sexual reverie. A voice said, 'Well, fancy seeing you.'

When Paul looked round and saw who it was, he had one hell of a surprise. Good God Almighty, who would have thought it!

Chapter Four

IT WAS TONY HARRISON of all people. Tony and Paul had been roommates when they'd both been at Sussex University studying for their respective degrees – Paul's in English Literature, Tony's in Economics – and they'd been close friends at the time. But they'd not kept in touch after they'd graduated and gone their separate ways. Paul hadn't seen or heard from Tony for seven, eight years. He looked smarter than he remembered him, neatly dressed in a business suit. There was the same dark hair but a little shorter, better cut. There was the same handsome aquiline face and vivid blue eyes and slim, athletic form. He was different but he was the same. In fact he looked very like – *extremely* like – Paul himself. People at university had constantly remarked on it. They'd said that the two of them could easily pass for brothers, twin brothers at that. And that remained the case.

'Tony, what a surprise!' Paul exclaimed with a broad smile. 'How great to see you.' He motioned for him to take a seat. At the same time he felt the butt-plug shifting inside him again and experienced another twinge to his cock within the tight chastity device. He panicked momentarily, as if Tony could somehow know what he'd been up to a few seconds ago, that he knew also that his steamy masochistic fantasy had been being nicely assisted by what he had lodged up his backside and locked around his genitals. But that panicky sensation was unfounded, he realised. How could Tony possibly know such things? He wasn't a mind reader, nor did he have x-ray vision.

A waiter approached the table, doing a distinct double-take at the remarkable physical similarity between the two men. Tony waved him away with a smile. 'I'm not stopping,' he explained amiably. 'Just spotted my old friend here when I was walking past, had to say hello.'

Tony then turned back to Paul and the pair of them made with the small talk. Paul asked Tony how he was keeping. Tony said he was fine, how was he? Fine too, Paul confirmed. What was Tony doing these days? He designed websites, he replied. He really liked his job which also paid well, he was pleased to say. And Paul? A copy-editor, he replied; it didn't pay much but it was OK. He worked mainly from home, which he liked. Tony could see the appeal of that, he said, although he was fortunate in that his own job, being freelance, allowed him quite a bit of flexibility too. Tony thought about him from time to time, he said, wished they'd kept in touch after university. They must put that right now, he added and Paul agreed.

'Hey, remember Laura?' Tony suddenly blurted out.

'How could I ever forget her,' Paul said, for it was true. He and Tony had shared a scruffy two-bed flat with her when they'd been roommates at university, Paul and Tony in one bedroom, Laura in the other. The place had had that general untidiness which you always seem to get when young people live together. There were rules for the flatmates that they adhered to, though, but not about tidiness. They were made by Laura.

'What a tease that girl was!' Tony said with a laugh.

Paul agreed, smiling wryly. She'd been a tease, all right, a prick tease: Laura with the beautiful blonde hair, Laura with the great big pale-blue eyes, Laura with the irresistibly sensual mouth, and the curvaceous figure, and the way she had of exaggeratedly swaying her hips when she walked. Laura who was always wandering barefoot around the flat in a *just*-long-enough T-shirt, her stiff nipples visible beneath the flimsy fabric, no panties. Laura who never wore underwear, she just *happened* to mention. Laura who had spelled out the rules to the guys when the three of them had moved in together and agreed to split the rent three ways. She was out of bounds, she explained; look but don't touch; try anything on and there would be trouble.

She'd driven Paul and Tony mad with unrequited lust, Laura the prick tease had. And they'd resorted in desperation to regular mutual masturbation sessions in their bedroom in increasingly vain attempts to try to get her out of their systems. They'd lain naked on their adjacent beds and pumped their hands over their own shafts simultaneously on these occasions. Their movements had been synchronized from frantic start to even more frantic finish as in twin eruptions of silvery cum they released all that

14

pent up frustration, all that constantly deferred desire ... until the next time the callous little cock teaser drove them to repeat the process.

'Why didn't either of us ever make a move on her?' Tony asked although he must have known the answer well enough, Paul thought.

'Because she told us not to,' Paul replied simply.

'We were both so submissive when it came to Laura,' Tony sighed. 'When it came to most girls, come to think about it.'

'I still am,' Paul said, looking him directly in the eye. 'Very submissive.'

'Me too,' Tony admitted.

'What do you do about it?' Paul asked, gazing intently at him now. 'I'd really like to know.'

'Are you sure you *really* do want to know?' Tony replied, meeting his gaze with a challenging look. 'It might well shock you.'

'I'm willing to take the chance,' Paul said, thinking: You want to know about shocking, you ought to know my shameful secret.

'I visit a professional dominatrix two or three times a week,' Tony said. 'She's an exceptionally good one, I might add.' Tony spoke *sotto voce* in order to avoid being overheard by any of the other diners. He needn't have been concerned though. There was no one in their immediate vicinity any longer, the lunchtime rush having by then largely dispersed.

'That's not an option I could possibly afford,' Paul said ruefully. 'I envy you, I really do.'

'What do you do then?'

'Are you sure *you* really want to know?'

'I'm sure.'

'Self-bondage and masturbation,' Paul said, also keeping his voice down. And I've got a butt-plug shoved up my arse and I'm locked into a chastity device even as we speak, he almost added but there was such a thing as too much information.

'Seems such a waste,' Tony said.

'What else can I do?' Paul replied with a resigned shrug. 'Beggars can't be choosers.'

Tony looked thoughtful for a moment. 'I'll talk to Mistress Nikki. She's the pro-domme I go to,' he said. 'I'll see if she's got

15

any bright ideas.'

'Thanks,' Paul said. 'That's good of you.'

Tony then looked at his watch and gasped. 'Listen, I've got to fly,' he said. 'I've got an important appointment I'm going to be late for if I don't get a major move on. And that simply wouldn't do. You see, it's with Mistress Nikki!'

'Don't let me keep you,' Paul said with a smile. 'But please do keep in touch.'

'Oh, I will,' Tony assured him as he got hurriedly up from his seat. 'And I meant what I said about talking to Mistress Nikki about your situation.'

'Thanks again.'

'Do you have a card?'

'Yeah, somewhere here,' Paul said, digging into the inside pocket of his jacket. 'It's got the address of my flat, phone details … all the usual stuff.' He handed his card to Tony who rushed off, reiterating as he went that he'd definitely be in touch.

Soon afterwards Paul too left the café. It was time to go back to work. It had started raining again, spitting, but he barely registered the fact. He was in a daze. What an altogether unexpected, altogether *surreal* way to get reacquainted with his 'twin' after nearly eight years.

Paul wondered when and how Tony would get in touch and what bright ideas, if any, this Mistress Nikki might come up with to help him resolve his predicament. As far as that last was concerned Paul didn't hold out much hope. In the world of the professional dominatrix money talked, that was obvious. And he had barely enough of the stuff to raise even a whisper.

Chapter Five

PAUL WORKED LATE IN the office, knowing that he wouldn't be back for a few weeks and wanting to get everything done there that he'd planned. After leaving, he took the underground train home. He walked the short distance from the station to his flat, picking up some takeaway food from the Chinese restaurant on the corner. The rain was still spitting and the streetlights in the side street where he lived gleamed on the wet parked cars, his own small aged Fiat included.

Opening the front door to the flat and then the door to the living room, he switched on the overhead light and surveyed the scene before him. The room was tidy and it was clean, its decorations plain and faded. It had cheap wall-to-wall carpeting and was sparsely furnished, what furnishings it had being more than a little threadbare. There was an old television set and a music centre of similar vintage, a black leather suite that had seen better days, a small scuffed table and two chairs, and a bookshelf full of dog-eared paperbacks and a handful of old hardbacks. There was also a telephone and an outdated personal computer, which had a weathered bottle-green leather office chair in front of it.

Paul got the central heating going straight away, made a quick trip to the bathroom, and pulled all the curtains around the flat. He then checked the answering machine and booted up the computer, checking to see whether he'd received any phone messages or emails during the course of the day. He hadn't received anything of any substance, just a telephone message from a cold caller and a couple of junk emails; he deleted the lot. The central heating kicked in fast, as it invariably did, and the place soon started to warm up nicely. Paul opened a bottle of beer from the fridge and sat down to eat his takeaway in front of the television. He watched the news, which was filled with the usual misery and mayhem. Then he watched the weather report. More rain was forecast for tomorrow in London and the rest of the south-east of England.

Paul finished his dinner, switched off the TV and went into the little kitchen to wash up. Then he returned to the living room and pondered what to do with the rest of his evening. Not that there was much to ponder. Paul already knew exactly what it was that he wanted – he knew exactly what it was that he wanted to have done to him, exactly where in his flat he wanted it done, and exactly the type of woman he wanted to do it to him. Well, two out of three wasn't bad, he said to himself sardonically. And looking to the future, maybe, just maybe, Tony and this Mistress Nikki person might be able to help him make it three out of three. And maybe not. He wouldn't hold his breath.

He'd live for the present, that's what he'd do, Paul told himself. And what he had in mind for himself presently was in itself a thrilling prospect, setting his heart beating like a metronome. Paul went into the bedroom and stripped off all his clothes but leaving the butt-plug and chastity device where they'd been all day. He went to his Fetish wardrobe to select the various other items he wanted, which he carried to the living room.

Paul double-checked that the curtains were pulled tight. He then sat down on his leather couch and took hold of a length of black bondage rope, which was one of the items he had extracted from his wardrobe. He bound his ankles, knees and thighs together with the rope, pulling it so tight that it bit into the flesh.

Paul put his leather wrist cuffs on next and attached a metal trigger to the one on his left wrist, leaving the trigger hanging for the time being. Then he gagged himself with the same ball gag he'd worn the night before, buckling it securely behind his head. Next he put earplugs in. The earplugs were very effective, cutting out all sounds; and the soft black leather blindfold he buckled into place after that had the same effect on light. Then he brought his hands behind his back and clipped his wrist cuffs together with the metal trigger. Finally Paul shifted himself on the couch so that he was lying flat on his stomach along its length. This manoeuvring of his body caused the butt-plug to move inside him and his cock to pulse within the restricting chastity device. These motions brought an electric sensation of pleasure that rippled through his body.

In his self-imposed bondage, Paul couldn't speak, couldn't see, couldn't hear, and could barely move. Before too long he would lose all sense of time, so disorientated would he become, and he would be able to disappear completely into his own personal world of fantasy. In that fantasy world normal logic did not apply and everything was the opposite of what it first seemed to be.

In that fantasy world he was the captive of a dominatrix who in her extreme cruelty was able to work a paradoxical kind of magic upon him. By keeping him bound so tightly, she set him as free as a bird. By taking away all his choices she took away all his guilt about his perverse sexual desires as well. And by bringing him great pain she brought him pleasure beyond belief.

But it *was* a fantasy, no more than that, a niggling voice inside Paul's head reminded him. He was a thoroughgoing fantasist, that was all. He was the fantasists' fantasist. And he was alone – completely alone. In reality he had nobody. He had no one to make him her prisoner and subject him to her every cruel whim. He was all trussed up, sure, but a sadistic Femdom hadn't done that to him; he had done it to himself. He was still in complete control. That was the plain unvarnished truth of the matter. Paul wanted so much for someone else – a dominant and sadistic woman – to be in complete control of him. Only then would he find true fulfilment. Only when he was *genuinely* helpless, held bound and gagged and blindfolded and sexually tortured by a ruthless dominatrix day after day after day, would he find the inner peace that he sought. And when, if ever, would that happen, Paul wondered despairingly. Perhaps never. Be honest, *almost certainly* never. Sometimes it all seemed so hopeless.

Paul told himself to ignore that dissenting, depressing voice that had managed to insinuate itself into his brain, it would ruin everything. Think positively. Better still, don't think at all; fantasize. That's what he did best after all. And that's what he did now. He blanked out that nay-saying voice and concentrated instead on his fantasy, making it as extreme as he could. He struggled and squirmed in his bonds, pretending to be terrified, pretending that at any time now his ruthless captor – his Mistress of Torment – was going to have her wicked way with him.

And it worked. The fantasy took over after a while, took over completely and with a vengeance. Paul's heart began crashing in his chest, frightened, aroused, quickened by need. What exactly *was* his captor going to do to him? What was she going to do to her *creature*? Was she going to be really excessive this time, go all the way? Was she going to beat him right into the ground, or tease him to death? Or what? How could he possibly know? How could he have even an inkling? He couldn't see anything at all, couldn't hear anything at all either. And how long had she been holding him captive like this anyway – an hour? More than that? Less than that? He didn't have a clue. He realised that he'd already lost all sense of time. He felt genuinely disorientated now. A strong sensation of unreality started to descend, began rolling over him like a dark mist. He began to feel woozy, felt himself drifting away …

Chapter Six

PAUL LAY NAKED ON his front, with his genitals locked tightly inside a chastity device and with a butt-plug lodged deep in his anus. Both had been in place since early in the morning. His legs were tied tightly together with bondage rope, he was gagged and blindfolded, and his arms were cuffed behind him. He'd done all that to himself this evening; he knew that well enough. But he had no way of knowing how long ago that had been.

There was something else, though, something that was in a different league altogether from losing all sense of time, something that was genuinely alarming. At some point since he'd put himself into this latest bondage – somewhere in the black nowhere space that he'd been occupying for who knows how long now – things had changed. For one, the leather couch felt different somehow. It felt harder, bigger. Was it his couch? Was he in his living room? It didn't feel like his living room. It felt more – what was the word? – cavernous.

His imagination was playing games with him surely, that had to be it. But no, that wasn't it, it simply couldn't be. Because here was the decider, here was the clincher: *He wasn't alone any more.* There was someone else in the room with him. Paul could hear him or her moving about. But how could that be? How could he hear the person? How could he hear anything? He had earplugs in. Or he'd *had* earplugs in. The person in the room with him must have removed the plugs from his ears to let him know he was no longer on his own.

Paul could hear the click-click-click of the person's high-heeled shoes or high-heeled boots or whatever it was he or she was wearing, moving around the room. But how could he hear that sharp, distinctive noise? His living room was carpeted throughout. This could mean only one thing. He'd been drugged in some way and then carted off elsewhere, *abducted*. The knowledge of this frightened him witless. He could feel sweat

21

gathering at his brow and his heart began beating like a jack-hammer.

The woman in the high heels, whoever she was, was holding him as her helpless captive here. But where exactly was here? Where had he been taken to, for Christ's sake? Maybe it was to a dungeon of some kind. Wherever he was he was obviously there to undergo some form of painful – probably *very* painful – torture. The prospect of this frightened, no, terrified him, and that terror rapidly began to consume his mind. He felt panic sweep over him, felt blood throbbing through his temples.

He heard again the click-click-click sound of the high heels coming at him from the surrounding darkness. The noise was getting louder. His captor was getting closer to him all the time, striding over to him with measured steps. She was coming to torture him with great cruelty, Paul was sure of it. The woman didn't say so, though. She didn't say anything, which made her all the more terrifying.

The footsteps stopped and where they stopped told Paul where the woman was, that she was now standing beside his prostrate, tightly trussed-up form. She immediately began to beat his backside with a whip. And it hurt like hell, each vicious lash smarting vividly. Paul tried to twist away from the blows that were landing on him with ever increasing frequency. But his efforts were futile and the searing pain continued to burn into his flesh. Then his tormentor, his *torturer*, started to lay into his backside with even more ferocity. Each of her blows was a sharp stab of fire that steadily accumulated, becoming an angry red heat that permeated his whole body. On and relentlessly on she lashed Paul's punished backside, stroke after searing stroke, until the furious pain he was suffering was becoming unendurable and he sobbed in agony beneath his gag.

But that only served to encourage his torturer to be even more vicious, making her beat him with even greater savagery. Over and over she whipped him with more and more ferocity until the fierce red pain he was enduring had become a fury burning agonizingly into his flesh. Then all of a sudden the agonizing pain he was suffering started to dissolve, started to turn into something else entirely: overpowering desire.

Paul suddenly felt on fire with lust, overwhelmed by it,

consumed by it. Intense sexual arousal took him over, making him writhe and buck against his bonds in erotic delight as the lashes continued to land across his rear. He was getting closer to orgasm and a guttural moan came past his gag. Paul's sexual arousal had by this time become agonizing, desperate. His tightly encased tumescence was throbbing like mad. He could feel every nerve in his body, felt as though waves of electricity were surging through him each time the savage whip landed.

The blows stopped abruptly and Paul was left breathing heavily with pain. Yet as he drew breath after shuddering breath, he felt himself on the very brink of climaxing, the waves spreading, filling him with wild pleasure.

And then he was past the point of no return, completely out of control. He felt his cock swell and pulse within the chastity device as he reached his peak. He tensed his trussed-up body, his trussed-up cock, and then gave himself up to the surging sensations that had taken over his body.

For a while Paul thought the surging wouldn't ever stop, that he would pulse like this for ever, every atom in him electrified. But finally the sensations subsided. The storm was over and he lay there trembling, his breathing ragged, his heart thudding rapidly in his chest. He was dizzy with the combined effects of his wild thrashings and the after-effect of the powerful orgasm he had experienced.

Eventually Paul's breathing and heart-rate slowed and the dizziness passed. He felt sticky dampness beneath him and knew that it had to be his own ejaculate seeping out of the drainage channel of the chastity device. He could feel the wetness spreading between his thighs. The mushroom odour of his release was sharp in his nostrils.

Paul lay still while he recovered from his orgasm. He became aware of the present once more. He was on his leather couch, in his living room, trussed up and blindfolded and gagged and unable to hear a thing. And completely on his own, as he had been all along. He had no idea of the time. He might have been bound and blindfolded and gagged like this for many hours. Who knew? He thought he'd better find out. With shaking fingers he unclipped his wrist cuffs from behind his back, began to get himself out of his bondage.

Once Paul had freed his wrists he took off his blindfold. The digital clock on the living room wall told him that it was after midnight, 12.25. That had been a long session and an exceptionally intense one, he said to himself with satisfaction. What a powerful erotic imagination he had! He'd *willed* himself to orgasm; that's what he'd done. And what an amazing orgasm it had been. He had been remonstrating with himself earlier for being a thoroughgoing fantasist. But if being such a fantasist meant he could give himself incredible experiences like that, then long may he remain one.

Paul removed his earplugs, unbuckled his ball gag and untied his legs. He cleaned his cum off the leather couch and went into the bathroom where he unlocked and removed the chastity device from around his genitals. After that he removed the butt-plug. Feeling the rubbery base of the object, he slowly extracted it from deep inside him. Oh, the pain! Oh, the relief! Paul carefully washed and dried the butt-plug and the chastity device as well as the ball gag and the earplugs. He then put all the items he'd used on himself that night back into the Fetish wardrobe in his bedroom.

Paul drew the bedroom curtain aside slightly and gazed out at the dark street: rain like mist around the streetlights. All was quiet outside although there remained in the background the familiar hum of traffic on the move; the city never truly slept. It was time Paul did though, time he went to bed. He had a quick shower, cleaned his teeth, and climbed naked under the duvet, cleansed, tired. He fell asleep almost as soon as his head hit the pillow.

Chapter Seven

PAUL SLEPT DEEPLY AND dreamlessly that night – and for a long time too, catching up on all the sleep he *hadn't* had the night before. He woke late in the morning and ran himself a hot bath, the rush of the water breaking the silence of his flat in a pleasant way. He enjoyed a good long soak, dried himself, and got dressed slowly. He then went to the kitchen and had some juice followed by a leisurely brunch, which he washed down with several cups of good strong coffee. It was gone two in the afternoon by the time Paul had finished his repast, washed up, and started to think about how to spend the rest of the day. He'd work naked and in bondage at his computer; that seemed like the best bet. He wondered in passing when Tony would get in touch. It wouldn't be for a while, he guessed. He was no doubt a very busy guy.

Paul glanced through the net curtains. The weather forecast had said there'd be more rain today and it had been right. But the rain had stopped for now. The sky had cleared to a dull blue and the sun was shining on the wet street outside. Paul decided to go out for a brisk walk, enjoy the sunshine and the break in the rain while it lasted. After that he'd strip off, get into some form of bondage and knuckle down to his work for the rest of the afternoon and quite possibly for much of the evening too.

Before he had a chance to do anything at all, though, the doorbell rang. He went to the front door, opened it and ...*Wow* – he found himself face to face with a woman of quite spectacular beauty. Her shoulder-length hair was flame-red and lustrous. She had large emerald green eyes, full sensuous lips and strong features with almost Slavic cheekbones. The woman, who was tall, was wearing a silky cream blouse and over that a tailored grey suit that managed to be both severe and yet also show off her lissom form and long bare legs to stunning effect. She had on black high-heeled shoes and was carrying a leather hold-all of the same colour.

'You are Paul Cooper, Tony's friend, I assume', the woman said, looking him up and down coolly.

'Y … yes,' Paul stammered.

'It's uncanny,' she remarked, raising an eyebrow. 'You really do look an awful lot like him. Hell, you could *be* him. Tell me, are you on your own at the moment?'

'I … eh … yes.'

Before Paul could say anything else the woman had crossed the threshold of his flat and shut the door behind her. She strode into his living room, with Paul following meekly in her wake, and put her bag down on the floor. Then she turned and stared directly at Paul. 'I am Mistress Nikki,' she announced, her green eyes boring into him. 'And you will do whatever I tell you to do.' What she said and, more to the point, the *way* that she said it – the tone of her voice, that look in her eyes – made it clear that she would brook no argument at all. 'Say, "Yes, Mistress",' she added.

'Yes, Mistress,' Paul replied without even thinking. He was already trembling with excitement and there was a hollow feeling in his chest. Could this really be happening to him?

'Strip naked for me,' she commanded next, maintaining her disquieting hold on his eyes.

'Yes, Mistress,' Paul said, and obediently stepped out of his clothes. By the time he was nude his cock was standing rigidly erect and was already covered with glittering wetness.

'Let's see what we've got here apart from an amazing Tony look-alike with a nice big overexcited cock,' Mistress Nikki said, and as she spoke she ran her gaze over Paul's body, over the ripples of muscle and sinew. Paul had a fine body, fluid and toned, without an ounce of excess. She cast an expert eye over places which, handled by a woman with her special skills, would make him squirm and squeal. And that would be just for starters. That would be even *before* she started torturing him.

'You'll do nicely,' Nikki said, concluding her inspection. She got on to one knee and began to rummage in her bag, pulling out two black silk scarves, a set of clover clamps and two pairs of metal cuffs, one pair slightly larger than the other. Paul gazed wide-eyed at what she was doing. His breath was coming quickly, his cheeks flushed. He felt on fire with sexual excitement.

Nikki got back to her feet. She put all the items she'd taken from the bag onto the table with the exception of the two sets of cuffs, which she kept hold of as she stood behind Paul. 'Put your hands behind your back,' she told him.

'Yes, Mistress,' Paul replied, his hands trembling as she locked the smaller of the pairs of cuffs on to his wrists. She then cuffed his ankles with the larger pair and put the keys to both sets of cuffs into the breast pocket of her jacket.

What was going to happen next? Paul wondered breathlessly. But in a sense, he felt, it didn't matter. Mistress Nikki was a professional. He was safe in her hands, could relax and let her take this in whatever direction she wanted to. He stood as still as he was able to and waited for her next instruction.

Mistress Nikki positioned herself in front of Paul, her luminous green eyes staring right at him again. 'Kneel down and kiss my feet,' she commanded, kicking off her high-heeled shoes.

Paul dropped to his knees straight away like a felled tree. He leaned forward, pressing his lips to one of the domme's beautiful bare feet. Paul kissed and licked it eagerly, tracing little circles over all its toes and every inch of its outer and inner surfaces, progressing to the ankle and all the way round to the back. Then she raised her foot, allowing him to lick and kiss a warm trail over its sole and lap at its heel like an obedient puppy. Next she placed her other foot to his lips and he repeated the process, feeling his cock tauten more and more all the time. It was all so *deliciously* humiliating.

'That's enough,' Nikki said in due course, getting back into her high heels.

'Yes, Mistress,' Paul replied submissively. He loved the sound of those words as they rolled off his tongue. *Yes, Mistress*.

'Stand up,' the dominatrix ordered next and Paul got unsteadily to his feet. She strode over to the table and picked up the clover clamps and the two silk scarves. She attached the clover clamps to Paul's nipples, which made him shudder with pain, the clamps gripping like burning pincers. His nipples throbbed painfully, the sensation sending sparks of electricity straight to his pulsing erection. He moaned softly with pain and pleasure.

'Now I'm going to blindfold and gag you,' Mistress Nikki told Paul. She blindfolded him with one of the silk scarves and then said, 'Open wide.' She pulled the second silk scarf tightly between his teeth and knotted it behind his head. Paul found it hard to get his breath. He swayed, feeling his knees go weak. He felt faint with excitement, close to passing out, dizzy with the knowledge that this woman could do anything she wanted to do to him.

Paul could feel something cold and hard, he didn't know what, being pressed against the underside of his erect cock, just beneath its bulbous head. At the same time one of Nikki's hands moved to the nipple clamps attached to his chest and she pulled very hard indeed, yanking viciously at them. Paul thought he really was going to pass out this time, the pain was so excruciating. But he didn't pass out. Instead he climaxed, he simply couldn't stop himself, couldn't restrain that aching sexual intensity for a second longer. He shuddered and shook, moaning from beneath his gag, as a racking orgasm took him over. Cum spilled from his cock and out of control spasms spread through his body like a mighty wave.

Finally Paul shuddered to a halt. He could no longer feel the object that had been pressed against the underside of his cock right up to that point. In the aftermath of the huge orgasm he'd just experienced, Paul stood shivering, blindfolded, gagged, his nipples clamped, and his wrists cuffed together behind his back, his ankles cuffed together too. He reflected in awe-struck wonder upon the strength of his reaction to what Mistress Nikki had done to him. The experience had been far better than anything he'd ever been able to achieve with his own resources, and for one very simple reason – it had been the *real thing*. And she'd hardly done anything at all to him this time. Just think what it would be like if she really went to town on him. He had to find out what that would be like, *had to*.

Paul knew what had happened to him, had always known it would happen to him if he allowed himself to succumb to a professional dominatrix of this calibre. He had become an instant addict. Oh fuck, he thought, and repeated the question to himself that he'd asked earlier: What was going to happen next?

Chapter Eight

WHAT HAPPENED NEXT WAS that Mistress Nikki removed Paul's blindfold and gag and the nipple clamps, and put them back in her leather hold-all. She then showed him something she'd evidently extracted from that hold-all as soon as she'd blindfolded him. It was a shiny silver goblet that now contained the jism that he'd just ejaculated. So a mystery had been solved, Paul said to himself. *That* had been the object that Mistress Nikki had held against his cock immediately before yanking with such viciousness at his nipple clamps and making him cum so copiously.

The dominatrix held the goblet to Paul's lips. 'Drink,' she ordered sharply. And Paul did as he'd been told, drinking down his own ejaculate – not the first time he'd swallowed cum, he recalled. But don't think about that, he told himself quickly. Don't go there ...

Mistress Nikki then took the goblet into Paul's small kitchen where she washed and dried it. Upon her return to the living room, she put it back in the hold-all. After that she stepped behind Paul and ran her fingers along the musculature of his shoulders for a while. Her touch was electrifying and he felt his breath begin to quicken once more. She moved her fingers down his back then and unlocked the cuffs from around his wrists, only to place his hands in front of him and relock them. She dropped the key to the cuffs back into the breast pocket of her jacket.

'Where's your front door key?' she asked. 'In the lock?'

'Y ... yes, Mistress,' he replied, a tremor in his voice.

'It won't be for much longer,' she announced matter-of-factly. 'It's going away with me. Bye for now, Paul.' And with that she picked up her leather hold-all and turned briskly away from him. She opened the living room door with a flick of the wrist and left the room, shutting the door behind her.

Paul heard the front door shut next and realised that he was alone and in bondage. And this was *real* bondage, different entirely from the self-inflicted facsimile he had been practicing for so long. Mistress Nikki had gone off with the keys to the manacles that were locked around his wrists and ankles, and it would be impossible for him to free himself. She had his front door key too, so could come and go as she pleased. No such option was open to him. Unless Paul wanted to make himself a laughing stock he could not leave the flat, nor even answer the door. He really was the captive of Mistress Nikki and would have to wait patiently for her to come back to free him ... or do whatever else she wanted to do to him.

Before the stunning flame-haired dominatrix had stridden into his flat and gone on to turn his world upside down he'd had plans for the day, Paul reminded himself. He had intended to go for a brisk walk and, upon his return to the flat, to strip naked, put himself into bondage and get on with some copy-editing at his computer. The walk was now out of the question of course, but working nude and in bondage at his PC wasn't. He therefore hobbled with difficulty in his ankle cuffs over to the computer and sat down to make a start.

Paul had worked naked at his home computer with his wrists and ankles cuffed many times before, enjoying the severely restricted movement between his ankles and the fact that even when he only needed to use one of his hands, he *had* to use both of them. But this was different because now he couldn't get the cuffs off his wrists or ankles even if he wanted to, which he didn't.

He was a virtual prisoner in his own home; correction, he was an *actual* prisoner in his own home, a hostage. And he was waiting on his captor to return and release him, correction, *punish* him. Because that was what she was going to do, wasn't it?

When Paul thought of it his pulse began to race and he became sexually excited again, all ideas of working at his computer rapidly beginning to disappear. And as he felt his cock stiffen to throbbing hardness once more he reverted to type. Paul the arch-fantasist started to fantasize again, letting his imagination rip, letting it run riot.

His captor, cruel Mistress Nikki, would come for him soon, secure in the knowledge that he could not possibly have managed to get free of his shackles, that it would have been pointless for him to have even tried. But would she come for him soon? The dominatrix hadn't said when she would return so he might be manacled like this for a long time. That excited Paul even more, making his heart drum louder, his cock throb more. Anyhow, come what might, she was bound to come for him eventually. And then what? Anything could happen.

Paul imagined Mistress Nikki returning to his flat and opening the living room door. He imagined her coming into the room with a whip in her hand and this time wearing a different outfit: a skin-tight black leather cat suit with a gigantic strap on dildo jutting from the crotch. He could see so clearly what the dominatrix would do then – She would instruct him to stand up in his shackles and to turn round and bend over. She'd go on to whip him hard (*Whip! Whip! Whip! Whip! Whip!*), making him shudder with pain.

She would redouble her efforts after that, whipping him even harder, her leather flogger penetrating his skin so deeply that it was like a blade. He would be sobbing desperately as she kept on tearing into his naked shackled body with the savage whip.

He was sure that Mistress Nikki would go even further after that, sure that she would make him kneel on all fours and then sodomize him brutally with the gigantic strap-on dildo. She would plunge into his narrow anus, then withdraw, then plunge in again, his insides screaming in protest.

Next she'd withdraw the strap-on dildo and stride to the living room door and open it to reveal that she had brought another dominatrix back to his flat with her. The other woman would come into the room. She was even taller than Mistress Nikki, a gigantic muscular blonde-haired Amazon who was also in a tight black leather cat suit with a strap-on dildo as huge as the one jutting from her own leather-clad crotch.

Mistress Nikki would then blindfold him again and let the other woman sodomize him, or was it her? Or were they taking it in turns? He was blindfolded, he didn't know. He would never know whether it was her ploughing deep inside him with a strap-on or the other woman, the blonde Amazon.

Paul couldn't tell which of them was tearing him apart because he couldn't tell one of their 'cocks' from the other. His body was so marked, so stretched, so damaged. It felt as if it was broken in

31

pieces. The excitement was too much, too much …

Paul's ever more demented sexual fantasy was interrupted abruptly by the noisy rattle of the key in the front door lock. Mistress Nikki was back.

Chapter Nine

THE DOMINATRIX STRODE INTO the living room, leaving its door wide open. She wasn't wearing a skin-tight leather cat suit or a gigantic strap-on dildo, that was clear. She hadn't arrived back at his flat accompanied by another domme or anyone else, that was equally clear. She was on her own and she was wearing the same severe grey suit, carrying the same leather hold-all. She had the same lustrous red hair, the same big glittering green eyes, the same full sensuous lips, the same knock-out body: curve to curve to curve. She was real, not a fantasy. And she blew his mind, drove him crazy with desire. His breath quickened. His mouth went dry. He could feel his heart pumping hard. And as for his cock …

Mistress Nikki took several steps towards him, her hips swaying provocatively. 'Get to your feet, Paul,' she ordered, staring unblinking into the deep blue of his eyes. 'Then shuffle towards me.'

'Yes, Mistress,' Paul said. He got up shakily from the chair and took several hobbled steps towards the dominatrix. His cock was achingly erect, so urgent that there was already pre-cum moistness at its tip.

Nikki put down her bag and walked a slow circle round Paul, inspecting him again, letting her gaze sweep over his fine smooth body. She allowed her gaze to linger over the nice tight arse, the broad shoulders, the lean but muscular frame, the thick erect cock sticking up so insistently and pulsing so enticingly. His cock was gleaming wetly with pre-cum once again, she noted with a lascivious smile.

Finally she shifted her gaze from Paul, took a couple of steps and grabbed hold of the top of the chair that he'd just vacated. She swivelled the chair round so that it backed onto the PC, pulled it forward and told Paul to sit back down on it in its new position. She took the keys to the manacles from the breast pocket of her jacket and rummaged in her bag, bringing out another set of the larger metal cuffs that she'd used on Paul's ankles.

Mistress Nikki then unlocked the metal cuffs that were around Paul's wrists. 'Put your hands behind you,' she ordered and when he'd done this she pulled them through the chair-back and locked the cuffs again. This left him manacled to the chair by his wrists. Next she unlocked his metal ankle cuffs, only to use the cuffs to manacle his left ankle to the corresponding chair leg. Nikki used the set of metal cuffs she had just removed from her hold-all to manacle Paul's right ankle to the other leg of the chair. She put the keys back in her jacket pocket.

Paul was left with his arms locked behind him, his thighs spread widely apart and his ankles locked to either side of the chair. He was powerless to prevent whatever she intended to do to him and the thought of it thrilled him immensely. He could hear his breath coming in short, ragged gasps and could feel his erection throbbing. This was no fantasy, highly exciting though the one that Mistress Nikki had interrupted had been. This was the real thing. This was *actually happening*.

He watched in excitement, his blue eyes shiny, as the dominatrix rummaged in her bag again. She brought out the nipple clamps once more and immediately attached them to his chest. He jerked in his chair, groaning with both pain and pleasure, and his cock spat out a stream of pre-cum that landed wetly on his torso.

Paul had become very excited while fantasizing about Mistress Nikki in her absence. Now that she was back and fantasy had turned to what he really wanted with every ounce of his being – the real thing – he was even more excited, knowing that he was helpless and in her hands entirely. Paul surrendered wholeheartedly to the experience, wherever it might lead.

Mistress Nikki yanked at his clamps with her left hand, making him gasp and whimper with pleasure-pain. He moved his shoulders, offering his clamped nipples to the fingers that had pulled at them. She yanked again, and again, and again. Paul began bucking his hips backwards and forwards in response, the muscles in his thighs tightening, as he strained against his restraints. He moaned continuously with the yanking movement of her left hand, the movement of his thrusting hips.

Nikki then brought her right hand to the hard throbbing flesh of Paul's cock while continuing to pull at the nipple clamps with her left hand. She started to rub her fingers fast and hard over his erection, which was now completely coated with pre-cum.

She was pulling the nipple clamps, pulling his hard cock, and it was making him frantic, making him moan louder and hurl himself about as far as his bonds would allow. Paul wanted to offer himself fully to Mistress Nikki but the manacles held him rigidly to the chair, adding to his torment and sexual excitement. The dominatrix yanked harder at the clamps with her left hand and stroked and pulled at his erection more insistently with her right, her fist moving furiously now.

What Mistress Nikki was doing to Paul with both of her hands combined with his own complete powerlessness drove him so mad with lust that he got very close to climaxing. Then she abruptly stopped. Paul didn't want that, didn't want that at all. He was *desperate* to come. But what could he do? Shuddering and jerking against his bonds, he sat gasping in the chair to which he was so firmly bound. He couldn't believe the incredible intensity of excitement he was experiencing at the hands of Mistress Nikki. He was hooked on her, no doubt about it. I am an addict now and that is that, Paul said to himself.

But *no, no, no* – that is *NOT* that, he shouted inside his head. He mustn't let this happen, he simply mustn't. He must nip all this madness in the bud before it was too late.

'I can't afford you,' he cried out suddenly.

'You must always call me Mistress,' was the only reply he received.

This is absurd, Paul thought. 'I can't afford you, *Mistress*,' he cried.

Chapter Ten

MISTRESS NIKKI WAS FULL of surprises; there was no doubt about that. Disregarding what Paul had just said, indeed acting as if he hadn't actually uttered a solitary word, she began to slowly undress. Off came her high-heeled shoes; off came her severe grey suit; off came her silky cream blouse. She hadn't been wearing a bra and her breasts were magnificent: twin orbs of sheer perfection with dark nipples as hard as stones. Nikki was now naked except for one item of clothing, which consisted of a buckled black leather belt that went round her narrow waist. A strap that was in a V-shape hung down from the front and went up snugly between her shapely thighs.

'It's a double dildo strap-on harness,' she explained to her slack-jawed captive. 'It already has one of the dildoes in place, the one facing inwards. And let me tell you, Paul – it feels divine.'

Nikki then rooted about in her leather hold-all and pulled out a tube of lubricant, which she put on the table. After that she took from out of the bag a black rubber dildo, which she affixed to the outer fitting on the strap.

And there the dominatrix stood before Paul's seated, manacled, nipple-clamped and throbbingly erect form – the black rubber shaft jutting from between her legs, another dildo inside her. She grasped the external shaft and caressed it, letting out a moan of pleasure as its twin shifted inside her sex.

Nikki thrust the strap-on dildo in Paul's face. 'Suck it,' she said. And he did, with relish. He wrapped his lips around the rubber shaft, swirling his tongue around its head, before taking its length into his mouth. Paul moved his lips up and down the shaft, tasting every inch of it, licking and sucking at it until finally Mistress Nikki pulled away from him.

'Enough,' she said impatiently. 'Let's get you out of bondage now.'

She unlocked and removed the metal cuffs from his wrists and ankles but she did not remove the nipple clamps, which continued to bite painfully into his chest.

'Get onto all fours,' Nikki ordered and Paul immediately got up from the chair and just as quickly knelt down in position on the floor, a rivulet of pre-cum trailing from the head of his cock. He began breathing very rapidly. Paul knew what was going to happen to him all too soon now, and he wanted it to happen, *couldn't wait* for it to happen. He felt a shiver, an electric pulse, course through his body.

Getting Paul to place his forearms flat on the floor so that his backside stuck up in the air, Mistress Nikki knelt behind him and liberally applied lubricant to the strap-on dildo. She placed the end of the dildo against his anal hole and pushed gently against the tight ring of muscles. She then used her hands to part the cheeks of Paul's backside, and the black rubber shaft slid part way into him before his anal muscles clamped down. The dominatrix didn't force the dildo in when she felt this resistance. Instead she waited for Paul's anal muscles to relax, and when they had she pushed the dildo a bit further until the next spasm of resistance caused the muscles to clamp down again. By a series of gentle thrusts and pauses like this she eventually got the dildo planted firmly inside Paul and he sighed when it finally slid all the way home. It was time, he knew, for him to be seriously buggered.

Nikki folded herself forward, with her magnificent naked breasts against Paul's back. She began a slow thrusting motion that caused the rubber shaft to slide in and out of his anus as the other dildo moved inside her. Each time the dildo slid in and out of Paul he groaned aloud. He was extremely aroused. His face was flushed, his eyes and mouth wide open, his breathing laboured.

Paul pushed his hips back on the rubber dildo that the dominatrix was thrusting into him with such skill, feeling it slide in and out as they both moved. These movements caused spears of pleasure to shoot through him as the implement made contact with his prostate gland. He threw back his head and groaned loudly with pleasure at each stroke, which made Nikki sodomize him faster and then faster still. This in turn made the dildo inside her slide ever faster too, which caused her to feel the beginnings of her own orgasm.

Mistress Nikki built up further momentum as she sodomized

Paul, grinding her hips over and over as he bucked beneath her. She pounded the dildo in and out of his anus, fucking him hard to the rhythm of his groans of pleasure. Then her orgasm came with full force and she shuddered convulsively in release.

At the same time Paul climaxed with violence, shivering and shaking as he spilled out one thick spurt of hot cum after another. He felt like he never would stop coming this time. He didn't think of anything except the waves of sensation spreading through his body as he spilled his cum in juddering spasms.

After his orgasm had finally subsided Paul felt like a limp rag, exhausted. But he was jarred alert when Mistress Nikki briskly removed the clamps from his nipples, causing a sharp burst of pain as oxygen rushed like quicksilver back into the previously constricted flesh. She next extracted the dildo from his anus and the implement came free with a wet, sucking noise.

Then the dominatrix spoke. 'Close your eyes tightly shut and do not open them in the slightest or even move a muscle until I've left your flat,' she ordered and Paul did as he'd been told. He knelt there on all fours, trying hard to stop his chest from moving, his eyes closed tight.

Remaining on his hands and knees as motionless as he could on the living room floor, lubricant trickling out of his gaping anal hole and down his thighs, Paul could hear Nikki moving around the room. Then he heard her go into the bathroom and the sound of taps being turned on and off, heard her come back into the room, heard the light rustling sounds of her getting dressed, of her leather hold-all being zipped shut. Then he heard something he hadn't expected to hear. It was the tapping sound of her typing something at his computer. Finally he heard the sound of the front door creaking open and then shutting with a resounding bang.

Paul immediately blinked open his eyes, got up from his kneeling position on the floor and went straight over to look at the screen of his PC and the Word document that Nikki had created on it. There he read the following message: *I've put your front door key back in the door. My visit to you is completed. Now it's your turn, Paul. Come to my address tomorrow at seven in the evening.* The message went on to give her address, which was in one of the smartest parts of nearby Camden Town.

But I told her I couldn't afford her, Paul said to himself in exasperation. I couldn't have made it any clearer if I'd tried. He knew he'd obey her, though. There really was no question about it, none whatsoever.

Chapter Eleven

TWILIGHT WAS JUST STARTING to shift into night as Paul drove his Fiat past a glimmering stretch of the Regents Canal and up towards the big, high-walled house in Camden Town that was his destination. He pulled the car to a standstill, switched off the ignition and sat listening to the tick of the engine for a few moments as his fingers played nervously along the smoothness of the driving wheel. His mouth was so dry he couldn't swallow; his heart was racing, the palms of his hands damp. Paul glanced at his watch. It was almost seven, time he made a move. He took a long deep breath to try and calm his nerves, and stepped from the car.

Paul walked through the high gates and up to the entrance, rang the bell and a few anxious moments later the door was answered by Mistress Nikki. The sight of the beautiful redhead made Paul let out a gasp of desire. She looked magnificent in a figure-hugging black leather dress, which was so incredibly short that it hardly covered her sex. She was also wearing a tight-fitting pair of tall boots with pointed toes.

Nikki led Paul into her spacious, elegantly furnished living room. And there, seated on a black leather couch and beaming a welcoming smile at him, was none other than Tony – Tony who'd promised faithfully that he'd be in touch with him and indeed who already *had* been in touch with him, it appeared, albeit indirectly.

Paul was about to say a warm hello to his friend but Nikki stopped him from doing so by speaking herself. 'I'm going to discipline you 'twins' together,' she said. 'But I'm only going to charge Tony for the privilege. Understood?'

'Yes, Mistress,' they replied in unison, exchanging glances. From the knowing look he saw on Tony's face it was evident to Paul that what Nikki had just said had come as little if any surprise to him and that he was more than happy with the arrangement. Perhaps, Paul thought, he'd actually suggested it in the first place.

'Now, go into the changing room and strip naked without delay,' Nikki ordered, pointing in the direction of the room in question. 'And don't say a word to each other while you're about it, not one word. Just strip off and get back to me *tout de suite.*'

As they both hurriedly took off their clothes in the changing room, Tony sneaked Paul another smile which he returned. Paul felt incredibly excited. He could see that Tony was excited too because once his pants were over his hips his cock started to engorge. He noticed that Tony's body was much as he remembered it from university days: slim but muscular and well formed and nearly hairless, like his own in fact. Paul's cock also began to swell at the sight of his 'twin', his doppelganger, as he too stripped naked.

The two men, their erections bobbing before them, followed Mistress Nikki down a long corridor and into the big dark chamber at its end. Paul's eyes widened and his erection throbbed at the sights that met him there. The large windowless room was decked out beautifully with high quality dungeon equipment, all polished wood, soft leather and gleaming metal. It included a St Andrews cross, a horse, a whipping bench, two sets of adjacent stocks, an upright torture chair, and a leather-covered bondage table. In addition there was a metal cage and also several chains hung from the ceiling with spreader bars attached to them, some with manacle attachments and others without. Up against one of the room's dark walls there was a rack upon which hung a large collection of canes, whips, paddles, chains, clamps and other disciplinary implements.

Nikki rested her hand firmly under Paul's chin and pulled his face towards her. 'Do you like my dungeon?' she asked.

'Yes, Mistress,' Paul replied in a croak. Did he like it? He *loved* it.

Nikki took her hand away from Paul's face and turned towards his companion. 'You like my dungeon too, Tony, don't you,' she said. 'After all, I've disciplined you in it enough times.' She was smiling as she spoke, just a slight touch at the corner of her mouth.

'Yes, Mistress,' he smiled back.

'Now, while I decide exactly what I'm going to do to you two,' Nikki said, 'I want you to play with each other's cocks.'

41

Paul had to be honest with himself and admit that he found no great hardship in obeying Mistress Nikki in this. She was pushing against an at least partially open door with him and, he suspected, with Tony too by giving such a command. It would be like it had been when he and his old roommate had masturbated together back at university while fantasizing over Laura the prick tease. But this time they could do what they'd both felt inhibited from doing back then.

As instructed, the two of them started masturbating each other, their hands moving in swift urgent rhythms over one another's hard cocks until they were dripping with pre-cum moistness.

Then Mistress Nikki told them to stop. 'That's enough pleasure for you two,' she said. 'Now for some pain. Lean over the horse right away, side by side.'

Here it came, what Paul had fantasized about so obsessively for such a long time but had never yet experienced: a damn good beating. And Mistress Nikki did not disappoint. She used her hand first, delivering six blows to his backside, each smack a sharp sensation of fire, then six to Tony, then back to Paul for another six, and on and on. For a long while the dungeon echoed with the sound of hand on naked flesh and their cries of pain as she followed one stinging blow with another in quick succession.

Nikki switched to a leather paddle then, using the same 'six to one and half a dozen to the other' sequence she'd used when she'd been spanking them. She brought the paddle down onto their backsides with remorseless energy, each blow landing like an explosion and smarting vividly. Both of them tensed and squirmed and cried out with pain as the searing heat burned their flesh.

Mistress Nikki then demanded that the two men grovel at her feet and lick one of her boots each. They got onto their knees, bent their heads low, pressed their lips against the pointed toes of her boots and slid their tongues along the pure leather. Paul obviously didn't know what was going through Tony's mind at that time. All he knew was that as far as he personally was concerned he thought he'd died and gone to heaven.

The dominatrix next told them to remain on their knees and instructed Paul to crawl to the front of Tony and suck his cock. Paul hesitated for a moment in alarm. This was something that he would never have been prepared to contemplate doing before, he reminded himself – not since that time when he'd … but again he thought: don't go there … he didn't have a choice, though. Mistress Nikki had *told* him to do it and to have disobeyed her would have been unthinkable.

So Paul did what he had to do. He got onto all fours, opened his lips and pressed his mouth to the head of Tony's pulsing shaft, tracing his tongue under it at first. Then he closed his mouth around his cockhead, sucking on it. As he did this he heard Mistress Nikki's voice above him, informing him in dulcet tones that he was about to be caned.

Paul listened to the low swish as she drew the cane back and the louder one as it descended. He suffered the sharp sting of its first searing stroke to his rear as she brought it down hard across the middle of his cheeks.

The second swipe hurt even more, a white flash of pure pain. Then she brought the cane down a third time and there was that white flash of sensation again, then a fourth time, harsher and sharper still.

In trying desperately to withstand the pain Mistress Nikki was inflicting on him Paul began to suck Tony's cock more and more voraciously. He worked his mouth up and down until Tony was groaning with desire. Paul didn't let up though, *couldn't* let up, he was in too much pain. The pace with which he was fellating Tony got increasingly frantic in response to Mistress Nikki's remorseless caning. Paul's backside ached so much, the smarting impact of each blow blazing through his body as he sucked and sucked.

Nikki stopped caning him eventually and told him to take Tony's cock out of his mouth. 'Did you enjoy it when I fucked you in the arse yesterday, *cocksucker*?' she said, grasping Paul by the hair and gazing into his eyes with laser-like intensity.

'Yes, Mistress,' he replied, his voice trembling.

'Good, because I'm going to do it again and this time you're going to enjoy it even more because you'll be *sucking cock* at the same time.' Why did she keep emphasizing the words like that, Paul asked himself. Did she somehow know what he'd done that time he couldn't bring himself to think about? But how could she? He must be imagining things, he decided.

Mistress Nikki took hold of the double dildo strap-on harness she'd worn at Paul's flat, both of its black rubber shafts already in place this time. She doused both of the dildoes with lubricant and first inserted the internal one into her naked sex, letting out a lustful moan as she did so. The other end extended from her pubis, a thick erect shaft that was identical to the one she'd just put inside herself. Then she buckled up the leather harness of the strap-on and was ready for action.

She ordered Tony to lie flat on his back on the dungeon floor and for Paul to straddle his face so that they could sixty-nine one another. As they obediently did this, Nikki positioned herself behind Paul and gently worked the thickness of the dildo in and out of the opening of his anus a few times, pushing against the clenched ring of muscles. She pushed it in a little further with each thrust, stretching his reluctant sphincter more and more. He suddenly felt the dildo spasm right into him until his anal ring was right against its base. At the same time his cock sent a throb of pre-cum into Tony's mouth.

Mistress Nikki began to sodomize Paul, slowly at first and then increasing in vigour until she was riding him really hard. His anal muscles squeezed and released deliciously around the large dildo she was pounding into him. Her rhythm was strong, each thrust going deeper into his anus, filling him, penetrating him. And all the while Tony and he sucked one another's cocks for all they were worth. By now the dominatrix and the two men were locked together in lust, giving each other ever more pleasure until they each in turn tumbled over into orgasms that racked their bodies with spasms of delight.

First Nikki climaxed with a long animal-like moan, shuddering deliriously at the sensations she was receiving from her internal dildo as she buggered Paul harder still with the strap-on. He began to tremble uncontrollably and climaxed, sending copious amounts of cum into Tony's mouth. Then Tony climaxed, too, filling Paul's mouth as he emptied one thick spurt of hot cum after another over his tongue and into the back of his throat. Paul sucked and sucked at this deluge, gulping down the cum over and over again until at long last he had sucked Tony dry. Only then did Mistress Nikki stop sodomizing Paul.

'Tony's got an appointment with me tomorrow at the same time, Paul,' Nikki said then, her strap-on dildo still buried deep in his anus. 'I want you to come along too. It'll be the same deal: he pays for my services, you don't, and neither of you are allowed to talk to the other during the session. There's more, though,' she added sternly. 'Don't communicate with each other *at all* between now and then. I mean, don't even catch one another's eyes.'

Driving home to Islington through the evening traffic, his body aching and his anus sore and the taste of Tony's cum still in his mouth, Paul found himself in a reflective mood. He and Tony had just been more up-close-and-personal with one another than either of them would have dared to have contemplate back in their university days during those Laura-inspired mutual masturbation sessions. Paul thought it was ironic that, after having the incredibly, the *outrageously* intimate experience that had just been forced upon the two of them by Mistress Nikki in her dungeon, they were not permitted to communicate with each other in any way, shape or form. Still, if that was what she wanted, that was clearly the way it had to be.

Chapter Twelve

DUSK WAS JUST SETTLING, blue-black, over the metropolis when Paul and Tony arrived for that next eagerly awaited appointment. They had done precisely what Nikki had told them she required. She'd said that she wanted them standing together at her front door exactly on the hour of seven, not a second late, and they had obeyed. They had also obeyed to the letter her instruction not to communicate with one another at all. They had each been very careful to avoid making eye contact, both when changing back into their clothes and leaving her premises the day before and also when they'd arrived there today.

As soon as Mistress Nikki opened the door to the two men Paul, for one, was hypnotized. The dominatrix looked absolutely stunning in an outfit guaranteed to set the pulse racing of any submissive male. She was wearing leather boots with exceptionally high heels and her shapely legs were perfectly outlined by extremely tight leather trousers. Every curve and swell of her backside and the slit of her sex were delineated and defined by the black leather. It was obvious that she was wearing nothing under the trousers or the skin-tight sleeveless black leather top she also had on, which followed the contours of her beautiful breasts and erect nipples like a second skin.

Mistress Nikki took Paul and Tony directly to the changing room this time and told them to strip naked. Then she led them down the long corridor to her dungeon. Once there, she got them to stand next to each other underneath two adjacent spreader bars with leather manacle attachments, which hung from the ceiling by chains. She told them to stretch their arms out, and then manacled their wrists to the spreader bars.

Their stiffly erect cocks told Mistress Nikki that they were ready for whatever she had in mind from this point on. And what she had in mind was to attach very tight metal endurance clamps to their nipples, making both men shudder with pain as the clamps gripped like red-hot pliers. She then began slapping their clamps with the leather tip of a riding crop, doing this so viciously that they flinched and winced in pain. But she was just getting into her stride.

'I'm going to break you two cocksuckers today,' she announced ominously, her gleaming green eyes going from one to the other of them, pinning them back with her gaze. She then went behind them and started to take a leather flogger to their backsides.

Initially every one of her skillfully aimed lashes was very painful indeed, intensely sharp and stinging. Paul thought it could only get worse but in reality the reverse happened. As she continued to bring the whip down, he felt the pain he was suffering start to melt away, becoming a suffused red heat that seeped through his body, connecting with the pulsing hardness of his cock.

Looking over at Tony's body he saw that his cock was also fiercely erect, a silver stream of pre-cum seeping from its head. He saw as well that he was doing the same thing as him – raising his backside to each blow in welcome anticipation. Nikki carried on beating the two of them for some time and the resounding crack of each blow mingled with their moans and muffled grunts of pleasure. If this was what being broken was like, Paul thought, she could break him any time she liked. What an idiot he was to have had such a thought, he said to himself afterwards. Mistress Nikki was always full of surprises and he was about to receive a very nasty one indeed.

'That was merely a warm up. Now to business,' she said, coming to the front of Paul and Tony and gagging them with identical blue ball gags. 'I want you firmly gagged,' she explained, her eyes fixing on one and then the other of them again with frightening intensity. 'That way I won't have to listen to your screams of agony.'

Nikki told them to spread their legs, after which she attached painful anchor straps to their scrotums. She added metal weights to these, which she proceeded to both pull and swing to and fro, causing the most searing pain imaginable. The two men's bodies shook, every agonized twitch involuntary. Their gags could not entirely muffle their piteous cries and their erections shrank pathetically as their nerves were flayed ragged by the agony she was inflicting on them.

Eventually the appalling weight and dreadful pressure they were feeling in their groins left the two men weeping. Tears rained down their cheeks in rivers before falling to the dungeon floor. So that had been what she'd meant by 'breaking' them, Paul thought. Jesus, it hurt. Everything inside him was crying out in agony. Mistress Nikki was torturing his balls. Hell, the woman was breaking – yes, literally *breaking* his balls. She was breaking Tony's balls too, Paul could tell, for it was obvious from his tears and the sobs coming from beneath his gag that he was in equally withering pain.

But the dominatrix did take pity on Paul and Tony at long last, removing their clamps, straps and weights with surprising gentleness and taking off their gags. Now that she had stopped torturing them in such an extreme way their erections began to come to life again.

Mistress Nikki released Paul from his spreader bar but left Tony suspended where he was. 'Get onto your knees and give Tony a blow job while bringing yourself off into your hand,' she ordered and Paul moved to obey immediately, didn't even think about it for a moment this time. What a difference a day makes!

He opened his mouth and closed his lips around the hot tender flesh of Tony's cock. He circled his tongue around its wet, swollen glans before starting to blow him. At the same time he took hold of his own hot shaft with his right hand. He tightly encircled it with his fingers and started to masturbate, his hand coming and going in brisk short strokes. Paul's cock became increasingly smeared with pre-cum until his pounding fist was covered in the fluid.

Then Mistress Nikki started beating Tony on the backside with the flogger again, laying into him so hard that each stroke made him cry out and jump and shudder within his bonds. It wasn't long before Paul felt Tony's hard cock in his mouth swell and pulse as he reached his climax, tensing his body and then yielding to the ecstasy of release. He called out a wordless explosion of pain and desire as his cock erupted, flooding streams of cum deep into Paul's throat, which he swallowed down greedily. The moment Paul extracted Tony's spent shaft from his mouth, out-of-control spasms began to shake his own body and he stroked his hard throbbing cock to a gushing climax. Squirt after squirt of cum leaped out of his shaft and spilled in pools into the palm of his waiting hand.

'Eat that too, cocksucker,' Mistress Nikki ordered. 'Lick your palm and all your fingers clean.' And Paul obeyed, licking up and swallowing all the pearly cum in his palm feverishly. Then he sucked hard on each of his cum-covered fingers, lapping his tongue over them sensuously, wallowing in his own degradation. He felt thoroughly debauched and degraded. And he adored feeling that way, was completely in awe of the woman who'd *made* him feel that way.

'I have some further instructions for you both,' Mistress Nikki told Paul and Tony once they had dressed and were ready to leave. 'I do not wish to see you together again and I absolutely forbid you to have any further communication with one another.' She turned to Paul, locking eyes with him. 'I understand your financial difficulties, Paul,' she said. 'And I am prepared to continue disciplining you free of charge as long as you always come running when I summon you and always do as I instruct.' She added, pointing a finger at him for emphasis: 'You are forbidden to ask me why I am doing this for you. Merely be grateful that I am.' Mistress Nikki concluded by instructing Paul to return the next day at three in the afternoon.

When he left Nikki's house Paul went straight to his Fiat while Tony wandered down the road to … where exactly? Paul certainly didn't know, hadn't the faintest idea in fact, and wouldn't have been in a position to ask him. He couldn't say thank you to him either. Paul had been denied the opportunity of thanking Tony for what he'd done for him and he regretted that of course. Even so he drove away in a state that could only be described as euphoric. He was as elated as any heroin addict living on the skids would have been if he'd been told that future supplies of his drug were going to be provided to him regularly and free gratis. Paul the addict could envisage all those hits to come. He could envisage hit after hit after hit after hit after hit.

Chapter Thirteen

FAST FORWARD TO MID afternoon the following day. Paul's first solo session *chez* Mistress Nikki had hardly even got under way but he was already finding it a deeply thrilling experience ...

The flame-haired dominatrix, her flawless body completely – wonderfully – naked on this occasion, was seated on a black leather easy chair in her living room. Paul, who was also nude apart from the red leather slave's collar she'd buckled around his neck, was on all fours on the floor beneath her. Mistress Nikki was gently masturbating while Paul was licking and kissing her bare feet just as she had told him to do.

Nikki reached out her free hand to pick up a riding crop that was resting next to a thick leather strap on a small mahogany table to her side. Continuing to masturbate, she began to idly spank Paul's backside with the crop's leather tip. As she did this she contemplated what torments to inflict upon her new 'client' for the remainder of this session. Paul was in a state of delicious erotic anticipation of the punishment to come. His breathing was hard ... and so was his cock.

Eventually Mistress Nikki spoke. 'You can stop worshipping my feet now,' she said. 'Follow me into the dungeon on all fours.' She then got up from her seat, at the same time putting the riding crop back on the side table and picking up the leather strap in its place.

Paul crawled behind the domme's shapely nude form along the lengthy corridor and into the dungeon. Once there, Nikki stopped and turned to look down at Paul, standing over him in all her naked majesty. He gazed back up at her, the pupils of his blue eyes wide with a mixture of desire and fear.

'Worship my feet again,' Nikki said, feeling the weight and suppleness of the thick leather strap that she was holding in her hands. She then began to beat Paul on the backside with the strap while he covered her bare feet with a shower of kisses, worshipping them with his lips once again as he had been instructed.

Mistress Nikki continued to thrash Paul with the heavy strap and did not stop until his backside was shining a roseate red and he was trembling with pain. Nikki then told Paul to stop worshipping her feet and to stand up. When he had done this, she attached vicious metal clamps to his nipples, which caused him to tremble even more with pain.

Next she attached a chained lead to Paul's collar and took him across the dungeon floor to the leather-covered bondage table. While Paul remained standing, Mistress Nikki, who was still holding the lead, placed herself on her back on the table and opened her legs. She used the lead to pull Paul's face towards her pussy, and he watched the lips of her sex open up before him like two beautiful wet petals. 'Lick me,' Mistress Nikki commanded and Paul immediately obeyed, his tongue darting hot and slick over her clitoris and labia.

'Now use your fingers on me as well,' she demanded. Paul slid a finger to her clitoral hood and teased it round and around. He then pushed two fingers inside her wet pussy and masturbated her furiously at the same time as flicking his tongue over her shiny clit. Nikki moaned rapturously as she climaxed, her body shivering with delight.

The naked dominatrix, briefly sated, got to her feet and removed Paul's lead but not his painful nipple clamps. She told him to lie on his front on the bondage table in a spread-eagled position and she manacled his wrists and ankles to its four corners. Nikki selected three implements of correction: a big studded leather paddle, a tawse of equally heavy leather and a rattan cane. She proceeded to use each in turn to beat Paul's backside remorselessly until it was a glowing, fiery red again and he was trembling once more with pain … and with pleasure.

Mistress Nikki paused to admire her handiwork, dipping her fingers between the wet folds of her pussy as she did so. She masturbated vigorously to another powerful climax as she devoured the sight of Paul, who was so hugely aroused himself now that he had begun wriggling and squirming uncontrollably in his bonds. He was desperate for sexual release by this stage, but knew that Mistress Nikki would allow him this only when she was

51

good and ready.

Nikki *was* good and ready. She unshackled his wrists and ankles and told him to get down off the bondage table. Then she removed his nipple clamps roughly, which caused him acute pain – pain that he knew would be well nigh unbearable if he were not so immensely aroused.

Finally Mistress Nikki told Paul to masturbate to climax while she caned him. She administered a severe beating to his backside with the rattan cane while he masturbated feverishly. He stroked himself more and more quickly while suffering a torrent of horribly punishing stripes from the cane that finally became completely unendurable. Paul emitted an excruciating cry of pain before gasping out in desperation, 'Mercy, Mistress … I beg you'. At the same time he climaxed violently, ejecting rope after rope of creamy cum into the air.

Nikki ceased caning him then and made him get back onto his knees. She used her fingers, fast and furious, to bring herself to a last shuddering climax. Afterwards she stroked Paul's hair gently, using the love-juice soaked fingers with which she had just masturbated. 'You're a good slave, Paul,' she told him softly.

These few brief words of praise from Mistress Nikki, coupled with the fact that she'd called him 'slave' for the very first time since he'd met her, filled Paul with delight. He was Mistress Nikki's slave now and she deemed him to be a good one. It was wonderful, he felt. *Everything* that had happened to him in the last few days had been wonderful. It was all an impossible dream come true. Mistress Nikki had told him the evening before that he was forbidden to ask her why she was doing what she was doing for him and to merely be grateful that she was. He was that all right – immensely grateful. Paul couldn't wait to see her again. He didn't have to wait as luck would have it.

Chapter Fourteen

IMMEDIATELY AFTER SHE'D FINISHED disciplining Paul and they'd both got dressed Mistress Nikki checked her phone to see if she'd received any messages while she'd been otherwise engaged. She'd had one from her next appointment, cancelling at the eleventh hour due to unforeseen circumstances.

The dominatrix therefore found herself with some unexpected time on her hands. She chose to spend it with Paul, chose *not* to send him on his way as she would otherwise have had no alternative but to do. She invited him back into the living room where she gestured for him to sit down on the black leather couch. 'Can I offer you a drink?' she said, going to the drinks cabinet in the corner of the room.

'It's a bit early for me, Mistress,' Paul replied.

'Me also,' Nikki said. 'I'm going to have something non-alcoholic – a glass of tonic water, I think. You too?'

'That would be fine,' Paul said. 'Thank you, Mistress.'

Nikki prepared the drinks and handed Paul his glass before seating herself on the black leather easy chair opposite him.

'So, you swing both ways, Paul,' she said bluntly, clearly alluding to what he and Tony had done together in her dungeon on the previous two evenings – what she'd *made* the two of them do together.

'I guess so, Mistress,' he replied, blushing furiously.

'It's nothing to be ashamed of, you know,' Nikki said, taking a sip from her glass. 'Some of my best friends are bisexual. I am too for that matter. Did Tony inform you of that?'

'No, Mistress,' Paul said. Tony had told him very little about this extraordinary woman.

'It came as quite a surprise to me to discover that about myself, I can tell you,' Nikki continued. 'You see, I was married at the time.'

'You were, Mistress?' Paul said. He took a swallow from his

glass.

'Yes and I'd always thought of myself as completely straight,' Nikki went on. 'The revelation that I definitely wasn't came to me like a bolt out of the blue and happened some years before I became a dominatrix. But as things turned out it definitely opened the way to my making that life choice further down the line. Tell me something, Paul,' she added, 'are you by any chance a good listener? You look as if you might be.'

'I like to think I am, Mistress.'

'Would you like to hear what happened to me?'

'It would be a privilege, Mistress,' he replied with obvious sincerity.

'Then I'll tell you,' Nikki said. She put her glass to one side and began her account. 'I remember it all as if it had happened yesterday. The woman's name was Samantha – Sam for short, and I'd known her for ever …'

Nikki and Sam had been best friends since their school days. Sam was lively and outgoing, confident, shrewd, witty and highly creative. She was also a natural beauty, with creamy alabaster skin, feline cheeks, big pale blue eyes, and long blonde hair. And, if that weren't enough, she had a figure to die for as well. She was as statuesque as a dancer, an exotic one.

Upon completing their further education the two young women had embarked on successful careers. Nikki was doing well in merchandising, although the work did not engage her with any great passion. Sam was different – her work did. She was a talented and successful fashion designer. After a few years the name of Samantha Burrell had come to be spoken of in the same breath as the likes of Stella McCartney and Roland Mouret.

Nikki had fallen in love with a man called Mark Jameson, who was handsome and intelligent but who'd also turned out to have an exceptionally driven personality. Mark was a rising star with the prestigious marketing agency, Simpson and Gray, and had become intensely ambitious to get to the top in that organisation. Mark's burning ambition and the workaholic way of life that increasingly went with it had started to take an inevitable toll on his relationship with Nikki.

Sam had not married and for very good reason – she was

unashamedly gay. When asked a very pointed question about her sexuality once by a fashion journalist her reply, repeated with monotonous regularity in the media ever after, had been typically sardonic. 'Put it this way,' she'd said. 'I'm not interested in anything with a tassel.'

It hadn't always been the case. She'd had plenty of boyfriends when she and Nikki had been younger; 'boy mad' their parents had said they were in their teens. Nikki had been surprised when Sam had come out as a lesbian. It had been shortly after her own marriage to Mark and she'd wondered illogically if it had something to do with her being in the fashion industry. It seemed to Nikki that it was virtually a statutory requirement for the men in the world of fashion to be gay. Was it perhaps the same with the women?

But no, that didn't make any sense at all. Sophie Dahl wasn't gay, nor was Naomi Campbell. Kate Moss wasn't gay either. But hadn't Nikki read somewhere that Kate had enjoyed some dalliances with her own sex, threesomes and the like? Maybe it had begun like that with Sam, starting as a bit of experimentation and ending with her conclusion that she 'wasn't interested in anything with a tassel'. No matter, if Sam was gay, she was gay. It didn't effect their friendship at all. But that, of course, is exactly what it ended up doing.

On the day it all started Nikki had been driving round the centre of London. She was stuck in a slow conga of seemingly interminable traffic, as she tried to find a parking space. When she finally succeeded it happened to be only a stone's throw away from where Sam lived and she decided on a whim to see if she was in. If she was, she thought perhaps she'd like to join her in what she'd originally been intending to do on her own: have a bit of a shopping spree. She was feeling rather low and thought it might lift her spirits.

Once she'd parked the car and fed the meter, Nikki walked past a classy boutique hotel and a short terrace of up-market shops to Palling Court. She arrived at the tall red-brick apartment block where her friend had lived for the last couple of years. Sam had always said she wanted to be 'where it was at', right at the heart of things in London. She'd found that with Palling Court, which was in the middle of the West End.

It was an overcast day, the sky the colour of a fogged negative, and there was a damp feeling in the air. There was just starting to be a spatter of rain as Nikki approached the block. Shit, she thought. I haven't brought an umbrella. Perhaps I can borrow one from Sam – if she's in, of course. She pressed the number of her address on the door entry system and hoped for the best.

'Hello,' she heard Sam say.

'It's me, Nikki.'

'Great,' came the friendly response. 'Come on up.'

There was a sharp buzz and Nikki pushed open the front door of the block and made for the lift area. She entered the lift and stared at the wan reflection of her face in the lift's smoked-glass mirror. She decided to put on a brave face for Sam. There was no need to burden her friend with her marital troubles. She emerged from the lift on the tenth floor a few moments later and walked down the spotlessly clean corridor. She stopped outside number 53, where she pressed the bell.

After a few seconds the door was opened by Sam. Nikki thought she looked even more stunning than usual, not least because of what she had on. Her shining blonde hair hung down over the shoulders of an absolute killer dress. It was a clinging little black number with spaghetti straps. Her breasts were almost falling out of its top and it was so short that it only just skirted her thighs.

She was bare-footed and, if Nikki knew her friend, bare-arsed under that dress, which she guessed might well be one of her own designs. Yes, she looked stunning. She smelled stunning too, some very classy perfume Nikki thought she recognized. It was musky, sexy.

'That's a nice dress you're nearly wearing,' Nikki joked, rolling her eyes.

Sam put her hands on her hips and smiled at her. 'And hello to you too,' she said. 'To what do I owe this unexpected honour?'

'I was in the area,' Nikki said. 'I thought I'd try you on the off-chance. I hope I haven't caught you at an inconvenient time.'

'Not at all,' Sam assured her. 'Actually, I've just this minute made some coffee. Want some?'

'Sure, thanks.'

Nikki followed Sam down a longish corridor in the direction of the kitchen and allowed her eyes to linger on the sway of her friend's hips, the way her hem kept riding up her naked thigh. She suddenly felt horny, could feel her pussy tighten. That was funny, she thought. Sam had never had that effect on her before, no girl had. She was straight, not even a bit bi, right. *Right?* Perhaps it was just the effect of that killer dress. Looking at her friend in it was making her mouth dry. She felt she needed that coffee.

'Did you design your dress?' she asked, taking Sam's arm.

'Un huh.'

'What look were you going for?'

'Haute couture meets trailer trash,' Sam replied giving her a sideways look, her eyes shining with mirth.

'You succeeded,' Nikki laughed.

When they got to the kitchen Sam grabbed a couple of mugs and they sat down at the table opposite one another. Sam poured them both coffees from the glass pot on the table and added milk from the jug next to it. They drank quietly for a few moments before Nikki asked, 'So, how are things with you?'

'Very good,' Sam said, taking a sip of coffee. 'Give it another year or two and I'm confident of being bought out by Versace or Dior or one of the other heavy hitters in the fashion business.'

'And you want to be bought out like that presumably,' Nikki said.

'Oh yes,' Sam replied. 'That way I'll get backing, advertising, money for my shows, accessories, support, it'll be great. It will mean that I'll be able to do the stuff I like doing, and offload what I don't. And it will mean I'll get more time to spend doing other things outside the fashion industry, like spending time with friends like you.'

'That sounds marvellous,' Nikki said. 'I hope it works out for you.'

'Well, there's a little way to go yet but everything seems to be proceeding according to plan so far,' Sam said. 'And it's a goal worth going for. After all, there's more to life than work.'

'God, I wish Mark could get himself a deal like the one you're aiming at,' Nikki said with feeling. Whether Mark wished that himself, of course, was quite another matter. Nikki was coming increasingly to the view that her husband preferred spending time at his high-flying job with Simpson and Gray than being with her.

He desperately wanted a place on the company's board of directors and was working so hard towards that end that it had completely killed his libido. That's what he told her anyway. In any event, he couldn't get it up these days and they hadn't had sex in months.

Sam took a swallow of her coffee. 'He's really busy, is he?' she asked.

'Extremely,' Nikki said. 'I work hard at my job but, like you, I think there are limits. You've got to have a life too. The hours Mark has to put in these days are ridiculous. I've barely seen him in the last few months. It's like he's married to Simpson and fucking Gray rather than me. I try to be philosophical about it, though. He's so exceptionally busy at present because he's working on a big project that could well mean a major promotion for him, get him on to the board of directors no less.'

'It can't go on for ever then,' Sam said and Nikki shrugged in a noncommittal way. 'Any end in sight?' Sam persisted, parting her lips quizzically.

'Nope,' Nikki said. 'Well, not at the moment anyway. To tell you the truth, Sam, it's really starting to get me down.' She hadn't meant to say that, had meant to keep her own counsel, keep her matrimonial problems to herself.

'I can see that,' Sam said. 'I thought you were looking pretty stressed-out as soon as I saw you, Nikki. Your little joke about my dress didn't fool me, I know you too well.'

'You're a good friend,' Nikki said softly. 'The best.' She drank some more coffee and then put her mug on the table.

The two women were quiet for a time, neither talking nor drinking. Then Sam lifted her mug and took a long sip of coffee. After that she rested her mug on the table and stared at Nikki for several long seconds, frowning. Finally she said, 'I know what you need.'

'A bit of retail therapy,' Nikki said, brightening slightly.

'Wrong,' Sam replied, with a shake of the head.

'What *do* I need then, wise one?' Nikki asked with a slightly forced smile.

'One of my massages,' Sam said, not skipping a beat. 'It'll do you the world of good, believe me, untense all those muscles. You'll leave this apartment a different woman.' Nikki would remember those words.

'A massage, huh. Do you do 'relief'?' Nikki joked, doing the quotation marks in the air gesture with her fingers.

'Why?' Sam countered. 'Do you feel in need of relief?' She smiled and looked at Nikki, her pale blue eyes engaging with hers for just a fraction longer than was necessary.

'Don't ask,' Nikki chuckled. Mark might not want sex these days. But she sure as hell did and she was feeling thoroughly deprived. She hadn't had sex for ages and ages and she resented Mark for that. But no, she scolded herself, she wasn't being fair. It wasn't his fault that he couldn't get it up these days, poor guy. Anyway, the point was it had been three whole months since he'd so much as laid a finger on her, and she was a very highly sexed woman with, well, *needs*, for God's sake. She felt a twinge of frustrated desire inside her sex, by no means the first she'd felt over the last twelve weeks.

'Come on,' Sam said, getting to her feet. 'Follow me.'

Nikki quickly finished the remains of her coffee, set the mug on the table and followed Sam as she sashayed to her bedroom.

Like the rest of Sam's apartment it was neat and tidy and furnished in a minimalist style. There were low bedside tables either side of the neatly made double bed and at its foot was a wardrobe with well-finished louvered doors. Against the wall beside that was a high-backed chair. There was a chest of drawers with an uncluttered surface up against another wall.

'Off with those clothes,' Sam said in a tone of theatrical command.

'Yes, Miss Dynamic,' Nikki said with a laugh that she was conscious was a little too loud. She undressed, folding her dress over the back of the chair and lining her shoes together under it. She squirmed out of her thong. 'I wasn't going commando like I bet you are,' she said, giving her friend a grin.

'You're not wrong there,' Sam said with a straight face.

'Shameless,' Nikki laughed.

Sam narrowed her eyes and smiled to suggest that maybe she was right in that assessment. She didn't say anything though. Instead she stopped and stared for a moment, in appreciation, at Nikki's naked form.

'Who are you staring at, mate?' Nikki said mock-aggressively in a ridiculous 'mockney' accent.

Sam raised an amused eyebrow at Nikki's impersonation. 'I love your figure,' she said, letting her eyes sweep over Nikki's body once more. 'It's so shapely, such a refreshing change from all the stick insects I work with all the time in my trade.'

'You're not so bad yourself,' Nikki replied, tilting her head back a little and lowering her eyelids, letting her gaze go up and down that floaty-clingy-sexy dress, appraise that lovely figure, those beautiful unbound breasts, those shapely thighs.

Sam gave her more than an appraising look as she did this, which did not go unnoticed by Nikki. She wants me, Nikki found herself thinking. I never realised that before. And I want her. I *certainly* never realised that before. She could imagine tonguing her friend's pussy, could imagine putting her fingers inside her. She was getting turned on and could tell that behind the impassive, slightly amused expression Sam was wearing she was turned on too.

'Get onto the bed and roll over on to your front,' Sam said, ostensibly all business. 'I'm going to knead your back from neck to ankles. You'll really feel the benefit.'

Nikki lay on her stomach on top of the bedspread and her red hair fell loosely across her face. She tucked her arms under one of the pillows, leaving the swell of her breasts visible where they pressed against the mattress. Her back sloped downward to the valley at the base of her spine, and then rose again at the graceful curve of her backside.

True to her word, Sam started at the top, touching the back of her neck. From there she moved across her shoulders, kneading the muscles there. It felt great, really relaxing, and Nikki gave herself to the experience. Next Sam began stroking gently down the top of her spine and over her shoulder blades, gliding her hand gently over her skin.

Then she planted a small kiss on Nikki's neck. 'It's so lovely to see you,' she said softly. 'You're adorable.' Nikki gave a little shudder in response. She could feel herself go wet between the legs.

Sam massaged her back some more – a kind of soft pummelling, awakening the skin, warming the muscles. 'Mmm,' Nikki said dreamily. 'You're so good at this.'

Sam moved down to her feet then and began to softly caress her calves, stroking them, feeling her slim muscles. Nikki imagined her friend kissing and licking her calves, each of her toes, *worshipping* her feet. The thought of it created an ache between her legs and her clit began to twitch.

Then Sam knelt on the bed and moved up her thighs. 'Your skin is so soft here,' she purred. The ache between Nikki's legs was getting more acute. Her pussy felt slippery. Sam pushed Nikki's legs apart to make room for herself and Nikki nearly climaxed there and then. She could feel her blood singing in her veins and her breath was coming quicker. Sam trailed her fingers lightly over her thighs. Nikki was now soaked

And then it happened. Sam plunged her fingers into all that wetness between Nikki's legs, making her groan with desire. She began pushing her fingers in and out of her pussy fast and hard and, God, it felt *so* good.

Then Sam did something else. She brought her mouth to Nikki's rear cheeks and pressed her lips to her anus, licking her until she trembled with desire. And all the while her tongue was flicking its magic over Nikki's anus she carried on masturbating her, making her clitoris pulse with a moist insistent throb until, all her nerves singing, a powerful orgasm shook her to ecstasy.

Finally Nikki's orgasm faded and she fell back down to earth. She rolled over then, revealing her naked breasts and erect nipples and the copious wetness between her thighs. She brushed her long red hair from her face and looked into Sam's eyes. 'Your turn now,' she said.

Sam's eyes were shining and her breathing shallow as she pulled her dress off, exposing herself entirely to her friend, her lover. Her body was perfect, Nikki thought. She pulled Sam down into her arms and pressed her lips to hers and kissed her hard as she rolled on top of her. Sam kissed her right back and the kiss felt fantastic.

Nikki then put her lips to Sam's throat and licked a gentle trail down to her sex and began kissing her there. Her pussy was as wet and gleaming as her own and Nikki subjected it to a persistent licking. Sam groaned deeply and ran her hands up over her stiff nipples as Nikki licked deep inside her. She cried out in total abandon when she licked her to a blissful orgasm.

Then Nikki slithered back up the bed and the two women looked at each other. They held the look, their eyes locked, and then they both smiled. No words were necessary. They kissed for a very long time after that, losing themselves in the kiss. Then they lay quietly on their backs, Nikki's arm under Sam's neck, Sam's head on her left shoulder. Their naked bodies were damp from their recent efforts.

'I love you,' Sam said 'I always have, you know. I love everything about you.'

Nikki sighed. 'I love you too,' she said. It was true. She'd always loved Sam as the closest of friends and now they had enjoyed the most incredible sex together as well. What was that but romantic love? Or *was* it just sex? It certainly wasn't any old sex, that was for sure. This was the kind of sex she'd been denied for too long – mind blowing, ecstatic, out of this world. She loved Sam for it. She needed her for it. She ached for it. They made love again. And again. And again, over and over.

It was only when they finally stopped and Sam, all passions spent at last, lay slumbering peacefully by her side, that the guilt began to set in with Nikki. What on earth was she going to do about Mark, she wondered anxiously. She looked up at the ceiling, her face clouded with concern. One thing was certain, she told herself. She must not tell him about what had happened between her and Sam. It was essential that she keep quiet about that. It would have to be her guilty secret.

And that was what it remained for the next three months as her affair with Sam raged like a forest fire. Finally Sam gave her an ultimatum. 'It's him or me,' she told her simply. Nikki was fed up with all the deception, all the lies she'd been telling Mark about non-existent business trips she was going on all the time, the fictitious conference she'd attended in Paris, the other in Milan. Not that he took any real notice of anything she said these days.

Things really were at their lowest ebb between Nikki and her work-obsessed husband. She saw Mark very rarely indeed now and when she did, he just wasn't there. He was present in the flesh, sure, but it was like his mind had travelled to another planet – the planet Simpson and fucking Gray. He was completely and utterly consumed by his work now, by his overwhelming ambition. 'It's him or me,' Sam had said. Nikki made her choice

Chapter Fifteen

'IT WAS THE RIGHT choice too, Paul, no doubt about it,' Nikki said, continuing her account. 'Because it was through Sam that I first discovered my great passion for erotic domination. In exploring that passion to the maximum I've also ended up making a very good living out of it. And a very enjoyable one as well – I truly love my work. Sam taught me that too, taught me that if you really love what you do you're more likely to make a success of it. You could say that all in all I owe that woman a great deal. But it certainly didn't feel like it at the time, that's for damn sure. I'll explain why.' And that's what she proceeded to do …

Nikki gazed out of the bedroom window of number 53 Palling Court, the tenth-story West End apartment that she'd shared with her lover Sam for the last two years. It was getting dark and was raining slightly, specks pattering on the glass. Through the misty rain Nikki could see the thick clots of cars, their headlights on now, that filled the streets of central London. She looked over in the direction of the River Thames, its grey waters more than usually sombre in the darkening light. Nikki switched on the bedside lamp and shut the curtains. She thought about changing her clothes but decided she wouldn't, not yet. She was wearing a dark blue denim mini-dress. It was cinched at the waist by a leather belt, which was black like her high-heeled shoes. Sam was having a shower, cleaning off the grime of London. Or so she said

Nikki didn't trust Sam any more, didn't trust a thing she said. Her instincts told her she was up to no good. Things had started to happen that had made Nikki increasingly suspicious. Sam was out more and more for a start, apparently extremely busy at work. By rights though, the take-over of her fashion design company ought to have led to the opposite happening. That had been the whole point of the merger, Sam had said. Her manner a lot of the time had also become oddly furtive, sullenly unforthcoming, which wasn't like the old Sam at all. It was as if she'd become a different person, completely different from the one Nikki had known as a lover these past two years. Sometimes when they were having sex, Nikki was almost certain she could smell the scent of another woman on her. She caught a hint of something else as well, something slightly acrid. The acid aroma of guilt, that's what she thought it was.

Nikki had got to the point where she didn't just suspect Sam was cheating on her. She knew. She just fucking knew. She was almost certain who it was she was cheating on her with too.

When Lisa Graves had become Sam's stylist six months ago, Sam hadn't stopped extolling her virtues to Nikki, saying what a find she'd been, how great she was. She had an excellent eye, Sam said, had great taste, was proving hugely instrumental in shaping Sam's latest collection. She was more than her key adviser; she was her creative muse, on and on.

Nikki found a lot of this sort of talk difficult to take seriously. She thought Sam was trying to elevate her trade to the level of high art. Nikki begged to differ. She'd got an insight into the fashion business as a result of her relationship with Sam and the people she'd met in that world and she found an awful lot of it – and them – facile beyond belief. The world of high fashion was full of parasites, as far as she was concerned. And she reckoned Lisa Graves was one of them.

What set Nikki's antennae twitching was when Sam stopped banging on about Lisa all the time, when she stopped talking about her at all. That made her uneasy, suspicious. Now she was more than suspicious. She was certain they had become lovers. Or almost certain. Nikki decided that she'd challenge her about it as soon as she came out of the shower, and that's what she did.

Sam padded into the bedroom naked, fluffing her blonde hair with a towel.

'What are you up to?' Nikki asked, throwing a combative gaze Sam's way. She noticed, averted her eyes

'Finishing drying my hair,' she said, painting an innocent expression on to her face. 'Trying to decide what to wear tonight.' She folded the wet towel neatly over a radiator.

'You know what I mean,' Nikki said, deliberately staring at her, forcing her to meet her eyes.

Sam brazened it out. She looked at her blankly as if she had no idea at all what she was talking about. 'I'm sorry,' she said. 'But I don't know what you mean.'

'I repeat,' Nikki said, her eyes darkening further as she fixed her with her most penetrating gaze. 'What are you up to?'

'Look, I don't know what you're talking about,' Sam said, still doing the Miss Innocent act. 'I'm not up to anything.'

Nikki stepped in closer, shifted her weight from one foot to another. 'You're fucking someone else, aren't you.' It wasn't a question.

Sam shook her head. 'You're out of your mind,' she replied in an affronted tone, moving seamlessly into righteous indignation mode. 'I don't have to put up with this.'

'Tell me the truth,' Nikki persisted, straining the words through her teeth

'It is the truth.'

That was when Nikki slapped her round the face. She did it very quickly. And hard. And twice. She delivered one hard crack to her left cheek and then another even harder one to her right cheek. The second slap was so hard that it sent her staggering backward. A dark flush smudged across Sam's cheekbones. But she said nothing, just began sobbing.

Nikki grasped her hair and put her face very close to hers. 'Tell me the fucking truth,' she rasped, her green eyes flashing with anger.

No reply. More sobs

'Quit blubbering!' Nikki ordered sharply. Sam swallowed back another sob, coughing.

'You're fucking someone else aren't you,' Nikki said, gazing at her with all the warmth of a rattle snake. 'You're fucking Lisa, or would it be more accurate to say that Lisa's fucking you?' Sam tended to take a passive role in lovemaking, didn't have much choice but to do so when Nikki was having sex with her.

Sam finally capitulated. She nodded yes. Her eyes were teary and red.

Bingo, thought Nikki. She'd had her suspicions confirmed. 'Say it, bitch,' she commanded.

'Lisa's fucking me,' Sam said softly, almost soundlessly.

'Why?' Nikki asked. 'Why Lisa?'

'She does things to me I like, kinky things.' Sam replied, not meeting Nikki's eye. She was trembling all over.

'What sort of things?' Nikki said, grabbing her chin, making her look at her.

'Honestly, Nikki,' Sam said in a wheedling tone. 'You really don't want to know.'

'Yes I do,' Nikki said. 'Tell me.'

'She pisses on me,' Sam said quickly.

So *that* had been it, Nikki thought. It had been the acid aroma not of guilt but of urine that she'd been picking up on her bed mate when they were having sex. 'No kidding?' she said.

'No kidding,' Sam replied.

'What else?'

'She ties my wrists up and blindfolds me and … and …'

'And what?' Nikki hissed. 'Spit it out.'

'F … fists me.'

'What else, bitch?'

'She spanks me.'

'*Spanks* you?' Nikki said incredulously, emphasizing the word. 'That's a bit tame, isn't it?'

'How do you mean?'

'Doesn't she whip you, take a belt to you?'

'No, she never has.'

'Why for Christ's sake?'

'We didn't want to leave any marks,' Sam explained. 'We didn't want to make you suspicious.'

'Didn't work, did it,' Nikki said with a snort of derision.

'No,' Sam said quietly. She bowed her head in apparent shame.

'Would you like *me* to beat you?' Nikki asked.

'Y … yes,' Sam said falteringly, but she was starting to look shifty, expectant.

'Punish you for what you've done?'

'Yes.' Sam's eyes had begun to light up.

'Really?'

'God, yes,' Sam gasped. It had only been a matter of moments but she had done a complete *volte-face*. She was almost drooling.

'Lay on your stomach on the bed,' Nikki ordered as she removed the heavy leather belt that she had around the waist of her denim mini-dress. She took off the dress, she was bra-less. She then removed her black shoes and her black thong.

Sam lay facedown on the bed, her face buried into the pillow, holding onto the iron head-board and twitching her thighs, waiting for Nikki to start beating her naked backside. She didn't have to wait long.

Nikki raised the black leather belt and swung it through the air. It landed with a crack on its target, causing Sam to gasp at the sudden pain that seared across her backside. She was still trying to draw breath when Nikki brought the belt down again. It was even more agonizing. A third and fourth stroke followed in swift succession and then she brought the belt down again. Each time Nikki struck Sam with it she made a noise into the pillow and her body twisted as if trying to get her grip loose from the headboard. She's loving it, the whore, Nikki thought. And so was Nikki. Her pulse was raging and there was a burning feeling between her legs. But that wasn't all. She felt liberated somehow, as if she was unleashing something deep within herself that she'd kept restrained for far too long.

As the savage beating continued, Sam began to tense and untense her thighs desperately to try and contain the furious pain, but to no effect. Nikki continued to thrash her backside mercilessly, causing numerous red wheals to appear there. Sam was crying and moaning into the muffling pillow. Her naked lacerated body glistened with sweat, her thighs with love juice.

Nikki finally stopped beating her and put the belt to one side. 'You like being fisted by Lisa, do you?' she said and Sam nodded into the pillow.

'Turn over,' Nikki instructed, her eyes still blazing but with something much more than anger now. Jesus, she was enjoying this. Her heart was pounding and her pussy was wet. Her nipples had become as tight as stones. She felt full of sexual energy, full of *power*.

Sam twisted, releasing her hold on the headboard as she rolled onto her back, her body arching towards Nikki. She was slack-mouthed and her eyes were glazed with lust, her pupils so dilated that she seemed almost to have no iris. She opened her legs wide apart, wantonly wide. Her pussy was wet and sticky and dripping with liquid.

Then Nikki put a hand down on her and started to rub, started to grind her fingers against her clitoral bud. She put two fingers into the slickness of her pussy, feeling the soft wet darkness of her insides. And Sam thrust her hips lasciviously against her probing fingers. She was in a delirium of lust, knowing more – much more – was to come.

Nikki's fingers were really working her pussy now and she twisted a third one in. She drove all three of them deep inside her, plunging hard into her wet sex. Sam was tight around her fingers as Nikki snaked her hand down to rub her stiff shiny clitoris again, this time with her thumb, and at the same time she inserted a fourth finger into her wet, wet vagina.

She forged deep into her wetness several times before she inserted her thumb. She had her whole hand inside Sam's sex now, plunged into the hot oozing wetness of her. Sam's breath was coming quicker and quicker. Her sex was soaking, drenched. Nikki's hand was drenched too as she pushed and pushed until Sam climaxed, shaking and moaning. Her face screwed up as her orgasm reached its peak and she cried out loudly. Nikki removed her hand. Her palm and wrist were soaked. The bedspread was wet with juice.

Now for that fucking bitch, Lisa, Nikki thought. She picked up Sam's cell-phone from the dressing table and threw it in her direction. 'Phone her,' she said

'Who?'

'Don't play dumb with me,' Nikki snapped. 'Lisa, who else?'

'What do you want me to say?'

'Tell her I'm away for a couple of days,' Nikki said. 'Tell her you need her now, this evening.'

'What if she says she can't come?'

'Do it.'

'I will but …'

'Just do it, bitch,' Nikki cut in. 'Tell her to be here in an hour's time.'

Sam did it, she made the call. Then she handed the cell-phone back to Nikki.

'What did she say?' Nikki asked.

'She said she'd come round.'

'In an hour?'

'In an hour.'

Great, Nikki thought. Fantastic. Enough time to do what she wanted to do. She left Sam on her back and went to the chest of drawers and put the cell-phone back on its top. She opened a drawer and took out three black silken scarves. She tied Sam's wrists to the bedstead with two of them and used the third to blindfold her. Last but not least, Nikki took hold of her own discarded black thong and stuffed it into Sam's mouth.

An hour later the silence of the apartment was broken by a sharp buzz. Nikki went to the panel by the front door to respond. 'Yeah,' she said in a passable imitation of Sam's voice. 'It's me,' Lisa said, announcing her presence at the apartment block's entry panel. Nikki buzzed her in so that she could push open the front door. A few moments later there was another sharp sound, the doorbell. Nikki was still naked when she opened the door. Lisa looked startled. She gave a sharp intake of breath not at Nikki's nudity but that it was her, not Sam, who had come to the door. Nikki had gone away for a couple of days, that's what Sam had said. What the hell was going on?

Nikki looked at the girl's confused face and then let her gaze wander down her body. She had to admit she could see why Sam had fallen in lust with Lisa. She was remarkably good-looking, a brunette with a small pretty nose, full lips and clean white teeth. She had a youthful face and unusual grey eyes. Nikki didn't like her eyes, though. They looked sly.

Lisa was dressed in a shiny dark grey top with no bra, her nipples stiff and sticking out underneath the fabric. She also had on a skimpy black leather skirt – no more than a pelmet – and flat black pumps. She was quite petite and her hands, their nails covered in dark red polish, were small. They were positively dainty, Nikki thought. She used one of those tiny hands to fist Sam. So fucking what!

'Where's Sam?' Lisa asked suspiciously.

Nikki gazed at her with a calmness she didn't feel. Then her lips slowly broke into a reassuring smile. 'Don't be concerned,' she said. 'Everything's OK. Sam's told me all about your affair with her and I don't mind.'

Lisa's mouth fell open. 'You don't?'

'No, not at all,' Nikki said, holding her with her green eyes, her winning smile, her *seductive* smile. Her voice remained perfectly calm, belying the seething emotions she felt within. 'I want you too,' she added. 'Sam and I both want you.'

Nikki watched her think, could see her breath quickening. 'You do?' Lisa asked.

'Un-huh.'

'Oh.' She was lost for words.

'Come into the bedroom,' Nikki said. 'Sam's waiting there for you – for us. Follow me.'

Lisa gasped in surprise and ill-concealed erotic pleasure when she was confronted by the sight of Sam in the bedroom, wrists bound to the headboard, blindfolded and gagged. Her eyes gleamed too and her breathing became short and shallow. Nikki could see her excitement, could tell she was turned on big-time. This was going to be *her* kind of sex.

'Take off your clothes,' Nikki said.

'Sure,' Lisa smirked. She tried to present a cool exterior as she undressed, like she did this sort of thing all the time, it was no big deal. But her eyes were even shinier now, her breathing even shallower and her face had become heavily flushed. She looked good naked, Nikki thought. She was well shaped and had high small breasts with nipples as hard as bullets. Her sex was shaven clean.

Lisa chewed at her lip and waited for Nikki to tell her what to do next. This was Nikki's show, Lisa had clearly decided. And she was more than happy to be a part of it.

'Time to play,' Nikki said, gesturing to Lisa to come over to the bedside. 'I want you to get on your hands and knees on the bed and lick Sam out.' Lisa obediently got on to all fours and brought her lips to Sam's sex. She was soon sucking and licking her pussy voraciously, making her shiver and squirm in her bonds.

Nikki buckled on a strap-on dildo and doused it with lube as Lisa continued to move her tongue hungrily over the slippery lips of Sam's sex, lapping at her, drinking from her. Nikki admired the way Lisa wiggled her backside in the air, admired the straining hollow of her hips, as she worked so energetically on Sam's pussy with her mouth and tongue.

Nikki didn't rush to start fucking Lisa but she didn't waste any time either. She eased the strap-on dildo into Lisa's tight moist sex, causing her to issue a pussy-muffled groan of pleasure. Nikki started to slowly pump into her from behind. All the while Lisa continued to lick and lap at Sam, her face glistening with her juices.

Nikki carried on fucking Lisa with the strap-on, thrusting in and out in a slow rhythmic motion, her hands on her quivering thighs as Lisa continued to lick inside Sam. Finally Sam groaned deeply beneath her gag and shuddered to an almighty climax.

Lisa hadn't climaxed though, Nikki knew that. But then Nikki wasn't finished either, not by a long chalk. She withdrew the strap-on from Lisa's wet pussy and, pulling her head back by her hair roughly, began to push the dildo into the opening of her anus.

Lisa squealed loudly. 'You're hurting me,' she whimpered.

'Good,' Nikki replied as she pushed the dildo through her tight sphincter and entered her fully.

She started to move in and out, pushing the dildo right inside each time, and before long Lisa began to push herself back on it as her excitement grew and her pain turned to pleasure. She moaned with the movement, luxuriated in it. Nikki had started slowly but soon speeded up her thrusts, pushing hard, and Lisa started to masturbate, using her fingers on herself to the same rhythm as the strap-on dildo going in and out of her anus. Nikki went faster still, penetrated her further, hammered into her until her body was shaking to its very depths. Finally Lisa began a long drawn-out moan and climaxed convulsively.

Nikki withdrew the dildo and Lisa collapsed, panting, onto Sam. She was now lying right on top of Sam – Sam her erstwhile secret lover, Sam, who was still in bondage, her wrists tied as securely as ever to the headboard, her blindfold and makeshift gag still in place.

Everything happened very quickly after that. Nikki unbuckled and removed the strap-on dildo. She climbed on to the bed and stood over Lisa and Sam with her legs apart. She unleashed a great golden stream of urine over the two women. The hot rain of piss saturated them. 'Hey,' protested Lisa, looking round and getting a burst of urine in the face for her trouble.

'Fuck you,' said Nikki.

Nikki climbed off the bed. She dried her soaking thighs with

Lisa's blouse and threw it onto the two piss-sodden women. She put on her dress and shoes. She stared at Lisa and Sam with quiet contempt as she was dressing, her eyes as hard as rivets. Nikki strode over to stand next to the bed. She took in a deep breath and let it out. Then she lifted Sam's piss-bespattered blindfold. Nikki looked for a long moment direct into Sam's startled, panic-stricken eyes. They were so wide she could see the whites above and below the pupils

'I'm leaving you, Sam, you cunt,' Nikki spat out finally, fixing her with her most withering gaze yet. 'We are no longer friends. In fact I don't ever want to see your treacherous face again. I think you're contemptible. I'll leave you to the person you deserve, this sly-eyed bitch – your ever so dominant lover. What a fucking joke that is!'

Sam's eyes remained as wide as saucers. 'Mnhhhh,' was all she could manage from beneath her gag.

'That's the most intelligent thing I've heard you say in a long time,' Nikki said with a dry laugh. 'Oh and Sam – my thong,' she added, pushing the makeshift gag it was being used for further into her mouth. 'You can keep it. Consider it a gift.'

Nikki slung her handbag over her shoulder and took hold of the small suitcase she'd hastily packed earlier while she and the blindfolded, gagged and bound Sam had been awaiting Lisa's arrival. As Nikki walked out of the front door of the apartment, she couldn't stop herself smiling, thin mirthless smile though it was. Revenge is sweet, she said to herself. And it's sour, too. As sour as piss.

Chapter Sixteen

THINKING ABOUT IT AFTERWARDS, it seemed to Paul that the moral of that story was a very simple one: Don't piss off Mistress Nikki unless you want her to retaliate in kind – a horrendous prospect at every level. *Eugh!*

Paul wasn't in any imminent danger of pissing Nikki off, though, quite the reverse. Because soon after he'd arrived at the Camden Town address for his next disciplinary session with the dominatrix she informed him that even though she wasn't actually making any money out of him he was definitely her favourite slave of the moment. He'd done it, she told him, and done it very quickly: he'd actually beaten his 'twin' Tony into second place in her affections.

Then she qualified her statement. He was currently her favourite *male* slave, she said. Her absolute favourite was a highly sexed, highly masochistic blonde-haired young sub called Sarah. Nikki said that Sarah had inherited a huge fortune from her filthy-rich father, who'd died several years ago.

Sarah could therefore well afford Nikki's undeniably expensive services, which she used frequently. Sometimes she came to see her alone, Nikki said, sometimes accompanied by her lover, Julie. Both women were bisexual, she added.

'Would you like to meet Sarah?' Nikki asked, her green eyes gleaming.

Is the Pope a Catholic? Paul thought irreverently. 'Yes, Mistress,' he replied.

'Good,' she said. 'Because she's due here in an hour. Incidentally, I've told her that she must be completely naked under her leather coat when she arrives.'

Paul smiled inwardly to himself and he felt his cock stiffen. Mistress Nikki was always full of surprises. And he was in seventh heaven …

*   *   *

73

Flash forward sixty minutes. Nikki was standing in her living room and was a vision of naked loveliness, wearing nothing but a pair of highly polished red leather shoes with high heels that were so sharply tapered they could easily have been classified as lethal weapons.

Paul was kneeling at her feet. His head, face and neck were encased in a black leather hood. It had apertures for the eyes, nostrils and the mouth. The mouth hole had been closed though, since Nikki had gagged Paul with a red ball gag as soon as she'd got the hood over his head. In addition she had cuffed his wrists and ankles with black leather cuffs, clamped his nipples painfully with clover clamps and buckled his erect cock into a tight black leather sheath.

There was a ring at the doorbell which, after taking a quick glance through the peephole, Nikki answered. Paul watched through the open living room door as Sarah presented herself to her Mistress exactly as instructed. Her body, which he saw was delightfully voluptuous, was completely naked under the long black leather coat that she immediately removed along with her high-heeled shoes, which were also black. She had short blonde hair that complimented her elfin face, big mahogany-brown eyes and plump full lips.

Nikki told Sarah to come into the living room. 'This is slave Paul,' she said, gesturing in the direction of the hooded, gagged and kneeling male with the clamped nipples and leather sheathed hard-on. Sarah nodded to him, giving him an engaging smile, her wide eyes sparkling. And Paul nodded back to her in all his horny, leather-hooded anonymity.

Mistress Nikki buckled a red leather slave's collar round Sarah's neck, and cuffed her wrists and ankles with red leather cuffs. Then she attached chained metal clamps to her nipples, causing her to gasp and her beautiful face to grimace in discomfort.

The dominatrix told Paul to stand up then. She led the two slaves out of the living room, down the long corridor and into the dungeon. 'Sarah,' she instructed. 'Lie on your front on the bondage table.'

Nikki put a soft red leather blindfold over Sarah's eyes and gagged her using a red ball gag identical to the one with which

Paul was gagged. She also used metal trigger clips to clip her wrist cuffs behind her back and her ankle cuffs together.

She then turned her attention to Paul. 'Lie face down on the bondage table next to Sarah,' she demanded before securing his arms and legs in the same way as those of the young woman. She left him ball-gagged as he was and used the eye-flap attachment on his leather hood to blindfold him as well. Both he and Sarah could now see nothing at all but blackness in the dungeon in which they lay together side by side in bondage.

Mistress Nikki went on to take it in turns to beat Sarah and Paul with a succession of paddles, floggers and canes, adding to the blazing heat of their pain by running a multi-spiked stimulator over the punished areas of their bodies as they struggled lamely against their bonds.

Nikki stopped torturing the two slaves in due course. She removed the eye flap attachment from Paul's leather hood, took off his ball gag, and freed his arms and legs by unclipping his wrist and ankle cuffs. She told him to get down from the bondage table and await further instructions.

The dominatrix then turned her attentions to Sarah again. She released her ankle cuffs but not her wrist cuffs, which remained clipped together behind her back. She told her to turn onto her back, upon which she removed her ball gag but not her blindfold or nipple clamps. She then instructed Sarah to open her legs wide, going on to clip her ankle cuffs to the chains on either end of the bondage table. This left Sarah's now sopping-wet pussy obscenely exposed.

'Lick her, Paul,' Mistress Nikki demanded and he immediately got into position and did as he'd been told. He leant forward over the bondage table, poked his tongue out of the mouth hole of the leather hood and began to perform cunnilingus on Sarah, making her moan with pleasure. He continued lapping at her sex, his tongue on her clitoris insistent as she moaned and quivered with passion within her bonds. Then Nikki told Paul to stop what he was doing and to get on to his knees.

'I want you back in bondage,' she said, looking down at his kneeling, hooded, nipple-clamped form. She clipped his wrist cuffs together behind him and his ankle cuffs together also.

Mistress Nikki went on to release Sarah's arms and legs and to remove her blindfold. Next she told her to stand up and, when she had, she carefully removed her nipple clamps. She then kissed Sarah full on the lips, a hard passionate kiss that forced the blonde girl's head back.

'I'm going to fuck you senseless now, Sarah,' Nikki announced, taking hold of a strap-on dildo harness, which she slipped into and buckled into place. She affixed a black rubber shaft to its front. 'Climb onto the bondage table again and lie on your back with your legs apart,' she instructed as she kicked off her lethal high heeled shoes.

Mistress Nikki came briefly over to the hooded, kneeling, bound and nipple-clamped Paul and gagged him with the red ball gag once more. She also replaced the eye flap attachment to his leather hood so that he was blindfolded as well. The dungeon for him was blanketed once more in impenetrable darkness.

He heard but could not see Mistress Nikki fucking Sarah noisily, energetically, lasciviously. He was shaking with excitement as he knelt in his bondage in the dark, unable to see or speak but able to hear and imagine only too well. It was such delicious torment for him.

Paul continued to suffer in silence and in darkness as he listened to Nikki having rampant sex with Sarah. With a dizzying orgasmic sensation that at first almost made him faint, he felt his leather-sheathed cock engorge further and ooze cum. It kept on oozing cum for a long, long time.

Chapter Seventeen

TWO DAYS IS A hell of a long time. It is anyway when you're counting virtually every minute, as Paul found himself doing until the next time Mistress Nikki had said she'd see him. At last that time had arrived.

It was just the two of them on this occasion, no Sarah, and Nikki didn't feel like disciplining Paul in her dungeon. She wanted instead for them to stay right where they were, which was in her living room, both of them stark naked.

Mistress Nikki was seated on her black leather easy chair, one hand languorously caressing her sex, the other holding the handle of the rattan cane with which she'd just beaten Paul. He was kneeling on the floor by her side, his backside covered in smarting welts, his cock stiffly erect.

'Confess to me something wicked you've done in the past,' Nikki demanded. 'I will then punish you for it.'

'What sort of punishment, Mistress?' Paul asked nervously.

'I don't know yet,' she replied. 'It depends what you confess. I'll make the punishment fit the crime.'

'I see, Mistress,' Paul said, his voice hesitant.

'Come on, slave,' Nikki pressed, a little impatient now. 'There must be something you did in your past that you felt was particularly wicked. Get it off your chest. Tell your Mistress all about it.'

There *was* something. Thinking about it was bad enough, Paul had found previously, and he'd always tried his best to avoid bringing it to mind. Talking about it would be difficult. It certainly had been all those years ago when he'd sought absolution for what he'd done from the parish priest in the confession box. But, that was then. This was now, and after some of his more recent experiences ...

Anyhow, he told himself, the fact was that Mistress Nikki had instructed him to tell her about it so he'd better comply – and pronto as well before she got annoyed. Paul took a deep breath and began his account. 'It goes back to when I was a teenager, Mistress,' he said. 'At the time in question I had hardly any experience of the opposite sex. I was also years away from recognizing my submissive and masochistic nature.

'I was a real late developer sexually and had only recently discovered masturbation. But I found it a guilty pleasure because I'd been raised as a devout Catholic, a religion that teaches that self-pleasuring is sinful. I'm not religious now, haven't been for a long time, but what I'm about to confess would certainly be regarded as wicked by the Catholic Church. In fact they would call it a mortal sin.'

'Go on,' said Mistress Nikki. 'You're beginning to interest me.' She put the cane to the side of the chair and started to pleasure herself in earnest, working her fingers rhythmically between the lips of her sex.

'It all started on a Sunday, Mistress,' Paul continued. 'I was looking forward to the week ahead as it was a half-term holiday. I was attending Mass as usual, but instead of worshipping God I was on my knees worshipping the pretty blond altar server – Jerry was his name – who was assisting the priest with the service …'

Jerry was a year older than Paul and lived a few streets away from him with his widowed mother. She and Paul's mother were friendly through their involvement with the church but Jerry and Paul were only passing acquaintances. On this occasion, though, as their mothers talked to one another after the service, Jerry and Paul also got into conversation and were getting on very well.

'What are you doing this week?' Paul asked.

'I've nothing planned,' Jerry replied. 'How about the two of us going swimming tomorrow afternoon?'

Paul said he thought this was a good idea and they made arrangements to meet.

That night Paul couldn't resist the temptation to masturbate as he imagined what Jerry might look like without clothes – he was about to find that out, and a hell of a lot more besides.

Paul and Jerry got together the next day and made their way to the nearby open-air swimming pool. As they walked along, idly chatting about this and that, Paul allowed his gaze to wander up

78

and down Jerry's body. He couldn't help thinking how good he looked in his tight jeans. He admired the perfect shape of his rear moulded into the denim, and the impressive bulge at the front.

Although the weather was reasonably mild that day, there were a lot of wet-looking clouds in the sky, and when the two young men arrived they found that the pool was only sparsely attended. There was a slight breeze that ruffled the water, which looked cold. They went into the changing rooms and, at Jerry's suggestion, shared a cubicle. As Jerry stripped off, Paul was surprised, and turned on, to notice that he hadn't been wearing any underwear beneath those tight jeans. Paul was aware that his cock was starting to swell when he slipped into his swimming trunks, and he found it a decided relief – an embarrassment averted – to run on ahead and plunge into the chilly water of the swimming pool.

Jerry and Paul stayed in the pool for about an hour, splashing about, and it gradually warmed up. Every once in a while the sun even deigned to reveal itself through a break in the clouds, allowing reflected light to dance on the rippling blue water. Jerry and Paul swam and played in the pool innocently enough. Well OK, maybe they did make physical contact a *bit* more than was strictly necessary in their games.

When they got out of the water the changing room was empty apart from them. They dried off in the same cubicle, still in their swimming costumes. However their bulges were becoming increasingly pronounced and when Paul took off his swimming trunks his cock sprang out erect.

'Mmm, that looks very nice,' said Jerry, who pulled down his trunks to reveal his own lengthening erection. 'Come on,' he said, his member now as full and stiff as Paul's. 'Let's wank off together.'

Feeling light-headed and extremely excited, Paul encircled his erect cock with his fingers as he watched Jerry bring a hand to his own erection. They both rubbed their cocks up and down vigorously, climaxing at virtually the same time. And equally lavishly too, spraying out streams of sticky wetness onto each other with great force. It was an amazing feeling for Paul – his first time masturbating with anyone else – and the most intense sexual experience that he'd so far had in his young life.

Paul and Jerry then showered, dried themselves and dressed. They headed for home, both of them more than a little subdued. They said very little as they strode along, lost in their own guilty thoughts. Just as they were about to part, however, Jerry brightened. 'Fancy coming round to my house tomorrow?' he said. He told Paul that his mother would be at work so they'd have the place to themselves.

'That'd be great,' Paul replied.

'It's a date, then. See you around eleven.' Jerry's face suddenly broadened into a grin. 'Hey and no more wanking until then.'

That proved easier said than done. Paul twisted and turned uneasily in his bed that night. His mind was in a whirl going over and over what Jerry and he had done together and what might happen tomorrow. According to his Church all these 'impure thoughts' were a sin but the feelings of guilt this caused just seemed to make his cock harder. He was excited as much as anything by the intoxicating shame of his own arousal. Even so, although it took a deal of willpower, he didn't touch himself that night.

The next day Paul killed time in the morning trying to decide what to wear for his 'date'. A clean white T-shirt and one of his pairs of jeans, he thought. On a whim, he removed his underwear at the last minute, taking a leaf out of Jerry's book, and squeezed into the tightest pair of jeans he possessed.

Paul set off, slightly nervous but very excited, the knot in his stomach no competition for the throbbing of his shaft. His growing sense of anticipation and the rough feel of the tight denim against his cock meant that he was in a high state of sexual arousal by the time he arrived at Jerry's house.

When Jerry answered the door Paul was struck anew by how attractive he was, with his blond hair falling over his forehead; that pretty face and lithe physique. He was wearing nothing but the jeans he'd worn the day before, which clung to his form like a second skin.

'Hi there, you're looking good,' Jerry said, reaching over and squeezing the bulge in Paul's jeans. Paul did the same to him, feeling the warmth of his cock beneath the skin-tight denim.

'Would you like a coffee or anything else to drink?' Jerry

asked.

'No thanks, I'm fine,' Paul replied.

'You sure are,' he said with a laugh. 'Follow me, we'll go up to my room and fool around.'

Once in his bedroom they hastily stripped and were soon on his bed mutually masturbating, their excitement growing and growing. They climaxed simultaneously in great bursting spurts, and then lay together in the afterglow, the cum on their bellies intermingling.

They washed themselves and put on their jeans, then went and had a snack and just hung out for a while. But it wasn't long before their lust erupted again and their swelling members were straining once more against the tight denim that covered them. Jerry began smoothing his palm over Paul's bulge, pressing it, teasing it. And Paul reciprocated. The two young men were soon naked and erect again, masturbating each other feverishly until the seed exploded from their hard cocks once more. And for most of the rest of that afternoon they simply couldn't keep their hands off each other.

'How about tomorrow?' asked Jerry, as Paul was about to leave.

'You bet,' he replied eagerly.

It seemed like an eternity to Paul until they met the next day. Jerry must have felt much the same way, he assumed, because as soon as he let Paul into the house he pulled him towards him. The two young men hugged while rubbing their bulging cocks together, getting more and more turned on. They then went up to Jerry's room, stripped naked again and began mutually masturbating once more. Then the mood changed …

'Kneel down,' Jerry said all of a sudden, his tone chilly with command. Paul, somewhat to his own surprise, obeyed in an instant. 'Now suck me off,' Jerry added, 'and make a good job of it.'

Paul was determined to do just that. He engulfed Jerry's stiff cock with his lips and swirled his tongue around its swollen head. His tongue laved his cock, licking the thickness, his lips kissing and rubbing against it so that it flexed and strained against his mouth. Next he began sucking on Jerry's shaft with slow regular movements, then faster, then slower, then faster still. Paul felt great: deliciously wicked, thoroughly debauched and perverted and – best of all – *sinful*.

Paul had been blowing him for a while when Jerry announced, 'I'm going to climax soon.' His voice was full of sexual tension but just as commanding as before. 'When I do,' he added, 'I want you to swallow my cum, every last drop.'

Paul wanted to do that too, yearned to do it. He could taste the beads of liquid seeping constantly from the slit of his cock and knew that they would soon be a gushing torrent. Then it happened. Jerry emitted a strangled moan and erupted to a shuddering orgasm, his cock gushing wad after wad of creamy cum deep into Paul's mouth. And Paul did exactly as he'd been told to do. His head still furiously pumping, he drew down every ounce of the semen that spurted onto the back of his tongue, taking it deep into his throat and swallowing.

'There's not a lot to add, Mistress,' Paul concluded, his face turned up to Nikki as he knelt before her. 'We carried on meeting in the same way for the rest of that week, and the following Sunday saw me at Mass on my knees again, my cock pulsing constantly as I worshipped that beautiful blond altar server. As a devout Roman Catholic I knew what I was feeling and what I'd done was sinful and wicked in the extreme, utterly depraved, but I just couldn't help myself. That, Mistress, is my shameful confession to you.'

Mistress Nikki had been pleasuring herself constantly throughout Paul's account, her fingers making an increasingly liquid sound. She removed those fingers, now sticky-wet with love juice, from between her swollen pussy lips. Then she stood up. 'That certainly was *extremely* wicked, slave,' she said, looking down at Paul, her green eyes shining. 'Is there anything you'd like to add to your account before I punish you for your wickedness?'

Paul thought for a moment before replying. 'There's this, Mistress,' he then said. 'After I'd got over my crush on Jerry I fell head-over-heels for my first girlfriend. Cathy was the girl's name and there was a really strong sexual chemistry between us. I vowed to myself after her that I'd never play with another guy's cock again and *certainly* never suck another cock. It wasn't a religious thing – I became a lapsed Catholic around that time. It was because I knew for certain, due to my sexual experiences with her, that I wasn't gay. And I stuck one hundred per cent to those resolutions despite certain temptations that came my way ...'

'Until I forced you to do otherwise,' Nikki interrupted. 'I love it. Doesn't make what you did with that altar server any less wicked, though, does it, slave?'

'No, Mistress.'

'I'm glad you agree,' she said. 'Now get on to all fours and prepare to receive your punishment.'

Mistress Nikki picked up the rattan cane she'd used on Paul earlier, gave it a couple of practice strokes through the air and then: swish! Paul suffered acutely the sharp sting of the cane's stroke as Nikki brought it down hard across the cheeks of his already punished backside. Swish! The next stroke was even more painful, as was the one that followed it and the one after that. For a long time the room resounded with the swish and crack of rattan against flesh. Nikki caned Paul's backside remorselessly until it was covered with clear stripes. But he gritted his teeth and took his punishment, took it until the pain lacing through him became so excruciating that in desperation he had to beg for mercy.

The naked dominatrix stopped caning Paul at that point and moved to his front. She placed herself on all fours, her rear splayed open, the pink opening of her anus twitching invitingly in his face. 'Lick my arsehole while I go back to pleasuring myself,' she instructed, looking at him briefly from over her shoulder.

Paul obeyed immediately and licked her pulsating anal hole with vigour. He darted his tongue in and out, feeling her anal muscles contracting around it as she continued to masturbate ever more furiously.

'Now bring yourself off,' she demanded, her voice throaty with desire. 'I want you to come over my arsehole and then lick it all up, swallow the lot.'

Again Paul did exactly as his Mistress told him. And as she used her fingers to bring herself, trembling ecstatically, to a violent orgasm, he too shuddered to a powerful climax. Convulsions shook his body as his cock erupted, pumping out a stream of ejaculate over her beautiful anus. Then, obedient slave that he was, he licked up and swallowed all that cum – every last drop.

Chapter Eighteen

THE NEXT TIME THAT Paul saw Sarah was the first time she saw him – without a leather hood covering his face, that is. When she arrived at Mistress Nikki's home for her next joint session with Paul and removed her long black leather coat, she revealed that on this occasion she had not been nude underneath it. No, this time she was dressed all in red leather: high boots, tight top and even tighter trousers. She looked luscious, incredibly seductive.

Mistress Nikki fell into the same category. What few clothes she was wearing – a halter top that barely contained her lovely breasts and a tiny skirt underneath which she was nude – were of soft black leather. Paul stood several paces behind Nikki and was buck naked, sporting a half hard-on. Sarah caught his eye and gave him a wicked grin. It made his cock twitch.

'If looks could thrill,' Nikki muttered dryly, the comment made almost to herself.

Sarah heard her, though, and immediately switched her gaze to the dominatrix. 'You look really lovely in that outfit, Mistress,' she said ingratiatingly, her big brown eyes aglow.

'Why, thank you, slave,' Nikki replied. 'You look lovely too in all that red leather you've managed to spray onto your body but I want you to take it off even so. Paul, go into the changing room with Sarah and help her to strip naked. Then both of you report to me – I'll be in the dungeon.'

Once they were in the changing room, Paul helped Sarah to peel off her skin-tight leather clothes and boots. Paul's cock began to swell increasingly and was fully erect by the time Sarah was as naked as he was. He eyed his curvy young companion, giving her a hot look. 'You look fabulous,' he said.

'Thanks, Paul. So do you,' she replied with another wicked grin, adding, 'My, what a handsome devil you are without your leather hood. Give me a kiss.' They kissed for a long moment, tongues flicking together, and Paul's cock became even more fiercely erect.

Sarah broke the kiss and started masturbating Paul, gripping her hand round his shaft and pushing her fist up and down. 'I'm going to bring you off before we report to Mistress Nikki in the dungeon,' she said with a giggle, starting to jerk more forcefully at his cock.

'No you're not, you minx,' Paul laughed, stepping with evident reluctance away from the blonde's seductive grasp. 'Now, hurry up. We mustn't keep Mistress Nikki waiting, you know that.'

The two of them hurried down the corridor and arrived, panting, in the dungeon. Nikki narrowed her eyes, taking note both of Paul's raging hard-on and of the pre-cum that liberally coated its tip. 'It is obvious to me that you two slaves have been playing with each other without my permission,' she said sternly. 'I will have to punish you severely for that, do you not agree?'

'Yes, Mistress,' came the nervous joint reply. Sarah *started* it, Paul felt like adding on his own behalf but the words sounded ridiculously whiny and childish in his head.

'Your punishment can however wait until I have taken my pleasure,' Nikki said. She then threw herself back onto the leather-covered bondage table, lifting and opening her legs wide. 'I feel so fucking horny today it's unbelievable,' she declared. 'Service me, slaves. You, Sarah, lick and finger my pussy. Paul, pleasure my arsehole with your tongue.'

The two of them immediately moved to obey. Sarah pressed her face into Nikki's sex, which was already gleaming with silvery wetness. At the same time, Paul planted a kiss between the cheeks of her backside, touching his lips to the tight opening of her anus. He pushed his sinuous tongue into Nikki's anal hole, pushing against the rim of muscles and going into her body. Meanwhile Sarah licked deep and hard into her pussy while stroking the domme's stiff clit with her fingers.

Nikki opened herself further, lifting her pussy to Sarah's all too welcome attentions. Sarah's fingers went deep into Nikki's sex, penetrating hard and fast. With her mouth she concentrated on Nikki's clit, teasing it with her pink wet tongue so that the dominatrix writhed with pleasure. All the while Paul was licking her anus hard, causing her to shiver with pleasure. Finally a shuddering groan escaped her and an instant later she climaxed convulsively.

After allowing herself a few moments to become composed, Mistress Nikki climbed down from the bondage table. She was all strict business once again by the time she'd got to her feet. 'Now we shall commence the severe punishment you two slaves have brought upon yourselves by playing with each other without my permission,' Nikki said, her eyes suddenly as cold as steel. 'You first, Sarah, over the whipping bench with you.'

'Yes, Mistress,' she said, a nervous catch in her voice, as she got into position.

'Paul,' Nikki said. 'Get on your knees and wait your turn.'

'Yes, Mistress,' he replied, hearing the break in his own voice.

Nikki began to whip Sarah with considerable ferocity. The lashes struck her backside in a regular harsh rhythm, and each time the whip cracked against her skin, Sarah cried out in pain. Nikki began to strike more quickly, inflicting ever more excruciating pain on her, and Sarah's cries came faster and faster. She began to sob, hot tears forming in the corner of her eyes and rolling down her cheeks in a constant stream. By the time Nikki stopped whipping Sarah orgasmic tremors were running through her body and her backside was bright crimson from its punishment. 'Get on your knees, slave,' Nikki ordered.

'Yes, Mistress.' Sarah sobbed, still shuddering from her agony-induced climax.

'Your turn now, Paul,' Nikki said.

'Yes, Mistress,' he replied tremulously as he got up from his kneeling position in order to change places with Sarah. He bent over the whipping bench, and awaited his punishment – correction, his *severe* punishment. That was what Mistress Nikki had said and she'd certainly delivered on her promise with Sarah. Paul's body was trembling with fear but his cock was rock hard and throbbing.

Mistress Nikki thrashed him as ferociously as she had flogged Sarah, whipping him over and over until the searing pain burned red-hot into his flesh and his aching backside was criss crossed thoroughly with the marks of the flogger.

The pain was extreme, it was excoriating, but still Nikki went on. Paul gasped and sobbed with agony and the cords stood out in his neck, it was so difficult to bear. In the end the only way he could cope with the intense pain was to block everything else out. He thought of nothing, imagined nothing, the vicious strokes that burned on his flesh his only reality. Paul felt himself on the verge of climaxing but he couldn't … It was hell. It was heaven. It was agony and it was ecstasy. It was unbelievably extreme, that's what it was, dangerously extreme.

And it couldn't go on surely, could it. *Could it?* It could go on, though, and it did go on. In fact all of this could almost be described as harmless fun compared to what Mistress Nikki had in mind for Paul in the future. It was child's play.

Chapter Nineteen

ADULT PLAY, THAT WAS what this place was all about. *Adult play for those of a kinky persuasion.* It said so on the door in neon lighting. It was a fetish store near Camden Market called *Consensual Kink* and Nikki had decided to take Paul there. She told him that she would be buying something for herself at the store and something for him.

As they paused together briefly outside the dark-windowed premises, Paul glanced over at his Mistress. He thought Nikki looked fantastic in the outfit she was wearing, which was of black leather: a short figure-hugging dress, high stiletto-heeled boots. Paul too was all in black. He had on a black T-shirt, snug-fitting leather trousers, and short boots. He was also wearing one of his AQL purchases. It was a chained collar with a padlocked front, which he had tucked discreetly beneath the neck of his T-shirt.

Paul felt a tremor of excitement when Nikki adjusted his collar so that the padlock was exposed. Then she touched his elbow and the two of them went into the darkened interior of the shop. Once inside, Nikki immediately greeted the proprietor by name. She was a beautiful woman of oriental appearance, and was wearing a purple leather mini-dress and thigh-length leather boots of the same colour. The woman was clearly a fellow dominatrix because Nikki called her Mistress Evie. 'This is Paul, my new slave,' Nikki said.

Evie's mouth settled into an approving leer. 'Very nice,' she said. 'Very nice indeed.' She offered Paul her hand and he kissed it, with a submissive bow of the head.

'We're just going to have a look round,' Nikki said.

'Feel free, my dear,' Evie replied. 'If you want any assistance let me know.' She shifted her eyes from Nikki and back to Paul then, giving him another leering gaze.

Nikki looked at him too and emitted a dry laugh. 'I think she likes you,' she said before taking his arm and steering him towards the part of the store that housed all of its BDSM items. There were whips, crops, handcuffs, clamps, various items of rubber and leather fetish-wear, masks, collars, reels of bondage tape, a variety of bamboo canes, harnesses, leads …

Nikki fingered several items before lighting on the one she wanted to buy for herself. It was almost a duplicate of the half dozen strap-on dildo harnesses she already owned. The difference was that this one had three dildo attachments. There was the strap-on itself and a pair of matching internal dildoes intended for the anus as well as the pussy.

'That's me sorted, slave,' Nikki said, picking up the item. 'Now you choose.'

There were various restraint devices in this part of the fetish store that had attracted Paul's attention but the one that appealed the most to him by far was a leather body bag. He felt himself go hot all over as he imagined himself being zipped and laced into it by Mistress Nikki and then tortured mercilessly by her.

He remembered many an occasion in the past when he'd gazed covetously at the body bags offered for sale on the AQL website, which were their most expensive products. He'd never seriously contemplated buying one, though, first because he wouldn't have been able to get himself in and out of it on his own, and secondly because of the expense. The first consideration wasn't a problem any more but the second one still was. He felt he couldn't ask Mistress Nikki to buy it for him because it cost so much. He didn't want to be presumptuous, didn't want in any way to take things for granted with her. The dominatrix, for reasons she was keeping strictly to herself, was already treating him with exceptional generosity by disciplining him regularly without charge. But she could pull the plug on the arrangement any time she chose, perish the thought. So, he definitely mustn't push his luck. Still, that body bag *was* very tempting.

Nikki gave him a sideways look. 'You like the body bag, don't you,' she said as if reading his mind.

'Yes, Mistress but …'

'It's yours,' she interrupted. 'And as soon as we get back to my place and into the dungeon I'm going to put you in it and drive you out of your tiny fucking mind.'

*   *   *

Mistress Nikki laid out the leather body bag on the dungeon floor and had Paul climb naked into it and lie on his back. It was obvious to the dominatrix that Paul was getting very excited indeed. His chest had started to heave and his cock was rigidly erect and pulsing. The body bag had two zippers, one starting at the feet, one at the neck and both ending at the waist. It had been designed that way so that a slave's genitals could be tortured without releasing him. Nikki zipped Paul in, leaving his balls and his throbbing erection exposed.

There were several large welded 'D' rings up and down the outside of the bag, so that rope could be threaded through them and the bag pulled more tightly around its occupant. Nikki picked up a length of black bondage rope and tied it tightly round the body bag. She pulled a thick black leather hood over Paul's head. It was the first time she'd used this particular hood on him. It had tiny nose holes but covered his eyes, ears and mouth, eliminating three of his senses. His sense of smell was informed with the wickedly sensuous aroma of leather.

The body bag had two tit flaps that were intended to expose a slave's nipples to torture when opened. Nikki opened them. She attached chained metal clamps to Paul's nipples and their teeth immediately bit hard into his chest. She then took two sterilized needles out of a box on the dungeon floor. She proceeded to puncture the skin of his clamped nipples with them, causing him to jerk spastically against his restraints at the indescribably sharp pain he was experiencing.

Mistress Nikki withdrew the needles but left the nipple clamps in place. She took hold of a small cat o' nine tails and began to whip Paul's exposed genitals, concentrating her blows on the head of his erect cock. When the whip landed for the first time, there was a hot flash of pain where it hit. The second wave of pain hit and the third and fourth and fifth, each time more agonizingly. Paul began to thrash around on the dungeon floor in the body bag, struggling helplessly against his restraints as the pain lanced through his body. Still Nikki went on though, and Paul's agony escalated even further until he was heaving and thrusting his body desperately and letting out pitiable cries, which escaped from under his thick leather hood.

And then something happened to him that was out of this

world. It wasn't an orgasm, not even an exceptionally intense one. It was something else, something distinctively different. An electric jolt began to radiate out from his punished genitals via his tightly clamped nipples to his brain where it exploded in a white hot brilliance that was as much ecstasy as agony.

Paul felt as though waves of electricity were surging through his body every time Nikki lashed the whip across his genitals. White hot pressure swelled within him, driving his mind out of his body. He could feel himself losing control of his own solar system, felt himself falling from its sphere. He was beyond reason now, floating free in infinite deep space, as far away from the real world as he could ever before have imagined possible, even in his wildest dreams, his wildest fantasies.

How could he ever have thought in the past that he could somehow replicate such a profound experience by means of self-bondage, Paul asked himself afterwards. Jesus, it didn't even come close. What he'd experienced this time had been the real deal. It had been what it was all about. It had been *nirvana*.

Chapter Twenty

PAUL FELT THAT THINGS were going extremely well for him with Mistress Nikki, given the fundamentally insecure nature of the relationship he had with her. He was acutely aware of the fact that she could terminate that relationship any time she liked merely on a whim. That notwithstanding, Paul was as confident as he could realistically hope to be that he remained in good favour with her.

When it came to how the dominatrix felt about him *together with Sarah*, however, he did not have the same confidence at all. What had happened the last time they'd been disciplined together had been predominantly Sarah's fault in Paul's view. But that was by the way. However one chose to read it, the fact was that as a pair he and Sarah had managed to blot their copy-book with Mistress Nikki.

Paul wondered whether, even though she'd already punished both of them severely for their transgression, the dominatrix would stop disciplining them together in her dungeon. And she did. She disciplined them together in her living room instead. It happened one weekday afternoon ...

Mistress Nikki was standing in front of the black leather couch, which on this occasion was strewn with various whips, paddles, canes, and other instruments of discipline. She had on a very high-cut basque that dug excitingly between the lips of her pussy, thigh-high boots and, oh yes, a pair of long gloves that were just a bit different: their fingers were decorated with tiny spikes.

Paul was held upright in bondage in a spread-eagled position. His leather wrist and ankle cuffs were clipped to the ends of two metal spreader bars, one hanging by chains from a ceiling hook, the other at floor level. Nikki had attached chain linked clamps to his nipples and scrotum, which gripped like pincers. Paul's mouth had gone dry and his heart was pounding with excitement. His cock was pounding too, jutting out from his body, rigid and throbbing.

Sarah was bent over a nearby table, her legs slightly apart, her arms in front of her and her wrists handcuffed. She was trembling with anticipation and her pussy was moist. Mistress Nikki looked at Sarah, then at Paul, then back at Sarah again, deciding finally that she should be the first to be disciplined.

The dominatrix started by running the spiked fingers of her gloves over Sarah's back and rear, causing her to tremble even more, this time with pain. Then she spanked her hard with both of her gloved hands, alternating the left with the right, admiring the way that the cheeks of her backside coloured more with each blow. She steadily built up the frequency and ferocity of the beating until Sarah's backside was prickly red and she could not help but let out an agonized cry of pain.

'Oh, don't you like that, slave?' said Nikki in a tone of mock concern.

'No, to be quite honest with you, Mistress,' Sarah said, wincing with discomfort. It had been a pretty ferocious start to her discipline, she thought – the very opposite of a gentle warm up.

Nikki pealed off the vicious spiked gloves. 'We'll try something different then,' she said, adding ominously: 'I've an interesting little array of disciplinary implements here that I intend to use on you two slaves this afternoon.'

Mistress Nikki foraged among the items of discipline on the couch and took hold of a red plexi-glass paddle. She immediately began to pound Sarah's rear with it, each blow an explosion of pure pain. The dominatrix carried on relentlessly until the cheeks of Sarah's backside were a blazing red. She then replaced the implement with a heavy wooden paddle and beat her backside with that until the pain that she was suffering burned even more hotly.

'You've told me, Sarah, that you don't like the feel of my spiked gloves,' Nikki said next, smiling sadistically as she foraged once again through the pile of disciplinary items on the couch. 'So, let's try this instead.' She put on a spiked leather spanking mitt and positioned herself behind Sarah once more. After giving her a harsh spanking with the mitt, she rubbed it over her punished rear, making her squeal with pain. She then removed the spiked mitt, got down on one knee behind Sarah and started licking and kissing her beautiful punished backside.

Mistress Nikki told Sarah to open her legs wider and went on to hand spank her with one hand while masturbating her with the other, her fingers penetrating the dampness of her sex hard and fast. Nikki then licked Sarah's pussy, which was gleaming now with juicy wetness, teasing her clit with her pink tongue and making her squirm. She went on to plant a kiss between the cheeks of Sarah's backside, touching her lips to her pouting anus. She pushed her tongue into her anal hole, pushing against the rim of muscles and going into her body, lick-lick-lick, as the slave groaned with pleasure.

Nikki next stood up, took hold of a cat o' nine tails and ran its handle tantalizingly over Sarah's wet pussy. She used the whip to thrash her back and rear with such remorseless ferocity that in the end it caused Sarah to scream like a banshee, her voice full of pain and anguish.

After giving Sarah a few moments to regain some of her equilibrium, Mistress Nikki told her to stay bent over the table but to put one of her knees up onto it. This made it easier for Nikki to kneel down and use her tongue once more to lick Sarah's pussy and anus, while also spanking her backside with one hand and her clit with the other.

Mistress Nikki next instructed Sarah to stand up, turn around and lie on her back on the table with her legs spread wide apart. She told her to put her handcuffed wrists behind her head with her arms outstretched. Nikki used heavyweight leather tails to whip her breasts and thighs until they were covered in wheals and sharp pain was burning into her flesh. She then buried her face between Sarah's thighs and licked her pussy again, making her moan with delight as she moved her tongue over and over, concentrating on her shiny clitoris.

'You know, Sarah,' Nikki said, 'I usually eat at this table'

Lick

Lick

Lick

'But I've never eaten anything here more delicious than your wet pussy.'

Lick

Lick

94

'Delicious.'

Lick

Lick

Lick

'Lovely.'

Lick

Lick

Lick

'So very, very wet.'

Lick

Lick

Lick

Lick

Finally Sarah could take no more of this delirious torment and shuddered to a tumultuous orgasm as wave after cresting wave of erotic bliss washed over her.

'You may get down from the table now,' Mistress Nikki said with an amused smile. She removed Sarah's handcuffs, told her to put her arms behind her back and cuffed her wrists again. 'Now, kneel down, slave,' she commanded. 'You can watch as I discipline Paul.'

Nikki strode over to the spread-eagled Paul and brusquely removed the painful clamps from his nipples and scrotum, which caused further pain to sear through him. She started masturbating him, rubbing his hard cock up and down vigorously. Then she squeezed hard and bit harder his already punished nipples, making him cry out with pain.

She continued with her discipline by flogging his chest viciously with a snake whip, each strike a hot flash of pure pain. Then she went behind him to give his backside an equally furious beating with a leather strap, delivering a solid slice of punishment each time she brought the instrument of correction down on its fleshy target.

'Some all-over attention now, slave,' she said next, taking hold of a dressage whip from the pile of items on the couch. She used this to cover his back, rear, thighs and chest with stinging welts, causing tremors of pain to run through his punished body. The dominatrix went on relentlessly like this until Paul was reduced to cringing and whimpering in agony. Only then did she cease whipping him.

'Stop snivelling, slave,' she commanded, her green eyes gleaming. 'Let's take your mind off your pain for a little while. Look above your head and tell me what you see there.'

'My wrists manacled to either end of a spreader bar hanging from chains, Mistress,' Paul replied, looking upwards as instructed.

'And what are the chains hanging from, slave?'

'A ceiling hook, Mistress.'

'That's right, and what a useful little device that ceiling hook is. You recall what I normally have suspended from that hook, don't you Paul.'

'Yes, Mistress – a hanging basket.'

'That's right,' Nikki said. 'You look better than any hanging basket, though.'

'Thank you, Mistress.'

'And what's more, you can give me so much more pleasure, hanging there completely at my mercy as you are,' she continued. 'You see, I can for example pull your hair as roughly as I want, like this.'

Yank

Yank

'I can give your face a good hard smack or two.'

Slap!

Slap!

'I can squeeze your nipples really fiercely, like so.'

Pinch

Pinch

'Spank your cock.'

Slap!

Slap!

Slap!

'Run my sharp fingernails down your thighs.'

Scratch

Scratch

Scratch

'I can give your backside a good old fashioned hand spanking, nice and hard.'

Smack!

Smack!
Smack!
'Or a paddling,'
Thwack!
Thwack!
Thwack!
'... Or a sound whipping,'
Whip!
Whip!
Whip!
Whip!
'And a severe caning.'
Swish!
Swish!
Swish!
Swish!
Swish!
Swish!

Finally overwhelmed by the escalating pain that had been inflicted on him by the cruel dominatrix and sobbing with agony, Paul begged for mercy. And she immediately ceased caning him.

After allowing him a few moments to recover himself, Mistress Nikki freed Paul from the spreader bars, handcuffed his wrists behind his back and led him over to kneel beside Sarah. 'Put your arses in the air and place your legs apart, both of you,' she commanded, adding impatiently: 'Come along, quickly now, slaves.'

'Oh, very nice,' she said when they were positioned to her satisfaction. 'Shall I tell you what you put me in mind of like that, slaves – two ornaments. Yes, two lovely ornaments, porcelain vases shall we say. And I do so admire that subtle red and white patterning,' she continued, warming further to her theme. She picked up a long, thin rattan cane, bending it in the middle as though to test it.

'But of course, there's one big difference between you two slaves and a couple of beautiful porcelain ornaments. What's that, I hear you ask. I'll tell you – one would have to be very careful not to break such exquisite pieces, whereas, you see,' she raised the cane high above her head, 'I really want to break you two ...'

Swish!
Swish!
Swish!
Swish!
Swish!
Swish!

'*Mercy, Mistress,*' the two desperate slaves both cried loudly, the excruciating pain caused by this brief but savage caning having rapidly become completely unbearable. Mistress Nikki stopped immediately.

'Well done, slaves,' she said with a sudden display of affection. 'You've done very well indeed and have really got me in the mood for some serious sex now. Stand up both of you so that I can release you from your handcuffs and in return you can help me out of these clothes.'

Shortly afterwards a nude Mistress Nikki walked the equally naked Paul and Sarah over to the black leather couch. She removed all of the disciplinary items that remained on top of the couch with a single sweep of her hand. On a small table next to the couch stood a candleholder containing two white candles and by its side a silver lighter and a purple dildo. Nikki lit the candles with the lighter and picked up the dildo.

'Let's play,' she then said, and she and Sarah began kissing sensuously. At the same time Paul got on to the couch where he lay on his back, his huge erection rearing up thick and ready and tipped with pre-cum.

'Now there's a sight for sore eyes,' said Nikki, breaking her clinch with Sarah. She then knelt down and, fastening her bright lips tight on Paul's cock and, tasting the juicy fluid leaking from its slit, she started to blow him with a will. Meanwhile Sarah came to his side, got onto her knees also, and kissed him passionately, her tongue wetly engaging with his.

Mistress Nikki then withdrew Paul's stiff cock from her mouth and stood up, telling Sarah to climb onto the couch and place her sex above his face. 'That's right, like that, Sarah,' she said, adding, 'Now stick that pretty arse of yours in the air and start sucking Paul's cock.' She obeyed with alacrity, widening her lips around his shaft and beginning to suck, her head bobbing.

Nikki moved behind Sarah and eased the dildo she was

holding into her wet pussy. She also snaked out her tongue and licked her anus quick and tight, making her squirm. Sarah brought a hand up to her own sex and rolled her fingers over her stiff clit as Nikki continued to pleasure her anus with her tongue and her pussy with the purple dildo. Sarah also carried on sucking vigorously on the hard flesh of Paul's shaft, which pulsed in her mouth as her head bobbed and bobbed.

Paul manoeuvred himself up the couch a little and replaced Sarah's masturbating fingers with the hot touch of his lips and tongue while she began sucking even more violently on his pulsing cock. Mistress Nikki carried on masturbating Sarah with the purple dildo, driving it in still further, plunging into her sopping wet sex as she also continued tonguing the pinkish hole of her anus, flick-flick-flicking at it just as Paul's tongue flick-flick-flicked at her clit.

Nikki also snaked a hand to her own sex and began masturbating hard, working her fingers feverishly between the folds of her own pussy lips. She rubbed herself all sticky with the hot liquid of her sex until her palm and wrist were soaked with the wetness of it.

The dominatrix then climbed off the couch and told Sarah to do likewise, leaving Paul laying on his back, his hard wet cock still rearing in the air. Nikki picked up the candleholder and took one lighted white candle herself, handing the other one to Sarah. The two women poured hot wax onto Paul's torso and chest, making him shiver in combined pain and pleasure as his cock squirted pre-cum into the air, which splattered back down onto his wax-covered body.

Nikki blew out the candles and returned them to their holder. She told Paul she was going to sit on his cock and fuck him. He sighed and put his hands on her waist as she straddled him. Nikki could feel the thickness of his cock impale her as she slid down on it, her pussy tight and moist. Paul moaned with her movement as she ground her hips down, his cock stiff inside her.

'Sit on his face, Sarah," Mistress Nikki instructed next and she immediately did so, bringing down her quivering thighs and guiding Paul's mouth to her sex where he straightaway began licking and lapping again. Sarah felt exquisite ripples of pleasure flow through her as his tongue moved over the lips of her sex.

Paul licked and licked at her, drank from her thirstily, his face shiny with her love juice.

Meanwhile Nikki shoved herself down on him ever more energetically, making him stiffen even more inside her. He began to thrust his hips upwards rhythmically while continuing to lick between Sarah's pussy lips like a man possessed. The two women began to moan and flush and rock back and forth on the licking, thrusting slave and all three of them got ever closer to the climaxes they knew would soon be devouring them.

The raunchy trio carried on making love in an increasingly frenzied way, pleasure pounding through their bodies, until they all climaxed simultaneously in an ecstasy of unbridled passion. They gasped and moaned in delight as muscular spasms ripped through them and Paul's liquid spurted out powerfully deep into Nikki's sex.

Mistress Nikki, Sarah and Paul lay together on the couch for a while after that, their damp bodies intertwined. Then Nikki made a move, getting to her feet 'Well now, slaves,' she said, looking down at them with heavy-lidded eyes, 'I think you'd agree, from the evidence of this memorably kinky session that we three have enjoyed together this afternoon, that serious discipline followed by serious sex is … seriously fantastic!'

'Yes, Mistress,' chorused the two sated slaves as they looked up rapturously at the beautiful red-haired dominatrix.

Chapter Twenty-one

BY THE TIME PAUL and Sarah emerged from Mistress Nikki's house the sun had set, although its glow was still lighting the sky to the west of the city. 'Serious discipline followed by serious sex has left me seriously hungry,' Sarah said with a laugh.

'Me too,' Paul replied, smiling.

'Do you think you can withstand the pangs of hunger for an hour or two longer?'

'Why do you ask?'

'My partner Julie and I are going out for a meal this evening,' Sarah said. 'I wondered if you might care to join us.'

'I'd love to.'

'Do you know *Marco's* in Knightsbridge?'

'I know *of* it,' Paul said. The place was *way* out of his league.

'It's on the opposite side of the road to Harrods.'

'It doesn't sound as if I could miss it.'

'Julie and I'll meet you outside the restaurant just before nine,' Sarah said. 'I've booked a table for two but I'll tell them to make it for three. Julie and I are well known there, so it won't be a problem. It'll be my treat, of course.'

'Thank you so much,' Paul said with feeling. He definitely couldn't afford to pay his way in a millionaires' haunt like *Marco's*.

'My pleasure,' Sarah said. 'I'd really like you to meet Julie and vice versa.'

A couple of hours later Paul, smartly dressed for the occasion in a dark suit, arrived at the entrance to *Marco's* and glanced at his watch: It was 8:45. He didn't see Sarah, didn't actually expect to see her for perhaps another five or ten minutes. Then he did spot her, crossing the busy road towards the restaurant. She was accompanied by another young woman who he assumed had to be Julie. She had brown hair cut short with a little fringe, big blue-green eyes and a full mouth. She also had a great figure, shown off to perfection by the snug-fitting short black dress she was wearing, which was almost a match for the red dress Sarah had on. Paul liked the look of Julie immediately, thought she was very attractive indeed, with bags of sex appeal.

Sarah made the introductions and the three of them entered the stylish restaurant together, a little early for their reservation, but that proved not to be a problem. The trio threaded their way through the other tables, nearly all of which were occupied, and were seated at their table by the waiter. It was in a corner of the restaurant and was set apart from the other tables, ideal for a private conversation. The table was spread with a starched linen tablecloth on which the cutlery and glasses were set. The waiter asked them if they would like a drink while deciding what they wanted to select from the menu. Sarah and Julie both ordered vodka tonics with ice and lemon and Paul scotch on the rocks. The waiter then hurried off to get their drinks.

Paul looked across the table, across the shiny cutlery and the sparkling glasses, at his two companions. He thought they both looked delectable, with their hair shimmering in the flickering candlelight and their eyes shining. The two young women were an absolute knock-out in his view: super-sexy, highly alluring. And they were here in this restaurant, which was one of the most exclusive in London, on a dinner date with him! The other diners couldn't keep their eyes off Julie and Sarah, Paul noticed, and it was hardly surprising – they were by far the most beautiful women in the restaurant.

Their waiter returned, bringing three drinks, ice cubes clinking. They then ordered the wine and decided on the food. 'I don't think you can beat the *menu de jour* in this place,' Julie said. Sarah agreed and they all opted for that, the main course of which was a delicious seafood salad.

The three of them ate their meal and drank their wine and chatted amiably. Paul could see both from their body language and the way in which Sarah often deferred to Julie in the course of conversation that the latter was the dominant partner in their relationship. Everything is relative though, he reminded himself. Julie was sexually submissive like her lover, he assumed; otherwise she wouldn't be one of Mistress Nikki's clients.

'That was fantastic,' Julie said, finishing her meal and wiping her mouth with a napkin.

'Up to *Marco's* usual superb standard,' Sarah agreed.

Paul finished eating last. 'Best meal I've ever had,' he said, adding his voice to the chorus of praise. 'Thank you again for inviting me, Sarah. I really do appreciate it.'

'You're more than welcome,' she beamed. 'Coffee everyone?'

'Please,' Julie said, Paul also, and the waiter was duly summoned.

'I gather from a comment Mistress Nikki made to me the other day that you and I have something in common, Paul,' Julie said when the coffees had arrived. 'Or rather we *had* something in common. Any idea what?'

Paul thought for a moment or two. 'None,' he said. 'Nothing that occurs to me off the top of my head at any rate, Julie.'

'Would you like me to tell you what it is?'

'I certainly would.'

'I say we *had* something in common because it goes back about five years for me,' Julie said. 'When I think about the way I was then it makes me realise just how much I've changed ...'

When Julie looked back at the person she'd been only five short years ago it felt strange – almost like a false memory of someone else's life. Had that really been her? Julie Ball had been so damn pleased with herself for 'coming out' as bisexual you'd have thought she was the first person who'd ever done it. She was so sophisticated, wasn't she? So uninhibited, so daring ... So deluded, more like.

The truth was that in her own way she was as repressed as some frustrated Victorian spinster. There was a whole dark side to her sexuality she hadn't even begun to come to terms with, let alone explore, for the simple reason that she'd yet to acknowledge that it existed at all. Let's face it, she'd said to herself afterwards wryly, you can't come out of the closet unless you've ventured in there in the first place. Julie learnt that lesson eventually, though, and in a very literal sense. It was a woman called Bridget who made it happen.

Soon after Bridget had broken up with her previous lover, a young woman called Maria, who happened to be one of Julie's oldest friends, she started making a move on Julie. Maria clearly didn't mind – her split with Bridget had been an amicable one, as Julie knew very well. The amorous interest Bridget was showing in Julie had been just fine as far as she was concerned as well. The truth was that Julie had always fancied Bridget like crazy, thought the tall, charismatic blonde with the short hair, glittering blue eyes and hour-glass figure was absolutely gorgeous.

Things developed quickly from the time Julie moved in with her. Bridget informed her early on that she was into kinky sex – whips and chains and clamps and the like – but Julie told her she wasn't interested. She really meant it too, or thought she did. The vanilla sex with Bridget was great, like nothing she'd ever experienced before and that was surely more than enough, she rationalized.

Bridget's bedroom wasn't short of clothes space and could easily accommodate the clothing Julie had brought with her. But here was the thing: the biggest closet in that room was always kept locked. Julie asked Bridget about it once and she just said, with a sly grin, 'Oh, that's where I keep all the stuff you're not interested in.' That did spike Julie's curiosity a little, she had to admit, but she didn't give it much more thought. She just blanked it out. Until, that is, one fine day when Bridget was out doing some chores …

Julie had just had a shower and had wandered back into the bedroom in the nude, feeling decidedly horny. She lay back on the bed, her head propped up by a couple of pillows, and began to masturbate. She was just starting to really enjoy herself, her fingers working away at the wetness that had begun to ooze from within her, when she noticed that Bridget's mysterious closet wasn't actually locked for once. Julie could tell because its door was slightly ajar. Her curiosity getting the better of her this time, she reluctantly stopped masturbating, swung herself off the bed and padded over to the closet.

Julie opened its door fully and what she saw then made her eyes widen like saucers. She was genuinely shocked – not so much by what she saw inside, although that was mind-boggling enough, but by its sheer volume. Hanging from the walls of that spacious closet were handcuffs, harnesses, chains, whips, paddles, gags, hoods, bondage rope, you name it – all the paraphernalia of

BDSM. Julie was also shocked by her own reaction to what she'd discovered in that closet because, despite herself, she was turned on by it – very turned on. The heady aroma of leather in there played its part as well, all but overwhelming her senses.

Julie shifted her gaze to the floor of the closet where she saw a pile of glossy black and white bondage magazines. There were some other items on the closet floor as well: a box full of different coloured pegs: black, red, purple, blue; a black leather slave's collar; and some wrist and ankle cuffs, also of black leather, which had metal trigger clip attachments; a red ball gag; and what looked at first sight like a blank video.

Julie got onto her knees, crawled into the closet a short way, and started to leaf through the pages of the bondage magazines, which showed numerous monochrome images of beautiful naked women being tied up and disciplined. Again she surprised herself because she found the striking photographs she was looking at powerfully erotic. As she gazed at those bondage photos she could feel the heat in her sex growing and growing until it seemed to permeate her whole body. Julie was soon playing with her pussy once more, imagining herself in the place of one after the other of the lovely women in those photos. She could feel her breath quicken and her nipples stiffen and her clit buzz as she wanked and wanked.

On a whim, she decided to try on the leather slave's collar that was on the floor. She liked the feel of it immediately. While she was about it, she thought she'd give the red ball gag a try too. As she buckled it into place the feeling of constriction it gave her sent a further rush of adrenaline to her brain and lust to her pulsating sex.

Julie began to play with herself even more energetically then, there on her knees inside the open closet. Her sexual imagination went into overdrive as in her mind's eye she became an amalgam of all the beautiful women she'd seen between the covers of those glossy black and white magazines.

She saw herself not only gagged with a ball gag, as she was now, but also bound, suspended from rafters, bondage rope digging into her pussy and rubbing excitingly against her clitoris. And all the while a tall, naked, dominatrix with short blonde hair – in Julie's mind she was Bridget – whipped her over and over again until her body was covered in agonizing welts.

Then Julie's attention moved away from the highly charged images in her head as she looked down and caught sight again of the video. Why was it there? Just because it was untitled didn't necessarily mean it was blank. In fact Julie now had a strong hunch that it wasn't.

She picked up the tape, climbed to her feet and took it over to the television in the corner of the bedroom. She fed the tape into the video player and pressed play on the remote control as she got on to her knees on the carpet. The TV flickered into life and what Julie saw next gave her such a surprise that she let out a gasp of amazement from beneath her gag. There on the screen was Bridget's previous girlfriend, Maria – one of Julie's oldest friends – laying face down and trussed up on the bed in that very room.

Maria's arms were pinned together behind her and her legs were held apart and knees bent with her ankles attached to her wrists. Julie noticed that the metal trigger clip attachments to the wrist and ankle cuffs she was wearing had been used to secure her into this position, that she'd been gagged and that purple clothes pegs had been attached to her nipples and pussy lips.

Not that Julie had given it anything more than passing consideration up to that moment (that denial thing again, she was to realise in hindsight) but she'd supposed it more likely than not that, once they'd become an item, Bridget would have got Maria into kinky sex. Well, here was irrefutable proof that she'd done that very thing. And to see it on film in this way inflamed Julie's overheated sexual imagination to fever pitch.

She went back to the closet, knelt down and buckled on the leather wrist and ankle cuffs with the metal clip attachments, which had been left on the floor. She also thought she'd go for it with the box of pegs. I mean, what the fuck! – In for a penny, in for a pound. She selected all the purple pegs she could find in there, ten in all, and then attached one each to her erect nipples and the remaining eight to her labia. Sure, it was painful – very – but in a way that Julie found she liked and in any event she was too far-gone in lust by then to care.

Julie then returned to watching that homemade video of Maria in her bondage. And as she did so she got back onto her knees on the floor and returned to pleasuring herself, this time even more vigorously. Her busy fingers, now thoroughly coated with sticky love juice, were making a constant rhythmic, wet sound, which was counterpointed by the clicking and clacking of the exquisitely painful pegs attached to her labia.

The film had certainly had a very powerful effect on Julie but there wasn't much happening in it. There was just a lot of Maria squirming in her bonds. And after a while Julie's mind drifted off again to what she'd like to have done to her.

She saw herself hanging from her wrists, gagged, Bridget beating her backside furiously with a leather paddle with one hand while she urgently masturbated her clamped pussy with the other … And all the time there was her camera whirring away at the side of the room, filming every perverted minute of it, creating an obscenely graphic record for anyone to see of Julie's depravity and degradation.

Julie was getting completely carried away by now, her fingers a wet click-clacking blur between the pegged lips of her sex, her thighs soaking with love juice. She was on the verge of a massive climax … when all of a sudden she was brought up short.

The door to the bedroom burst open and in strode Bridget … who was stark naked. Julie realised what must have happened: Bridget had sneaked back from the chores she'd so conveniently had to go out to do and then stripped off elsewhere in the apartment, only to appear now in all her naked splendor.

'Well, well, Julie,' she said with a smirk. 'And you told me you weren't interested in this sort of thing.'

Yeah, like she was surprised, Julie said to herself. God, she'd made it so easy for her crafty lover, fallen entirely for her devious ruse. She was already collared, cuffed, gagged, pegged, and in an incredible state of sexual arousal – *this* close to the most colossal orgasm.

Bridget pulled Julie unceremoniously up off her knees and pushed her just as roughly onto her front on the bed. She used the metal clip attachments on her wrist and ankle cuffs to pin her arms behind her back and her legs together, and there Julie was – at her complete mercy.

She lay there and waited for the inevitable, and waited … and waited. The only sound punctuating the silence was the tell tale click-clacking of her pussy pegs as she shivered and trembled ever

107

more uncontrollably with anguished anticipation of what she knew – just *knew* – was going to happen. Her backside and thighs started to quiver convulsively as the piercing ache in her pegged pussy (c*lick-clack, click-clack*) became unbearable, agonizing (c*lick-clack. click-clack. click-clack, click-clack)*

Bridget unbuckled Julie's ball gag. 'Tell me what you want me to do,' she ordered, knowing full well what she'd say. 'Tell me right now and I'll do it.' She pulled the gag from Julie's mouth.

'B … b … beat me,' Julie managed to stammer – and just getting those words out precipitated the first tremors of that too-long-delayed orgasm.

'Speak more clearly, Julie,' Bridget replied, her voice cold and harsh. 'I couldn't hear you over the sound of those pegs you've attached to your cunt lips, you *fucking pervert*.'

'Beat me,' Julie gasped indistinctly. She tried once more: 'beat me.' Here it came, that first wave of shameful delight.

'Still not clear enough, *pervert*,' Bridget taunted. 'Say it again.'

'Beat me!' Julie cried out, the full force of her climax hitting her now like a tidal wave, her body shaking and shivering in pure ecstasy as the sensations flooded through her entire being. 'Beat me! Beat me! Beat me!'

Chapter Twenty-two

'SELF-BONDAGE,' JULIE SAID, bringing to a close her much-abbreviated, much-censored account of this cathartic incident in her life. 'That's the thing we had in common, Paul.'

'He's still an aficionado,' Sarah said, her brown eyes twinkling with humour. 'I phoned him yesterday and got his answering machine. It said: "Paul can't come to the phone right now because he's all tied up."'

'None of that is true,' Paul laughed.

The three fell silent for a few moments as the waiter topped up their coffees. Then Paul spoke again: 'Stating the obvious, Julie, you and Bridget split eventually.'

'Yes we did.' Julie said. 'I thought she was too much of a control freak as a partner and actually not that good as a dominatrix – not imaginative enough, not *cruel* enough when it came down to it. And she said I was too wilful.'

'Perish the thought,' Sarah joked.

'I know,' Julie said with a smile. 'The very idea!'

Sarah turned to Paul, still teasing. 'Anything else you're just dying to know?'

Paul took a sip of coffee as he thought about the question. 'I'd be interested to hear how you two first got together?' he asked. 'But what I suppose I'd really like to know most of all is how you both came to be clients of Mistress Nikki?'

Sarah peered into her coffee cup and then looked over at Julie. 'Shall I tell him or will you?' she said.

'Why don't we both tell him?' Julie suggested. And that's what they did …

Julie and Sarah first met at a fashionable party in Chelsea that had been thrown by a mutual friend. There was an instant and powerful attraction between the two bisexual women, both of whom were unattached at the time. Julie thought Sarah was lovely, with her short honeyed blonde hair, wide dark brown eyes, small pretty nose, delightfully plump lips, and sumptuous figure. She thought Sarah was about as sexy as a woman could be just from the look of her.

But appearance isn't everything. It was Sarah's character that impressed Julie the most, that really got under her skin. She was amazed at how nice-natured Sarah was, given her financial circumstances. Julie wasn't exactly short of money – a generous trust fund had seen to that – but Sarah was something else. Julie's inheritance amounted to little more than loose change compared to Sarah's. She had been left *pots* of money – many millions of pounds – by her father and could all too easily have been a thoroughly spoilt bitch. But she was anything but that. Her character was playful, affectionate and sweet. It entranced Julie and, one way and another, she fell for Sarah hook, line and sinker in no time at all.

Likewise, Sarah was extremely taken with the lively, vivacious brunette she had only just met. She found her a major turn-on without a doubt. Sarah thought Julie was drop-dead gorgeous and loved her strong-willed character. The two women started a passionate affair, with Sarah invariably taking the passive role in their feverish bouts of lovemaking.

As they got to know one another better, Sarah became increasingly fascinated – and sexually excited – by Julie's accounts of her sadomasochistic experiences, particularly those at the hands of a professional dominatrix called Mistress Nikki.

Julie told her how, soon after she'd spit with Bridget, Mistress Nikki had picked her up at a kinky fetish club near London Bridge that she'd gone to. It was Nikki who'd introduced her to the delights of being erotically dominated by someone who *really* knew what she was doing – Bridget had been a rank amateur by comparison. Julie had been visiting her as a client ever since for regular bouts of discipline. She said she'd do anything, *anything*, that Mistress Nikki wanted her to, she had that much control over her

Sarah was totally fascinated. If Mistress Nikki could have that profound an impact on an alpha female like Julie, just think what she could do with her – someone who, as well as being highly sexed, was exceptionally submissive by nature. Sarah's only previous experience of erotic domination, though, had been of being spanked and subjected to some light bondage by an otherwise forgettable boyfriend.

BDSM was a mysterious world about which Sarah knew next to nothing but she longed to learn. She wanted so much to have more extreme sexual experiences of the kind that Julie had described to her. She imagined how erotically frightening it must be to be disciplined by someone like Mistress Nikki. Sarah desperately wanted to experience such sensations for herself. She told Julie this one day and asked her whether there was any chance that Mistress Nikki might be prepared to dominate her as well. She knew, because Julie had told her, that Nikki was regarded as one of the top pro-dommes in the capital. She was therefore understandably very fussy about whom she would take on as a client.

Julie agreed to ask Mistress Nikki as soon as possible whether she'd consider adding Sarah to her client list. In fact she said she'd raise the issue that very evening because she had a disciplinary session booked with her then. Julie gave her lover the hoped for answer that night when she climbed into bed to join her. Sarah thanked her in the best way she could think of – she threw off the sheets and buried her face between Julie's thighs. Sliding her tongue into her pussy, which was already wet from Nikki's earlier efforts, she licked her to a wonderful orgasm.

It was three evenings later that Sarah, accompanied by Julie, arrived for the first time at Mistress Nikki's high-walled house in Camden Town. The two young women were exactly on time, as Nikki had instructed them to be and, as also instructed, were naked beneath their leather coats – this was an instruction, Sarah was to discover subsequently, that Mistress Nikki was very fond of issuing to her female slaves. Sarah could not stop herself from trembling as she anticipated what the evening might bring. Her mouth was so dry she couldn't swallow and her palms were damp. Courage, Sarah, courage, she said to herself as she tried as best she could to pull herself together.

She and Julie walked through the high gates and up to the entrance. Julie rang the bell and a shortly afterwards the door was answered by Mistress Nikki herself. Sarah was mesmerized by her first sight of the tall dominatrix. She positively oozed sexuality and was hypnotically beautiful too, with her lush shoulder-length red hair, her exquisite bone structure that gave her such a look of sensuality and strength, her full lips and her luminous green eyes. It was those luminous eyes that did it more than anything else. They drew Sarah into an orbit all their own once they fixed on hers. One look from Mistress Nikki was really all it took. Sarah was completely in her thrall from that point on.

What the dominatrix was wearing that evening didn't exactly detract from the effect either. She was looking particularly exquisite in the seductive outfit she had on: a choker, a minute bra and an even tinier slit-sided skirt, all of kid-soft black leather. She was also wearing pointed shoes with very high heels. Sarah could feel herself getting very aroused. There was an ache between her legs and her pussy had become wet.

Mistress Nikki told Julie and Sarah to remove their coats and high heeled shoes. Having ushered the two nude women into her spacious living room, she went to the drinks cabinet in the corner of the room and mixed vodka tonics for the three of them. They sat and conversed and drank for a while. This was partly so that Mistress Nikki could break the ice with Sarah, who she could see was obviously nervous, but also so that she could familiarize her with some of the main ground rules of BDSM.

Among other things, she emphasized the importance of total trust and obedience on the part of the slave, of always calling the dominatrix 'Mistress', and explained the significance of the slave's collar. She also talked about the need for slaves to be able to exercise highly disciplined orgasm control whenever required to do so by their Mistress.

The dominatrix then put black leather collars on Julie and Sarah and also encircled their wrists and ankles with black leather cuffs. 'I'm going to start your punishment by giving you both a hand spanking,' she told them. 'As I am spanking one of you,' she elaborated further, 'the other must kneel by her side masturbating. The spanking will only stop when the slave who has been playing with her pussy has climaxed. Understood, slaves?'

'Yes, Mistress,' Julie said.

'Yes, Mistress,' echoed Sarah, trying to mask the nervous quaver in her voice. But in truth she was more turned on than nervous now. The ache between her legs had become more acute, her pussy felt slippery-wet.

Julie was the first one over Mistress Nikki's knee. Nikki paused for a moment to admire the curve of Julie's backside, so delightfully vulnerable, before beginning her spanking. She raised her hand and brought it down forcefully on her rear. The sharp slap was so hard that it left a distinct red mark on her flesh and made her cry out in pain. She spanked Julie a second time, lifting her hand high and then bringing it down swiftly to make contact with her backside, leaving another red mark on her flesh and making her cry out again. She delivered a third heavy stroke which smarted even more painfully. It made Julie cry out more loudly this time and left a deeper red mark on the cheeks of her backside. There was another sharp sound as Nikki's hand cracked down again on the curved cheeks with another harsh spank, and another, and another.

While Mistress Nikki was vigorously spanking Julie in this way, Sarah knelt by her side and masturbated with equal vigour, her frantic fingers sticky inside herself. Her face was flushed and her breath was coming shorter all the time. She was in such a high state of excitement that it was not long before she climaxed, sighing and gasping loudly. So Mistress Nikki stopped spanking Julie.

When it was Sarah's turn to be spanked Julie thoroughly enjoyed kneeling next to her lover and watching her comely backside colouring to a deep red. Mistress Nikki cracked her hand down on it relentlessly, beating hard flat strokes against the ever more punished flesh. Julie rubbed herself very wet indeed and her hand became coated with sticky love juice, as she gazed lasciviously at the delicious sight before her. But, to her surprise, she also found herself deliberately holding off her orgasm in order to lengthen Sarah's punishment. Nikki noticed what Julie was doing and looked over at her with a knowing smile. That look from her formidable Mistress was enough to tip Julie over the edge and, to the ringing sound of hand on naked flesh, she climaxed, her orgasm exploding through her in its intensity.

Nikki next attached leads to the collars of the two young women. She told them that she was going to take them to her dungeon. And down the long corridor to the dungeon the three of them went.

Mistress Nikki opened the heavy door and led Julie and Sarah into the large, dimly lit room. Sarah was both frightened and excited by the ominous gloom of the place. It was made more threatening to her eyes by the rack lining one of its dark walls, containing a terrifying collection of straps, whips, canes, clamps and other instruments of correction. And then there was all the sinister looking metal- and black leather-covered dungeon equipment …

Mistress Nikki ordered Julie and Sarah to kneel down and kiss her high heeled shoes before leading them on all fours to two adjacent stocks. She removed their leads and told them to place their necks and wrists in the stocks, which she locked into place.

Nikki used first a paddle, followed by a small whip, a tawse and finally a heavy leather flogger to whip Julie and Sarah with increasing force until their bodies burned with agony. She stopped whipping them when she considered that they'd had enough punishment for the time being. 'Spread your legs,' she told them. She proceeded to masturbate them both frantically to simultaneous orgasms that spasmed through them as they cried out their pleasure in unison.

The dominatrix then released Julie and Sarah from the stocks and led them over to the leather-covered bondage table. She told Sarah to lie on her back on it and spread her arms and legs. She clipped her wrist and ankle cuffs to the chains at the four corners of the bondage table. Sarah felt as horny as hell by this stage. Her pulse was raging, her eyes shining, her breathing shallow, her pussy soaked.

Mistress Nikki told Julie to position her sex over Sarah's face and to lick her lover's pussy as Sarah did the same to her. Julie and Sarah made love like this with great urgency, both covering the other's face with oozing love juice. And all the while Nikki beat Julie on the backside with a studded paddle. She didn't stop until both slaves climaxed again, trembling and moaning in ecstasy.

Next Nikki released Sarah's wrists and ankles and led her over to the St Andrews cross. The dominatrix secured Sarah even more thoroughly to this piece of equipment. She strapped her to it, face forward, at the wrists, upper arms, waist, thighs and ankles.

Mistress Nikki took hold of two large floggers and, to Julie's surprise, handed one of them to her, saying: 'I want you to whip Sarah's arse with this while I'm whipping her back.'

Julie's initial blows were quite tentative as this was the first time she had ever whipped anybody. However she soon picked up the rhythm, really got the knack. Did she ever! To her shock and surprised delight she found it intensely exciting to be thrashing her lover. As her excitement escalated, her blows became increasingly savage until Sarah, struggling in desperation against her bonds, begged for mercy, at the same time climaxing violently.

Mistress Nikki then grabbed hold of Julie, who was stunned by what she had just done. Nikki kissed her hard on the lips and finger-fucked her roughly until she, also, trembled to a convulsive orgasm. 'Quite the switch, aren't you,' Nikki informed the still gasping slave.

Nikki next released Sarah from the St Andrews cross and walked her and Julie over to two metal spreader bars that hung side by side from chains at the centre of the dungeon. She clipped Julie's wrist cuffs to either end of one of the metal bars and did the same to Sarah with the other one. 'Spread your legs,' she told them, and clipped their ankle cuffs to either end of the two spreader bars that she placed beneath them. Next she blindfolded them carefully so that neither of them could see a thing.

She began caning Sarah and Julie, at first quite lightly and then with increasing force until their backsides were covered with angry tram lines and it was evident that they were close to finding their punishment intolerably painful. When the caning suddenly stopped Sarah wondered in trepidation what new torment cruel Mistress Nikki had in mind for her and Julie next. She soon discovered what it was.

Nikki attached the most vicious clamps she possessed to their nipples. The experience was excruciating for both of them, an explosion of crimson agony that made them shudder and shake uncontrollably. While they were trying to cope with the extreme pain that they were now experiencing, Nikki placed one hand between Sarah's legs and the other between Julie's and masturbated them ever more furiously. She kept on finger-fucking them like this until they felt the pleasure explode through them once more and climaxed together convulsively with a series of shuddering gasps.

Then Nikki gently removed the clamps and kissed their punished nipples, removed their blindfolds and released their wrists and ankles. 'Kneel at my feet,' she ordered them and they hurriedly obeyed. 'What have you to say to your Mistress?'

'Thank you, Mistress,' Julie replied, her eyes gleaming.

'Yes, thank you, Mistress,' added Sarah, looking up adoringly at her tormentor, her Goddess. 'Thank you so much for the discipline.'

Nikki led Sarah on hands and knees to the metal cage and locked her in, leaving her kneeling on the floor. She took Julie over to the leather-covered bondage table, removing her own choker, bra, skirt and high-heeled shoes when she got there.

'It's time I had some pleasure now,' she said as she lay down on the table and spread her legs. She told Julie to lean forward and lick her pussy and she obeyed straight away. Julie clamped her mouth against Mistress Nikki's pussy and her sinuous tongue straight away began licking her clit. Nikki luxuriated in the sensation, running her hands up over her own stiff nipples as Julie continued to pleasure her with her mouth.

Sarah watched from the cage and knelt masturbating in a fever of lust. She rolled the fingers of her right hand over her stiff clitoris fast and hard, and then pushed them in and out of her soaking pussy.

As the fingers of her right hand plunged in and out of her sex, making her palm and wrist soaked, the fingers of her left started to pinch first one of her punished nipples and then the other as hard as she could bear. She felt insatiable, every sexual part of her swollen with desire.

Sarah had never felt so alive. Pleasure-pain spiked up through the fingers pinching her nipples while her other hand continued to plunge and plunge into the soaking wetness between her thighs. Blood was rushing through her veins from her self-ministrations and there was a roar like the ocean in her ears. Mistress Nikki had done this to her, had made her feel this way. The woman was a Goddess, a Goddess.

Chapter Twenty-three

GODDESS, THAT WAS THE name of the club to which Paul was being taken. It was a moonless, starless night and the air was warm. The black cab that had just picked up Mistress Nikki and Paul was taking them to an anonymous building in central London, not far from Liverpool Street Station. The cab driver didn't know the fact – extremely few people did – but it was the venue of an S&M club called simply *Goddess*. It was the most uninhibited Femdom Fetish club in Europe, Nikki had told Paul, and was extremely selective about who it would allow as a member. He would only be allowed in because he was her guest.

Mistress Nikki's outfit was borderline obscene but until they got inside the club she knew that it would remain covered by the long, enveloping leather coat she was wearing. Paul had on the all-black leather outfit Nikki had told him to wear: short boots, no socks; skin-tight jeans, no underwear; and a button-up jacket, nothing underneath.

He'd thought for a while that he might get away with it with the cab driver and pass for just another passenger, albeit one with a major penchant for wearing leather. Paul attempted this deception by doing up all the buttons on his leather jacket and keeping the collar up high. But early on in the journey Mistress Nikki insisted that he undo the jacket completely. The dominatrix then extracted a black leather slave's collar and a lead from her bag. She buckled the collar around Paul's neck and then attached the lead to it.

Paul was burning with embarrassment throughout this humiliating procedure, which Mistress Nikki deliberately dragged out for as long as she could. He was only too aware that the taxi driver could see what she was doing to him through his rear-view mirror. Paul remained in a state of red-faced embarrassment for the rest of the journey because Nikki insisted that he keep his jacket wide open. She also kept hold of the lead attached to his collar, wrapping it round her hand and holding it taut for the rest of the journey.

The cab driver took a turning off Liverpool Street, then another and parked besides the innocuous-looking building that housed the *Goddess* club. Nikki paid the driver and pulled Paul out of the cab by his lead. Paul, who was still acutely embarrassed, was careful not to look at the driver.

Mistress Nikki tugged at Paul's lead and led him through the entrance door and into the pulsating darkness of the club, where he very quickly lost all feelings of embarrassment. Understandably so; he fitted right in. The ambience at the club was great. The lighting was subtle and atmospheric. The dungeon equipment was superb. And the raunchy, throbbing music was where it belonged – in the background. Far more insistent was the non-stop sound of bare flesh being soundly thrashed.

The club was busy that night and, looking around, Paul could see that Mistress Nikki had not been exaggerating in her description of how uninhibited a place it was. Nearby, a dominatrix was sitting with her legs apart as a naked woman knelt before her, eating her pussy. In the corner a man was grovelling on the floor at another domme's feet, kissing and licking her pointed-tip shoes as she stood above him wielding a whip. A naked man was being led around on all fours by another dominatrix. The man's backside had been whipped red raw and numerous metal pegs had been attached to his genitals. Another naked male had been strapped on his front over a whipping bench and two more dommes, both of them masked, were taking it in turns to whip his rear ferociously with identical floggers. The two masked women were clearly vying with each other to see which of them could beat the man with greater ferocity.

Mistress Nikki led an increasingly excited Paul into the changing room, where she first removed her long leather coat to reveal that she was wearing a tiny red leather bra that showed off her décolletage to stunning effect, and a matching leather skirt that was miniscule and skin-tight and beneath which she was nude. She was also wearing knee high red leather boots with very high heels.

Seeing Nikki in this incredibly seductive outfit had a predictable effect on Paul. He could feel his cock harden and flex, pushing against the inside of his tight leather jeans. 'You look absolutely wonderful, Mistress,' he said, drinking in the sight of her.

'I know,' Nikki replied with a straight face. 'Now, let's get you undressed.'

She made Paul strip naked except for the slave's collar and also the lead, which she continued to grasp the short time it took him to remove what little he was wearing. After that she let go of the lead, but only in order to reach into her bag and pull out a black silk scarf and a thin leather belt. She rolled the silk scarf up into a ball, stuffed it inside Paul's mouth and held it in place by the belt, which she buckled tightly behind his head. Paul by now had become extremely excited – almost too excited. His cock was rigidly erect and throbbing and he was hyperventilating to such an extent that for a moment he came close to choking on his gag.

Mistress Nikki allowed Paul some time to calm down a little and then excited him all over again by twisting his arms behind his back and putting a pair of handcuffs on him that she had also removed from her bag. She grasped hold of Paul's lead again and led him, his throbbing erection on full display, back into the main room. She took him to a metal cage, put him inside it on his knees, and fastened his lead to its bars. The dominatrix then left him there, saying, 'I'm going to have a few words with my friend, Strap-on Jane.'

Paul watched wide-eyed as she strode across the room and started to talk to a woman who even in her bare feet was as tall as Nikki and who, truth be told, was as drop-dead gorgeous as she was too. She had long blonde hair, full lips and heavy-lidded eyes. She had smooth all-over-tanned skin and her body was fleshy and well proportioned with firm high breasts, which were gloriously bare. In fact the woman was as near as makes no difference completely naked, except for one thing – she was wearing a gigantic black strap-on dildo. Every so often she and Nikki would look over at Paul and it was obvious that they were talking about him.

Eventually Strap-on Jane left Nikki's side and strolled in Paul's direction. As the Amazonian domme got closer to his cage Paul found that he couldn't take his eyes off her strap-on. It was sizeable indeed, a good ten inches long and almost two inches thick.

Saying nothing, the dominatrix opened the cage door, unfastened Paul's lead from its bars and pulled him out of the cage. By yanking at his lead she indicated to him that he should get up from his knees. She then led him across the room, his sense of sexual anticipation growing by the second.

When the two of them had arrived at a leather-covered bondage table that nobody else in the busy club was currently using Strap-on Jane got him to stand fronting this piece of equipment. She told him tersely to bend as far forward on to the table as possible.

As he did as he'd been told she knelt down and secured his ankles to the chained manacles that were attached at floor level to either end of the table's base. She also picked up a bottle of lubricant that was standing by its side.

With his gagged face pressed against the leather table top, his arms pulled behind his back by the handcuffs, his legs manacled apart and the cheeks of his backside spread so wide that they fully revealed his pinkish hole to Strap-on Jane, Paul knew what was coming – anal penetration by that gigantic dildo.

And he was right. Breathing hard, his lungs burning in his chest and the blood coursing through his veins, Paul felt the dominatrix slowly ease the dildo deep into his rear, impaling him. She used a liberal amount of the lubricant she'd picked up but even so the dildo was so huge that when she pressed it into him he thought he'd split.

He let out muffled cries of distress from beneath his gag and tried to twist himself away to let Strap-on Jane know she was really hurting him. But she ignored him. She ran her hand against Paul's rear and began to thrust in and out in a rhythmic motion, pushing the shaft even deeper inside. Then she began pumping into his anus hard and furious, really giving it to him with the giant strap-on dildo.

Strap-on Jane pounded and pounded into Paul's anal hole. And as she continued to do this she brought her right hand to his aching cock and started masturbating him, jerking hard. She buggered him painfully and jerked furiously at his cock until a delirious combination of pain and pleasure exploded through him. Grunting noisily beneath his gag, he climaxed, spraying silvery strands of ejaculate onto the leather below him, while the dominatrix climaxed too with a cry and long ecstatic spasm.

At last both their orgasms had ebbed and Strap-on Jane withdrew the huge dildo from Paul's gaping anus. She released him from the bondage table, unbuckled the leather belt that was holding his gag in place and removed the black silken scarf from his mouth. She used the silk scarf to mop up all of the cum that Paul had spilled on the bondage table. She then stuffed the now thoroughly sodden piece of material back into his mouth and tightly rebuckled the belt to hold it in place. Finally she grasped hold of Paul's lead and took the handcuffed and gagged slave back across the room where she returned him to his Mistress.

Mistress Nikki and Paul left the club shortly after that on Nikki's insistence and Paul wondered why their stay had been such a relatively brief affair. It was because it had achieved its purpose, that was why. It was only an hour or so later, back in his flat on his own, that it dawned on Paul precisely why it was that Nikki had taken him to the *Goddess* club. It was in order to hand him over to another dominatrix to be used and abused by her, thereby demonstrating to him in the most explicit way possible just this: that submitting himself unconditionally to the will of his Mistress meant submitting himself unconditionally to the will of *anyone else* she wanted to pass him over to at any given time. The realisation of that and its likely implications for his future sent shivers of apprehension and anticipation right through him.

Chapter Twenty-four

PAUL WAS SEATED AT the computer in his flat doing what he was employed to do. But he wasn't naked and in self-administered bondage as once might very well have been the case. In contrast to what Sarah had jokingly claimed, the truth was that he'd completely lost the taste for it. He'd discovered that when you'd experienced the real thing it was impossible to go back.

He was hard at work. It really felt like hard work too. He was in the process of editing the poorly written and deeply uninteresting autobiography of a Z-list celebrity currently enjoying her fifteen minutes of fame. Paul was expected by his employers to lick efforts like this into some kind of publishable shape and he always seemed to manage it. But, with ever more of the raw material he had to work with being as uninspiring as the piece of trash currently before him on his PC, he couldn't say he was enjoying much job satisfaction these days.

The work paid peanuts as well, he reminded himself. But for all of its shortcomings it had one overwhelming advantage. It enabled him to be very flexible in how he used his time. It was true that to keep on top of his workload he had to put the hours in, but *when* he put them in was very much up to him. That meant that whenever Mistress Nikki contacted him and told him to jump, he was able to jump as promptly and as high as she demanded.

The phone rang and Paul's heart skipped a beat when he saw Nikki's number flash up. He picked up the receiver, saying, 'Hello, Mistress.'

'Drop whatever it is you're doing at the moment,' Nikki instructed. 'Go straight away to Earl's Hotel in the Earls Court Road. Ask for the key to room 35. Have you got that, slave?'

'Yes, Mistress,' he said, a lump rising in his throat. 'Room 35, Earl's Hotel.' What was this all about, he wondered excitedly.

'Once you've let yourself into the room go over to the bed and look in the top drawer of the table on its left hand side where you will find written instructions from me telling you what to do next. Got that too?'

'Yes, Mistress.'

'Good,' she said. 'Off you go now, slave.' Then the line went dead, she'd gone.

Paul didn't delay. Pausing only to go to the bathroom, he left his flat directly. He was reasonably au fait with the Earls Court area of London and knew where Earl's Hotel was located. Paul drove to the big Victorian building that housed the hotel and found a vacant parking space nearby. He parked the car, fed the meter and walked over to the quietly opulent hotel, which he entered. Paul obtained the key for Room 35 from the receptionist and took the stairs to the first floor. He walked down a long corridor and then a much shorter one that was at the back of the hotel. He let himself into Room 35, the last room in the corridor.

Paul walked straight over to the big four-poster bed, which was the most dominant piece of furniture in the room. He then went to the bedside table on its left where, in the top drawer, he found the written instructions to which Mistress Nikki had referred. Paul also found there several black leather BDSM items: a blindfold, a tongue gag and a pair of ankle cuffs, all of black leather. In addition he found a short length of chain with a snap trigger at either end, and a set of metal handcuffs.

Paul read the typed instructions from Mistress Nikki, which said: *Take off all of your clothes and then do the following – go to the end of the bed, buckle the leather cuffs around your ankles and, facing outwards, chain your ankles via the cuffs to the right leg of the bed. Then gag and blindfold yourself and handcuff your wrists behind you to the bedpost. After that, wait.*

As Paul stripped naked he wondered how long he would have to wait. And for whom. It might well be Mistress Nikki herself of course. And it might not – his Mistress was always full of surprises. Could she have arranged for it to be Strap-on Jane from the *Goddess* S&M club, he wondered. Maybe that Amazonian domme hadn't finished with him yet. The thought of what she might do to him this time, considering what she'd already done to him at the club, made him tremble with excitement. Or it could perhaps be Mistress Evie from *Consensual Kink*. She had made it very clear that she liked the look of Paul when they'd been introduced to one another in her fetish store. Maybe Nikki had decided to permit her friend to 'sample the goods'. Or it could be that mega-rich minx Sarah who might have paid Nikki enough money to let her have a one-on-one session with Paul but with a delightfully kinky twist. Or maybe it was Julie. That wasn't beyond the bounds of possibility. She liked him, that had been clear when they'd met for that memorable meal at *Marco's*, and she liked to 'switch'. Yes, thinking about it, it definitely could be Julie.

Or it could be none of these people. It could be anyone, anyone at all, who would walk into this hotel room and do anything they liked to him. *Anything*. Paul felt a tremor run up and down his spine and his breathing became short and shallow. He was naked now and very excited, his cock stiffly erect.

Paul took hold of the ankle cuffs, the short length of chain, the blindfold, the tongue gag and the handcuffs and went to the foot of the bed where he stood next to the right hand bedpost. He cuffed both of his ankles and clipped one end of the chain to the leather cuff on his left ankle. Squatting down with his back to the bed, Paul put the chain behind the leg of the bed and clipped the other end of the chain to his right ankle cuff. Then he stood up and fitted the open handcuff around his left wrist and put on the blindfold and gag. Finally Paul stood with his back up against the bedpost. He brought his arms behind him around the post and snap-locked the open cuff round his right wrist.

And then he waited ... for what seemed like a very long time indeed. And the longer he waited, the more agitated he became. Paul had put himself into bondage not dissimilar to this on countless occasions in the past. But this time what he'd done had been fundamentally different in its essence from those other occasions. Every time he'd engaged in self-bondage before he'd been very careful to ensure that he could release himself when the time came. But that wasn't an option on this occasion. He had less options open to him even than the time Mistress Nikki had put him into bondage in his flat and left him to stew for a while. That bondage had only been partial by comparison to the situation he was in now.

If he needed to on this occasion, Paul asked himself, could he remove his blindfold or his gag? No, he could not. Could he release his legs? No, he could not. Could he release himself from the bedpost to which his wrists were manacled? Absolutely not. The fact of the matter was that from the moment Paul had snap-locked those handcuffs together around the post behind him he'd put himself into a position he was helpless to alter. And that both scared and excited him in equal measure. It made his body tremble and his erection pulse.

It was very quiet inside the room as Paul continued to wait and wait for someone to arrive. At times he wondered if anyone would *ever* arrive. Then finally he heard the sound of the door opening and closing. It was Mistress Nikki, he thought. Never mind about all his conjecture earlier about who else it might be; he'd just been being fanciful. It had to be Nikki surely. But was it?

Chapter Twenty-five

PAUL'S VISITOR SAID NOTHING, not one word. He didn't hear anything else either after the opening and closing of the door. He didn't even hear the sound of footsteps. He thought that this was probably because the room had a heavily carpeted floor. But even so he would have thought he'd have heard *something*. Was the person who was now in the room with him actually Mistress Nikki, he wondered. If he hadn't been gagged he would have asked but he was gagged – and very effectively too – with a leather tongue gag and he couldn't utter anything the least bit coherent.

The silence inside the room continued interminably. Who was his visitor, Paul asked himself nervously. Who was she? Was it a she, though? He mustn't jump to conclusions. Was it actually a woman? Could his visitor be a male? Could it be Tony? There was a thought. Mistress Nikki had banned Tony and himself from communicating with each other for reasons best known to herself. But presumably that ban wasn't intended to be indefinite. He certainly hoped that wasn't Nikki's intention anyway. What a shame that would be. Maybe this was her way, weird as it was, of getting Tony and him back together. And maybe it wasn't. There was no way to tell who was in the room with him, no way to tell anything if the person wouldn't speak to him or even make a single sound.

The silence continued for what seemed like an eternity, broken only by the light clinking noises that his handcuffs and the chain attaching his ankle cuffs made from time to time. Paul made himself stand stock still so that he wasn't making even these small noises. He was hoping to catch some sound – anything – from his mysterious visitor. But he heard not a thing.

A thought flashed into his mind. Maybe no one was in the room with him. Maybe the door to the room had been opened and then hastily closed by a member of the hotel staff. It had been a startled chambermaid perhaps, who'd realised that she'd stumbled on to one of the establishment's kinkier guests. Paul had read *Hotel Babylon*; he knew that some of the bizarre sites the unwitting staff of big city hotels like this were confronted with on occasion would shock even the most jaded observer. Was that it? Had a member of the hotel staff made a quick appearance at the door and then hurriedly disappeared once he or she had seen him? Was that what had happened? Was he actually on his own in this silent and anonymous hotel room? Alone and blindfolded and gagged and naked. And in bondage so thorough that he could not possibly escape unaided. The thought of it was alarming. It was also deeply, perversely thrilling and he felt his erection throb more insistently.

The silence went on and on until nothing but darkness and stillness surrounded Paul and he'd almost convinced himself that he was all on his own. Then something happened all of a sudden. It was something that made Paul break the silence again, something that made him gasp in surprise from behind his gag. A hand suddenly gripped his erection. It seemed as if a spark of electricity leaped straight from the hand to his cock at the unexpected contact. Was it Nikki's hand? Was it Tony's hand? Was it ...?

He didn't know whose hand it was, simply couldn't tell. Tony's hands, like his own, were relatively slender. *Everything* about Tony physically was like him. It could be Tony's hand. It could equally well be Mistress Nikki's hand. Or Strap-on Jane's hand or Mistress Evie's hand or Sarah's hand or Julie's hand. Or someone else's hand. It could be the hand of a complete stranger. It was impossible to know whose hand it was or even whether it belonged to a male or female. Because it was covered by a tight-fitting leather glove.

The smooth fingers immediately began to pull on the hardness of his shaft, moving rhythmically. They were the fingers of someone's right hand. This meant that the person was right-handed or ambidextrous, Paul reasoned. No shit, Sherlock, he said to himself scornfully. That told him what exactly? Nothing at all, sweet FA, that's what it told him.

All he knew was that those fingers were doing what they were doing with consummate skill and that they were sending shock after electric shock to his erection each time they pulled at it. The fingers pulled slowly at first, rhythmically, and then began pulling faster, rubbing harder and harder all the time. Before long Paul found that they were working his erection ever more furiously. And, in doing that, they were making him frantic with lust. His hips thrust back and forth and he strained against his bonds in fevered response to the leather-covered fingers. Those fingers rubbed and rubbed until Paul was teetering on the edge of orgasm, about to go over. He was ready to burst, ready to come, right on the brink ... Then all of a sudden the fingers went away.

The room was silent – apart, that is, from Paul's painfully heavy breathing as he tried to get some semblance of control over his acute sexual frustration. His visitor made not a sound, but was still there, had to be there, watching him, waiting ...

After another eternity the leather-gloved hand returned to his erect cock and gripped it again, began stroking and caressing at the hardness. The strokes, slow and rhythmic at first as before, built steadily in pace until they were moving with increasing urgency. Paul's arousal was tightening into something painful, urgent now, and he began desperately writhing and twisting in his bonds. The leather-covered fingers that were wrapped around his cock were pulling him into a delirious state of sex and grip, faster and faster. Trembling uncontrollably and groaning through his gag, he was approaching the point of no return again. He was almost there, right on the very edge of the precipice ... when the fingers that had been moving so furiously over his throbbing stiffness stopped abruptly and withdrew once again.

Paul's heart was pounding in his ears and he was still shaking all over. He'd been even closer to climaxing this time – a hair's breadth away – and felt the most desperate desire for release. But he knew he could do nothing about it – *nothing* – and gradually he retreated from the brink once again, unsatisfied.

He went back to waiting. And waiting and waiting and waiting. Eventually, after an endless wait, the leather-covered hand returned. But not to his cock.

Chapter Twenty-six

THE LEATHER-GLOVED RIGHT hand, which was this time joined in its activities by a leather-gloved left hand, released the chain attaching Paul's ankle cuffs and unlocked his handcuffs with a key. Those same hands then turned Paul round firmly, reattached his wrists to the bedpost by snap-locking his handcuffs around it and re-secured his ankle cuffs to the foot of the bed by means of the chain.

Paul stood in the blackness, shackled to the bed once more but aware that he'd been repositioned so that he was now facing it. He listened to the pounding in his ears and felt the throbbing of his cock and wondered what was going to happen next. He soon found out. The leather-gloved right hand started to spank his backside – hard.

Smack! The crisp sound announced that the harsh spanking had begun. Smack! The hand cracked down again on his curved cheeks with another harsh smack. And another – Smack! And three more – Smack! Smack! Smack!

The owner of the hand (whoever the hell that person actually was) increased the frequency and harshness of the blows, continuing unremittingly, cracking the hand down onto Paul's backside with relentless energy, following one smack after another in swift succession.

And Paul was really feeling the effects of the spanking too. The cheeks of his backside smarted so much that it made him squirm within his bonds, and with each slap his squirming increased.

The hand did actually stop beating Paul for a short time and began to gently stroke his rear but only to quickly resume beating it, this time with even greater ferocity.

And with a paddle.

Thwack! The first blow with the heavy leather implement brought a blast of searing pain that nearly knocked the stuffing out

129

of him. Thwack! So did the second one. Thwack! And the third.

Thwack! Thwack! Thwack! Thwack! ... On and on the furious paddling continued until Paul felt as if his backside was on fire. And then the paddling stopped.

There followed another noise, that of a whip being wielded with real energy. It hissed like an angry snake when it was swung through the air and it landed with a crack on its target.

Crack! The sudden pain that seared across Paul's backside was agonizing. He was still trying to cope with that when – Crack! – the whip came down again. It was even more agonizing. Crack! Crack! Crack! – A third, fourth and fifth strike followed and then down came the cruel implement again.

As the savage whipping continued the cheeks of Paul's backside began to smart with a blazing sensation so acute that it made him buck and strain helplessly against his restraints. And as he bucked and strained he could feel the full effect of the whipping as it spread like wildfire through his body.

The whipping stopped as suddenly as it had started. But then there came another noise. It was the sound of a cane being swung vigorously. Paul listened to the sinister swishing noise the cane made as it sliced through the air and felt its painful sting as it cracked against his rear. Crack! Then it happened again. He heard a low swish as the cane was drawn back a second time, a louder one as it descended and then that Crack!

Strike three: Crack! He suffered again the sharp sting of the cane's searing stroke as it was brought down hard across the cheeks of his backside.

Then came strikes four, five and six, each more vicious than the last: Crack! Crack! Crack! Paul tried to cry out but his cries were strangled by his gag. He flung himself about frantically to the limits of his bonds as he tried to escape the stinging blows. It made no difference at all. There was no escape from the blows, no escape from the unbelievable pain.

This latest beating seemed to go on for ever as the room resonated with the constant crack of cane against naked flesh. Paul's mysterious torturer brought the cane down on his backside with unrelentingly hard rhythmic strokes until he reached a point where he didn't think he could possibly take any more pain. He felt as if he might faint at any moment.

Perhaps sensing this, the wielder of the cane stopped beating Paul and began to stroke the implement gently over his rear, rolling it tantalizingly over his backside and legs ... before recommencing the beating. This time the swipes of the cane inflicted onto Paul's rear by his mystery assailant were less frequent but also much harsher. His blindfolded eyes started to burn with tears as pain and fear collided in his punished body. He couldn't imagine more!

But there *was* more. The swipes of the cane became frequent again and harsher still. Three powerful blows in very quick succession – Crack! Crack! Crack! – left Paul whimpering in agony beneath his gag. His rear was now burning with a pain that was ferocious.

There came another torrent of blows from the hard rod. Crack! Crack! Crack! Crack! Crack! Crack! Crack! Paul felt like screaming, would have screamed if he could. The muscles in his throat were straining as he tried to cry out, but the strangled noises he made were barely audible from beneath his gag. The next series of sounds were certainly audible, though – all too audible.

Crack! Crack! Crack! Crack! Crack! Crack! Crack! Crack! This last vicious onslaught caused Paul to shake all over with excruciating pain, which morphed all of a sudden into a sensation of pleasure-pain of such incredible intensity that it began pounding through him. Paul knew he couldn't wait any more, that he was about to lose control. He came then, moaning deep in his throat, experiencing an orgasm that was long and violent. It was the most savage climax he had ever experienced in his life. He shot out his own liquid in spasm after spasm as sensations of agony and ecstasy ripped through him like a sound wave.

When at last his climax had finished Paul stood there in the blackness for a long while. He was trembling uncontrollably in his bonds and was panting into his gag. He felt shaken to the core. Then the leather-gloved hands unlocked and removed his handcuffs. He heard a few indistinct sounds after that, which he couldn't identify, followed by a sound he definitely could distinguish. It was the sound of the door to the hotel room opening and shutting.

After that there was nothing but silence. This time there really wasn't anyone else in the room with him. And now that his handcuffs had been removed he knew that he would be able to release himself from the rest of his bondage quite easily. So that is what he started to do.

Chapter Twenty-seven

PAUL FELT BEHIND HIS head and unbuckled and then removed the leather blindfold. He blinked rapidly several times, adjusting his vision to the daylight. The room seemed slightly darker than it had been before he'd put the blindfold on. He glanced over at the net-curtained window and saw that it was just starting to turn to dusk outside. This gave him some indication of how long he'd been in the hotel room. He reckoned it must have been about four hours. He'd lost all sense of time since stripping off, putting on the blindfold and other BDSM items and handcuffing himself to the bedpost.

Paul removed the leather tongue gag next and flexed his aching jaw from side to side. Then he squatted down on his haunches in order to free his ankles from the foot of the bed, removing the leather cuffs along with the chain to which they had been attached. He found that he needed to pee, which he went off to the en-suite bathroom to do. Given how long he'd been manacled to the bed, he needed to stretch his legs a little more than that short trip to the bathroom had allowed. He did this by wandering around the hotel room.

He wasn't wandering aimlessly though. He was taking the opportunity to look and see if his mysterious visitor had left him any clue at all as to who he or she had been. But he gave up the effort in the end. There was absolutely nothing – zilch – to indicate the person's identity. There wasn't even a lingering scent in the room that might have told him something he didn't already know. There were just the mingled odours of leather and of his own sweat and ejaculate.

He padded over to the full-length mirror, turned around and looked over his shoulder into the reflective glass at his punished rear. He winced at the sight. There were livid red marks where he'd been beaten and some areas of broken skin. Along with the external damage that he could see he could feel a dull persistent ache in his buttocks. Sitting down was going to be painful for the next few days, he told himself resignedly.

Paul went back to the bathroom and this time had a quick shower, warm water boring into him from all directions. It stung when it hit his damaged behind. He dried his body with one of the hotel towels, making sure he went easy on his backside. Paul got dressed then and was just putting the last of his clothes back on when the phone in the room rang. He answered it and recognized Mistress Nikki's voice straight away. 'Leave the hotel now, slave,' she said curtly. 'Drop the key off at reception and go home.' That was all she said before terminating the brief and entirely one-sided conversation.

Paul emerged from Earl's Hotel into a grey, chill evening and walked over to where he was parked. He got into his car – and yes, it certainly was painful to sit down – and drove off in the direction of home. Motoring through the endless, ragged chain of city traffic Paul suddenly felt ravenously hungry. He stopped off at a fast food place, loaded up on carbohydrates there, and then completed his journey to Islington. It was dark now, raining, the city a smear of lights.

Back in his empty flat Paul spent a distracted evening, not watching television, not looking at the computer, not reading, not listening to music, just thinking. He felt restless, couldn't get the experience in the hotel room out of his head. His mind was brim-full of questions about what had been done to him there. There was so much that puzzled and bewildered him.

Had his captor – his torturer – been Mistress Nikki herself, he wondered, or had she loaned him out to someone else, someone he already knew. Or to a complete stranger, for that matter. Paul would have loved to have known who it was that had done those amazing things to him – those amazingly *sadistic* things. The experience had been outstandingly intense. Just thinking about it made him shiver with excitement.

But who had his tormentor been for God's sake? Would he ever find out the identity? Maybe he never would. Who did he know that was capable of that degree of sadism, Paul asked himself. Mistress Nikki was the obvious answer. But it didn't add up somehow.

This fact was clear, though. Regardless of whether or not it had been Mistress Nikki in the hotel room with him, *she* had been the one who'd made it happen. Her hold over his life nowadays was extraordinarily strong and it was growing stronger all the time. She was his Mistress and he was her slave, so their relationship was by definition an unequal one. But it seemed to Paul that it was getting more unequal by the day.

He had no influence over Mistress Nikki whatsoever. He'd never had any influence over her and doubtless never would. In complete contrast, she had close to total control over him these days. Perhaps, Paul wondered, she'd had that degree of control over him right from the beginning and he just hadn't quite realised it at the time. But never mind her having *close* to total control over him, Paul thought on reflection. Perhaps that control *was* now total – and as much as a result of his attitude as of hers. Because he valued what he had with her immensely, fully appreciated its innately tenuous nature, and knew that he would never wittingly do anything that might possibly jeopardize it. Paul was more determined than ever before to always be the best of slaves to Mistress Nikki and simply couldn't envisage a situation nowadays where he would question one of her commands.

And yet, and yet … profoundly dependent, *recklessly* dependent though he now was on the flame-haired dominatrix who was always so full of surprises, the woman remained a complete enigma to him. Yes, she'd shared with him early on some of the experiences that had led her to become a dominatrix and he'd appreciated her doing that, of course he had. But what she'd said to him then didn't answer any of the questions he'd really like to be answered now – starting with why she had allowed him into her life in the first place. He'd presumed it had been as a favour to Tony. If that was the case why, then, would she not permit the two men to communicate with one another? It didn't make sense. Why had she decided not to charge him anything for her professional services, which would otherwise have been extremely expensive, *prohibitively* expensive? Where was her motivation in all this? What was her agenda?

Questions, questions, nothing but questions. But answers came there none. Paul's thoughts reeled as the unanswered questions swirled in his brain. He went to bed eventually, his mind a jumble of confused thoughts and unanswered questions. And as is the way of things sometimes when one least expects it, he fell unconscious almost instantly and slept like a log.

Chapter Twenty-eight

MISTRESS NIKKI WAS A highly enigmatic woman, Paul was well aware of that. She was also full of surprises. God knows, he'd had ample experience of that. It seemed to him sometimes that when she wasn't beating the living daylights out of him or otherwise sexually torturing him she liked nothing better than to toy with him, treat him as her puppet, her submissive plaything.

And she did it to Paul again: lured him stumbling into one of her traps. He'd waited patiently for days on end for her to summon him to her home, or to a hotel, or wherever. But what she did instead, when she finally condescended to get in touch, was to go right back to square one. She paid him a visit just as she'd done the very first time he'd met her. Unlike that occasion, though, this was the briefest of visits.

'Come on, slave,' Nikki said almost before she was through the front door of his flat. 'We're going on a little trip.'

'If you don't mind me asking, Mistress,' Paul said respectfully. 'Where are we going?'

'Not far,' she replied. 'Hampstead.'

As chance would have it, this was not an area of London with which Paul had ever become familiar to any extent. He knew of course that it was mainly residential and that it had a famous heath. Indeed he had a dim recollection from his childhood of being taken there once to fly his kite. He also knew that it was generally regarded as one of the most salubrious parts of the capital and that some extremely wealthy people lived there, a number of them high-profile media types and the like. And that was about the sum total of what he did know about the place. Anyway, he said to himself, Mistress Nikki telling him she was taking him there wasn't exactly helpful. In fact it didn't tell him a damn thing.

Paul followed Nikki out into the weak sunshine of a mild autumn day. He felt a sense of resignation mingled with sexual excitement, knowing that he was about to embark on another perverted sexual adventure that the dominatrix had devised for him. But what would it entail this time? He hadn't the faintest idea. She knew everything and he knew nothing. No change there then.

Mistress Nikki got into the driving seat of her car, which was a Mercedes. The vehicle was as big and new as Paul's Fiat was small and old. She leaned over and opened the door on the passenger side, gesturing to Paul to get in. As they drove off Paul sank into the leather upholstery and wondered again about what exactly would be waiting for him in Hampstead. A heady mixture of fear and sexual anticipation rose up inside him as they crawled through the London traffic, getting slowly nearer to their destination. Finally the traffic cleared and they got to a road sign that announced that they were now in Hampstead. They drove on for another five or ten minutes, the surroundings becoming ever more leafy and affluent as they went. 'Here we are,' Nikki said at last. 'Groveton Court'.

They had arrived at a large Georgian house that, Nikki went on to inform Paul, had been converted several years ago into a small number of luxury apartments, each worth millions of pounds. The block was set well back behind a high wall, the wrought-iron double gates of which were locked. Nikki got out of the car, pressed a number of buttons on the access panel that was to one side of the gates. These then whirred into operation, swinging back on their expensively automated hinges. Nikki climbed back into the car and took the vehicle up a tree-lined driveway to a circular parking area under an ancient plane tree, where she parked.

She and Paul stepped from the Mercedes and Nikki locked it, putting the key into her handbag. They went up the path to a massive black door with fine brass trimmings that was under a portico. The mild sunshine was starting to go now and a few dark clouds were gathering. In the shadow of the big Georgian house the day was cooling quickly. Paul felt very nervous but he also felt very excited too.

'The person we are going to visit is a woman called Alicia Germain. She lives in the penthouse apartment,' Nikki said. 'It's got great views over Hampstead Heath – not that that's going to be of any benefit to you,' she added cryptically, ominously even.

Entry to the property they were visiting was through the massive black door but admission was by buzzer. Nikki buzzed.

'Hello,' a woman's voice said.

'It's Nikki.'

The woman said nothing more but with another buzzing sound the black entrance door was unlocked from on high.

Nikki took Paul through the lobby, which had a vaulted ceiling and floorboards that were polished like glass. She summoned a brass-gated lift, which she and Paul entered. They alighted on the top floor and crossed an expensively carpeted landing lit by skylights. They arrived at an entrance door, which was the only one on the landing, and Nikki knocked at it.

The door was opened by a tall pale-skinned woman of considerable beauty and formidable presence. She had dark brown shoulder-length hair with a shiny fringe hanging over her forehead, big piercing blue eyes, strong cheekbones, and a wide fleshy mouth of extraordinary sensuality. The woman also had a demeanour that Paul found truly overwhelming. It was all in the eyes and the lips. She had extremely attractive eyes but a gaze that was so challengingly direct and yet at the same time unreadable that he couldn't help but be frightened by it. Similarly the set of her wonderfully sensuous mouth managed to be both generous and severe at the same time.

The woman excited Paul immensely and so did the way her shapely figure looked in the killer black leather dress she was wearing, which was very tight and very short. She also had on long boots of the same colour. When she raised her arms briefly to brush back her hair, the dress slid up her thighs seductively. Paul could feel his cock stiffening, straining against his pants.

Who was this amazing woman, he wondered. She had to be a dominatrix; you didn't need to be a brain surgeon to work that out. And she was a seriously rich one as well, that was clear too. But, those obvious facts apart, where exactly did she fit into the scheme of things? Paul wondered. Where was her place in the bizarre parallel universe that Mistress Nikki had created for him?

The woman had said nothing when she'd opened the door and caused time to stand still for Paul. After that brief eternity she stepped beckoningly backward, waving an elegant hand. Paul went into the apartment and Nikki followed him but did not shut the door.

'This is Mistress Alicia, slave,' Nikki told Paul. 'She is your Mistress now. Whatever orders she gives you, you must obey them.'

And that was *all* Nikki said to him. She mouthed a brief goodbye to Mistress Alicia and then she was gone, the door closing behind her as she left the apartment.

Chapter Twenty-nine

PAUL FELT THOROUGHLY CONFUSED, disorientated. What exactly had Nikki meant when she'd said that Alicia was his Mistress *now*? She must have meant temporarily, surely. She must have inadvertently missed out a word. What she'd meant to say was *for now*. He couldn't ask her to clarify because she'd disappeared from the apartment with something approaching the speed of light.

She couldn't have meant this new arrangement to be a permanent change, he said to himself incredulously. But perhaps she had meant exactly what she'd said. Full of surprises though she was, Mistress Nikki wasn't in the habit of saying what she didn't mean or of equivocating. She'd said what she'd said and it appeared to be unequivocal. Well, he couldn't be expected to stand for that. Mistress Nikki had gone too far this time. What she'd done wasn't reasonable. It was more than unreasonable, it was absolutely outrageous. That was it, Paul thought angrily, he'd had enough.

He should just walk away, that's what he should do. What did he mean 'should', Paul remonstrated with himself. Don't procrastinate about the matter, don't agonize over it. He must be decisive, he told himself. Do it, do it right now. He must make his apologies to the stunning leather-clad woman standing in front of him and leave. What was she going to do if she didn't like it – wrestle him to the ground? He should go home on his own. He didn't have transport with him but that wouldn't be a problem. This was Hampstead, not Outer Mongolia. That's what he'd do, then, no more vacillating – he'd walk away.

And where would that get him, the devil's advocate inside him asked. He knew for certain Mistress Nikki would never contact him again if he did that. And then he really would be in trouble. Jesus, worse than that, much worse – it would all be over. It would be finished; *he'd* be finished. Talk about burning your bridges! So, no, he mustn't do anything rash.

Nikki was testing him by handing him over to Mistress Alicia, that was it, Paul told himself. The very last thing he should do was to turn around and walk away, that would be disastrous. The right course was to show Mistress Alicia that he could take whatever she had to dish out to him. She would report back favourably to Mistress Nikki and, *voila*, all would be well – she'd take him back.

The dauntingly beautiful woman who was now Paul's Mistress – in his mind now, his *temporary* Mistress – looked him up and down appraisingly. Did she like what she saw, Paul wondered, or did she have doubts. He had no way of knowing. If Nikki was enigmatic, this woman was downright inscrutable.

Then she ushered him wordlessly into her living room. The huge room, its tall windows looking down over the verdant expanse of Hampstead Heath, was exquisitely appointed. The last remnants of the day's sunlight glinted on the deep dark patina of the furniture – all soft leather and highly polished mahogany – and the oil paintings on the walls were exceptionally fine. As well as being a person of considerable wealth, Paul said to himself as he looked around in admiration at his elegant surroundings, his new Mistress was obviously also a woman of consummate taste.

Alicia then broke the silence, uttering the first words she'd ever spoken to Paul and at the same time issuing her first command to him. 'Get undressed,' she said.

Was Mistress Alicia sexually excited now, Paul wondered as he started to remove his clothing. He simply didn't know since she remained self-assurance and inscrutability personified, her gaze continuing to be both frighteningly direct and yet at the same time completely unreadable. Paul tried to match her in coolness of approach but it was a humiliating failure – a deliciously humiliating failure, it has to be said. As soon as he'd stripped off completely his cock betrayed his obvious arousal. It was as hard as a rock.

What did Mistress Alicia think of Paul's big erect shaft standing up there in front of his taut abdomen? What did she think of his firm balls, his slim muscular thighs? Did the sight of him make her horny? Was her clit twitching? Was she all wet and sticky, soaked with the sap of desire? Who could tell? Her poker-faced expression certainly didn't give anything away.

Keeping the same unreadable expression on her beautiful face, Alicia brought the fingers of her right hand to Paul's erection and he gasped when she started to stroke it. Soon she had worked up a nice slow rhythm. And as she stroked and stroked his cock, pushing her fist up and down on it, he became ever more excited. His breathing became ragged and his knees started to buckle, he felt so weak with desire.

Then it hit him like a thunderbolt, a sudden shock of recognition. Paul recognized the insistent stroke of that hand. Leather glove or no leather glove, he'd have recognized it anywhere. 'It was you in the hotel room,' he said out loud. He hadn't *meant* to say it out loud, hadn't meant to say anything out loud. And he regretted it as soon as he had.

Mistress Alicia took her hand away from Paul's cock. 'I didn't give you permission to speak,' she said in a tight voice. 'I'm going to have to punish you for speaking out of turn.' And with that she hauled back and struck him twice across the face, open-handed. She struck first with the palm of her hand, which was glistening and wet with Paul's pre-cum, and second with the back of her hand. Paul's head rang like a bell and he felt stunned, both from the violence of the two swift blows he'd just received and the casual manner in which they had been delivered.

'You need to be clear about one thing right from the start, slave,' Alicia said sternly, her gaze penetrating through him like a laser beam. 'You are not permitted to speak to me unless spoken to and when you do speak to me you are always to call me Mistress. Otherwise you are not to talk at all.'

I'm sorry, Mistress. I'm so, so sorry. I didn't mean to speak, it just slipped out; please forgive me. That was what Paul wanted to say. But he didn't say anything. He wasn't *allowed* to say anything. Speaking without being spoken to and omitting to call Alicia 'Mistress' had been foolhardy, and what he had said had been even more foolhardy. He really regretted what he'd done. He would have liked to have got off on the right foot with Mistress Alicia but instead he'd made a stupid faux pas and had deservedly had to pay the painful price for that. Even so, he knew what he'd said had been right. It *had* been her in Room 35 of Earl's Hotel. *Hadn't it?*

143

Chapter Thirty

MISTRESS ALICIA TURNED AND left the room then, but she was not gone for long. She returned with a heavy leather flogger and several other BDSM items. These consisted of a blindfold and gag, both of soft black leather; and a pair of handcuffs and a pair of leg irons, both chained.

'Hold your hands out in front of you,' she told Paul and she locked the cuffs on him.

'Get over the footstool on your hands and knees,' she said next, pointing towards a leather-covered footstool that was nearby. Once Paul was in position she locked him into the leg irons and then she buckled the blindfold behind his head.

'Open your mouth,' Alicia ordered finally before gagging him with the soft leather gag.

Paul was almost certain about what was going to happen next. He wasn't wrong. But he wasn't right either in the sense that – more fool him – he hadn't anticipated the sheer ferocity of the beating he was about to receive.

There was a loud crack and another and another as three fearsome blows from the heavy leather flogger landed across the cheeks of his backside. The pain was unbelievable, like lines of fire on his flesh.

Then Alicia spoke again. 'The sound insulation in this apartment is superb,' she said, adding mysteriously, 'particularly in one part of it.'

Another noisy crack sounded as she brought the flogger down a fourth time with full force, causing Paul to squirm with pain. Then she delivered her fifth strike, which was so ferocious that it caused him to let out an explosive grunt of agony from beneath his gag. He bucked wildly, trying to twist away from the next blow as yet another line of fire was drawn in his flesh. Then came another full-armed swing of the flogger and another loud crack. And another. And another. Mistress Alicia continued to rain down the heavy blows until a florid pattern of agonizing pain covered his backside.

But even as he fought in vain to escape the vicious blows that landed on his rear, Paul's body was transmuting the pain into a fierce sexual pleasure. It began to surge through him like an inferno until he was certain that he was about to climax. He could feel the push of his hard cock against the leather surface beneath him each time the whip landed on his backside and he knew that he was now only a few seconds away from orgasm.

That was when Alicia stopped beating him. Paul was left hanging. He was so near and yet so far from climaxing. His breathing had become ragged and his mind a whirl of pain, humiliation and sexual excitement. He wished against wish that Mistress Alicia would start beating him hard again and that she would keep on beating him like that until he achieved the release he craved. But the dominatrix had other ideas.

She left the room again – Paul distinctly heard her open its door and go out – but, as before, she soon returned. And this time her return was silent. The first Paul was aware of her reappearance was when he suddenly felt her cool fingers on his wrists as she unlocked and removed his handcuffs. He then felt her hands on the back of his head as she went on to remove his gag and blindfold. She did not, however, remove his leg irons.

Paul looked up and shuddered with desire when he saw what it was that Mistress Alicia had done after she'd left the room this last time. She had taken off all her clothes and was now utterly, gloriously naked. And she looked incredible, magnificent, superb. She had a knock-out body: creamy-white and sumptuous and beautifully proportioned with firm breasts tipped with erect nipples, shapely legs and a prominent, hairless mound. The sight of her inflamed Paul, making his breath quicken and his erection pulse.

The naked dominatrix seated herself on the leather couch opposite him. 'I want you to kneel up from the footstool and then crawl over to me, slave," she said. "I would then like you to pleasure me. Would you like that too?' she added, parting her legs wide.

'… Mistress …' Paul gulped. He could barely speak. An intense feeling of desire had swept through him. The chains between his ankles clinked softly as he crawled on all fours towards her, his body burning with sexual arousal. His cock, which was stiff and throbbing between his legs, was drizzling precum.

When Paul had crawled into position before Mistress Alicia she shoved her hand into her pussy until it was wet with love juice. She then took her hand from her sex and thrust it towards Paul's mouth. She parted her own lips quizzically. 'Would you like to lick this?' she asked.

'Yes, Mistress,' he gasped and, sticking out his tongue he sucked at her fingers, licking her juices away.

'Worship my sex with your mouth,' she said next and he immediately obeyed, burrowing his face into her hairless pussy and kissing its plump mound. Alicia's hands clasped Paul's head, pressing his face further between her thighs until his mouth was pushed against her labia. He licked and sucked at the lips of her sex and slid his tongue inside. He licked persistently inside her pussy with a steady rhythm: lick, lick, lick.

And the dominatrix enjoyed it. Oh yes, she enjoyed it. The pressure of her hands on his hair told Paul that he was doing what pleased her. And there were other signs too: her thighs were quivering, her pussy soaking wet now. Alicia gasped with delight as Paul licked her and licked her, lingering over the hard button of her clitoris. She joined in too. She bucked and moved her sex more rapidly against the regular licking of his tongue.

He licked and she bucked until she climaxed. Shaking with excitement, Mistress Alicia cried out, coming in short intense spasms of erotic delight. Then she pulled Paul away from her sex by his hair and looked into his face, giving him a rapacious, vulpine grin. It made his breath quicken further, made his pulsing, drizzling cock stiffen even more.

'Want to carry on pleasuring me, slave?' she asked, getting up off the couch and onto all fours on the floor.

'Yes, Mistress,' he said, his breath coming even more quickly now.

'Kneel behind me,' she said. 'But not too close, understood?'

'Understood, Mistress.'

'Like what you see?' she said, wiggling her backside at him.

'God yes, Mistress.' He gazed at the glorious curve of her hips, at her wet open pussy, at the pink rosebud of her anus.

'Would you like to lick my arsehole, slave?' she asked, looking back at him seductively.

'Yes, Mistress,' he gasped.

'Then tell me so – say the words.'

'I would like to lick your arsehole, Mistress,' Paul said, his voice trembling with desire.

'Beg me.' Alicia brought her hands behind her and put one on each cheek of her backside, pulling them widely apart.

'Please let me lick your arsehole, Mistress,' Paul said, even more of a tremble in his voice as he gazed at her spread cheeks, her open anal hole.

'Once more with feeling,' she demanded.

'Oh, *please, please* let me lick your arsehole, Mistress,' he said, his eyes never leaving her anus. He felt inflamed with passion, in pain with lust.

'I'll have to think about it,' she said, flexing her anal hole enticingly.

After a long silence during which Paul felt tortured with excitement as he gazed at her inviting anus, Alicia said, 'All right, I'll allow you to.' She removed her hands from her backside and put them back in front of her.

Paul crawled forward, his leg irons clinking. He then brought his mouth into the space between the cheeks of Alicia's backside. Paul snaked out his tongue and began delicately probing the tight ring of muscles that was her sphincter, gently moving his tongue in and out. 'Mmmmmm …' he moaned appreciatively, wallowing in the task he had been given, his sinuous red tongue wiggling and wiggling.

'Do you like that, slave?' Alicia said. 'Do you like licking my arsehole?'

Paul stopped licking her for a moment. 'Oooh yes, Mistress,' he said before returning his tongue to her anal hole and redoubling his efforts, flick-flick-flicking away. The strokes of his tongue became longer after a while, electric, as he lovingly pleasured her anus.

'Is this making you excited, slave?' she asked.

'Mm-hmmmm …Yes, Mistress.' His hard cock was pulsing like crazy now and drizzling pre-cum constantly.

Mistress Alicia drew away. 'Lay down on your back on the floor,' she told Paul. 'I want to sit on your face.'

He did what she said and got into position, his ankles still hobbled by the chained leg irons. His erection was sticking up rigidly from his thighs. It was covered with glittering wetness, as if it had just been withdrawn from Alicia's soaked pussy.

'Are you even more excited, slave?' the dominatrix asked, looking down into his gleaming eyes as she started to straddle his face.

'Y ... y ... yes, Mistress,' Paul gasped. 'I ...' But he had no chance to elaborate as she shoved her crotch down firmly over his mouth.

'Worship my sex with your mouth again,' she ordered and he got to work once more, using his tongue to excellent effect. He flicked it over her clit and deep into her pussy as she ground her hips down on his face.

Paul continued to expertly tongue-fuck Alicia, licking up into her sex rhythmically. It made her shudder and moan and rock back and forth on his face. Then she brought her fingers to her clitoris. She began to rub out a frantic rhythm over her clit as he licked inside her pussy with his busy tongue.

Paul licked even harder and Alicia ground her fingers harder still over her stiff clit as she built towards her orgasm. Then it arrived and she surrendered herself to a climax so powerful that it made her quiver and jerk with pleasure over his mouth.

'That's me done,' Alicia announced all of a sudden. 'Which means that that's you done too.' She climbed off his face, which was now shiny with her juices, and got to her feet.

She couldn't mean it, Paul thought desperately, his mind now full of his own unrequited need. It was *his* turn now, surely. The hard wet cock jutting from his body was so thick and throbbing and ready by this stage that it looked as if it might burst.

'Oh, did you want me to fuck you?' Alicia said, her eyes widening. 'You *look* as if you want me to fuck you.'

'Yes please, Mistress,' he moaned, breathing heavily.

'You want me to sit on this?' she asked, leaning down and slapping his erection. It stung, but felt good at the same time.

'Yes please, Mistress,' he panted. His vision had gone all blurry he was so excited.

'Please what, slave?'

'Please sit on my cock, Mistress,' Paul groaned, his vision still flashing.

'You want me to sit on your cock and fuck you?'

'I'm *desperate* for you to sit on my cock and fuck me, Mistress,' he said, his voice beseeching as he looked up at her.

'What are you saying, slave?' Alicia asked with mock-incredulity. 'Are you saying that even though I am now sated and no longer want sex, you want me to sit on your cock and give you, what, a *pity fuck?*'

'Yes, oh yes, Mistress.'

'Beg me.'

'Please sit on my cock and give me a pity fuck, Mistress,' Paul begged. '*Please, please, please.*' His heart was pounding, his cock was pounding; his whole body was shaking, making the chains to his leg irons clink and clank.

'Say, pretty please.'

'Pretty please, Mistress,' he panted.

Alicia looked down at him for a long moment, her blue eyes shining. Then she gave him her answer. 'Certainly not,' she said sharply. 'Now, get back on to your knees where you belong.'

Chapter Thirty-one

PAUL DID AS HE'D been told, after which the naked dominatrix knelt down herself in order to adjust his bondage. She did not remove his leg irons but she did replace his chained handcuffs, cuffing his wrists in front of him and retaining the key in her hand as she stood back up. 'Keep your head bowed and follow me on all fours,' Alicia said and led him crawling out of the room, the chains from his handcuffs and leg irons clanking as he went. She took him on his hands and knees down an internal corridor, which was carpeted in deep red and at the end of which was a heavy oak door. She unlocked the door with the key in its lock but did not at first open it.

'Get to your feet,' she told Paul. 'But keep your head bowed. Understood?'

'Yes, Mistress,' he replied and got up, careful to keep his head down. He remained extremely aroused and his cock was still achingly erect. He watched as Alicia unlocked his handcuffs.

'Put your arms behind you,' she ordered next and relocked the handcuffs to his wrists. Then she opened the door and pushed him, hobbling, into the room beyond. She turned the overhead lights on and the large, windowless room they were now in was at once bathed in a pale radiance.

'I'll leave you to look round your new home,' Alicia said then and before Paul knew it she was gone, locking the door behind her.

The objects in the room became visible in the soft light and Paul began to wander slowly and stumblingly in his leg irons to take a closer look at them. His eyes widened and his erection throbbed at what he saw in the cavernous, windowless room in which he now found himself. The room – the walls, ceiling and floor of which were all black – contained a whole range of beautifully constructed dungeon equipment. This included a wall-mounted cross, a whipping bench and a suspension machine.

There was a leather-covered bondage table, a metal spreader bar with leather manacle attachments that hung from the ceiling by chains, and a large steel-framed cage. There was a black leather throne with a small table next to it on which there were several implements of correction. There were also two multi-strapped torture chairs, one of which was horizontal and the other upright. The vertical torture chair had a large black dildo strapped to its seat.

There was an open closet against one of the walls that covered most of its length and contained a huge collection of BDSM implements. From the sheer size and variety of the collection, Paul surmised that Mistress Alicia must have been several years assembling it. He felt a shiver of excitement as his gaze passed over all the straps, tawses, crops, whips, paddles and canes. There was a variety of chains, cuffs, and clamps as well as gags of several sorts, including one that was intended to be inflated after being placed in the mouth. There were also several dildo gags as well as a number of strap-on dildoes and the harnesses to go with them along with various different types of lubricant. There were leather slave harnesses with straps that buckled and locked.

There was also a leather body bag, identical to the one Mistress Nikki had bought for Paul and used on him so memorably in her own dungeon. There was in addition a leather hood almost identical to the one she'd put on him on that same occasion.

Paul leaned forward and examined this last item more closely. There were holes in the nose-piece to let air in, but the eye and mouth areas were closed. It had adjustable straps that buckled behind the head and under the jaw. Paul thought back to that amazing occasion when Mistress Nikki had strapped him inside the body bag and then covered his head with a leather hood very much like this one so that he'd been unable to see or hear or speak. He remembered how she'd then gone on to torture his nipples and genitals with such exquisite sadism that in the end he'd felt that he had entered another stratosphere.

That had been an extraordinarily intense out-of-body experience, mind-bendingly unforgettable. Paul shivered with the memory of it and his breathing became shallow and thin, as if suddenly there were not enough air in the room. His cock became more ragingly hard than ever too and he felt a strong urge to masturbate, bring himself off. But his hands were manacled behind his back, preventing him from doing any such thing. Anyway, he strongly suspected that Mistress Alicia would have frowned on him doing for himself what she had so patently not been prepared to do for him herself a few minutes ago – provide him with sexual release. Come to think of it, Paul said to himself, that was probably why she'd handcuffed his arms behind his back in the first place.

Trying his best to ignore his raging hard-on, Paul continued with his tour of what Mistress Alicia had described as his 'new home'. He wondered what exactly she'd meant by using that term. It hardly seemed appropriate. As far as he could see, this was a dungeon – a place exclusively of punishment, erotic or otherwise. It was a magnificent dungeon, true. It was even bigger and better and more expensively equipped than Mistress Nikki's dungeon, and that was saying something. But it was still a dungeon. It was not a home in any real sense.

Then Paul came to the end of the big dark chamber where he found an evenly spaced row of three doors that were as black as the walls that surrounded them. By the time he'd opened each of these doors and seen what lay beyond them he knew exactly what Mistress Alicia had meant by her words. Because behind the first door was a kitchen-dining room, behind the second a bathroom and WC, and behind the third a bedroom containing a single bed. All of the rooms were relatively compact and were kitted out neatly and cleanly. They were all spick and span, clearly ready for immediate use. None of the three rooms had windows but it was clear from the narrow vents he found that they were air conditioned. When he looked further he found that the same was true of the equally windowless dungeon area itself; it was air-conditioned also.

Another memory flashed into Paul's mind and with it came a swiftly dawning recognition. He suddenly remembered something that Mistress Nikki had said when they'd arrived at Groveton Court. It hadn't made any sense to him at the time but it certainly did now. She'd said that Alicia's penthouse apartment had great views over Hampstead Heath, 'not that that's going to be of any benefit to you.' So, he said to himself nervously, that was what she'd meant by that cryptic, that *threatening* comment.

Then he remembered something Mistress Alicia herself had said. It had been just after she'd started flogging him so viciously in her living room. 'The sound insulation in this apartment is superb,' she'd said, adding mysteriously 'particularly in one part of it.' There was nothing the slightest bit mysterious about that statement any more.

All of this gave Paul very serious cause for concern. What in God's name had he got himself into by coming to this place, he wondered with a tremor of fear. More precisely, what in God's name had Mistress Nikki got him into by bringing him here and leaving him to the anything but tender mercies of the formidable Mistress Alicia? Paul wondered too whether his throbbing erection would *ever* go down.

Chapter Thirty-two

'STILL STANDING PROUD, I see,' Mistress Alicia remarked sardonically, eyeing Paul's erection. Her words nearly made him jump out of his skin. He hadn't even heard her come back into the dungeon, so distracted had he been by the disturbing thoughts that had been racing through his mind.

'Follow me,' the naked dominatrix commanded and led Paul hobbling in his leg irons to the area of the dungeon where the metal spreader bar with leather manacle attachments at either end hung by chains from the ceiling. She went to the open cabinet of BDSM items and picked out another identical spreader bar with leather manacle attachments, which she placed on the ground directly beneath the hanging bar. She unlocked and removed Paul's handcuffs and leg irons and, in substitution, manacled his wrists and ankles to the ends of the spreader bars so that he was held standing in bondage in a spread-eagled position.

Then she went back to the open cabinet and selected several implements of discipline: a wooden paddle, a leather strap, a cat o' nine tails, a braided leather flogger, a swagger cane and – the implement she decided to employ first – a riding crop. Using the leather tip of the crop, she began to beat Paul's cock, concentrating her attentions especially on its swollen head. The pain was bearable at first, her beating initially quite restrained, but the severity of her blows rapidly escalated. The resultant pain was starting to become unendurable when, all of a sudden, she stopped.

Mistress Alicia put the crop to one side and went behind Paul. She began vigorously spanking his rear with her hand, and then moved on to beating it with the wooden paddle before switching to the leather strap. Alicia beat him at length and with ever-increasing ferocity, and then stopped suddenly. But this was only so that she could go to his front again where she returned to using the riding crop. She beat the head of his phallus with the leather tip of the crop ever more viciously until the pain was so extreme that Paul was certain that he could stand no more. And then, mercifully, she stopped. But only to go behind him again.

The dominatrix started to flay Paul's back and rear with the cat o' nine tails, causing numerous welts to appear on his skin like fresh-cut flowers. She followed this with the braided leather flogger that stung even more painfully than the cat and caused more welts to appear on his skin. Paul was in a state of agony now that was so acute that it had transformed itself into something close to ecstasy, his system by this stage being thoroughly awash with endorphins.

Then Mistress Alicia freed him from the spreader bars. 'I have one last instruction for you today,' she stated, standing before him in all her naked glory. 'I want you to bring yourself off while I give you a final beating, which I will do with this swagger cane. When I get to the tenth stripe you are to climax, but only after you have sought my permission. Understood, slave?'

'Yes, Mistress,' he replied, panting. Then he took his erection into his hand and closed his fingers around it. As soon as Alicia started caning him, Paul began masturbating. He could feel his cock throb and pulse against his pounding fist as the swagger cane swished down agonizingly again and again. Swish! Swish! Swish! Swish! Swish! Swish! Swish! Swish! Swish! Swish!

'Permission to come, Mistress,' he cried out frantically after the tenth agonizing strike, his backside feeling as if it was ablaze and his cock about to explode at any moment.

'Permission granted,' the dominatrix replied and he climaxed exuberantly, grunting in satisfaction with each orgasmic spasm as cum sprayed out of his cock in liquid abundance.

Then Mistress Alicia spoke to Paul for the last time that day. 'I'm going to leave you on your own now, slave,' she said. 'Sleep well,' she added, both the sentiment and the tone of voice she used to express it seeming to Paul to be uncharacteristically affectionate. Then she disappeared from the room as silently as she had arrived, although Paul did hear her lock the door behind her.

Chapter Thirty-three

THE FUNNY THING WAS that Paul did sleep well that night, very well indeed and dreamlessly too. It was only after he'd woken that his mind began to be assailed by disturbing thoughts again. During the course of getting out of bed and bathing and breakfasting in isolation in what Mistress Alicia had described as his 'new home' he agonized over what he might say to the dominatrix the first time she gave him a chance.

Paul decided that he would explain to Mistress Alicia with the utmost respect that while he would of course like to stay here with her he couldn't do so for any length of time. He would explain that this was because if he did he wouldn't be able to do his job, which would cause him to be sacked, resulting in the loss of his livelihood, his flat, his car, everything. He was sure she'd understand, Paul would tell her – when she allowed him to converse with her in any meaningful way, that is. It didn't look as if today was going to be the day for that, though ...

Mistress Alicia was back in the dungeon with Paul once more and was as naked as he was again. Paul was standing before her, his shaft rock hard.

'Go over there, slave,' Alicia said, motioning in the direction of the wall-mounted cross. She stood Paul with his face to the cross and strapped his upper arms, wrists, thighs and ankles to the equipment.

Paul could guess in broad terms what was going to happen next and knew that the most he could hope for would be some kind of warm up. But yet again there was no warm up. The dominatrix simply took hold of a heavy leather flogger and began to whip him hard with it straightaway. Each strike was a flash of pure pain that caused him to shudder and cry out as she used the cruel implement on his backside. The whip landed on each occasion with a sharp resonating sound and he felt its harsh sting time and time again as she swung it through the air faster and faster.

On and on Alicia whipped Paul, every lash striking his rear in a regular rhythm and each time bringing that flash of pain again. His flesh quivered constantly as she increased the momentum of the beating, showering him with blows. She did not stop until his backside was covered in lacerations and the pain that soared through him had become almost overwhelming.

Mistress Alicia then stopped beating Paul, who found that he couldn't stop himself from trembling. She detached him from the cross and told him to get on to his knees. 'I want you to worship my sex again,' she said, standing above him and parting her thighs.

Paul obeyed immediately, burying his face in Alicia's pussy, which was already wet with passion. He kissed the lips of her sex with his own hot lips and licked her clitoris, his tongue gentle and rough by turns. She let out a low moan of pleasure as he pushed his face further upwards and thrust his tongue deep into her pussy. His tongue played inside her sex, licking and sucking and probing with increasing force until he brought her cresting to a delirious climax.

'I want you to lick my arsehole again now, slave,' Alicia ordered next, turning around and bending forward slightly.

Again Paul complied straight away, touching his lips to Alicia's anus. Darting his tongue as far up her anus as it would go, he probed and prodded hard into her hole. Alicia squeezed the muscles of her anus around his tongue and at the same time brought her fingers to her sex, which was gleaming with silvery wetness. She stroked her clit before pressing two fingers directly into her pussy, sliding between the tumescent labia and penetrating fast and furious.

Paul's cock swelled even more and a stream of pre-cum began to seep from its slit onto the dungeon floor as he listened to the wet sound of Alicia's agile fingers working in and out of her sex. He brought his hands up to spread her buttocks further so that his tongue could cut a path even deeper inside her. He licked her anus more and more frantically, his pace growing faster in time with her masturbating fingers, until a shuddering moan escaped her and she climaxed deliriously again.

Mistress Alicia then told Paul to stand up and she led him over to the horizontal torture chair. She buckled his wrists behind his head, his knees up and his legs wide apart. '*Very* inviting,' she purred, admiring Paul's hard wet shaft, which was jutting into the air, and his arsehole which was pulsing constantly.

The dominatrix harnessed on a sizeable strap-on dildo and coated it liberally with lubricant. She went on to ease the dildo into Paul's anus. He let out a groan, his cock spitting out a throb of pre-cum as his sphincter adjusted to the large dildo. Alicia began to sodomize him hard and, as she built up ever greater pace, also started pulling on his cock. She masturbated him briskly, her hand moving with a swift, urgent rhythm.

As Alicia continued to bugger Paul energetically she worked her hand up and down his hard shaft with equal energy. Her fingers became increasingly smeared with pre-cum until they were covered with it. Then she abruptly stopped both buggering and masturbating him.

Mistress Alicia removed the strap-on dildo from Paul's anal hole and took off the harness. She picked up a set of chained metal clamps and attached them to his nipples, their teeth immediately biting hard into his chest. Then she pulled on the clamps, sending sharp jags of pain through his body and spasms of sensation directly to his pulsing shaft, which spat out another throb of pre-cum.

The dominatrix took hold of a small flogger and began to whip Paul furiously between the legs, aiming her blows first at the insides of his thighs and between the anus, and then at his genitals. She concentrated on his cock, which was now painfully engorged. Its wet bulbous head was becoming an increasingly furious purple in colour. Each blow to Paul's aching shaft made him shiver with pain and desire. When the blows landed it was as if his cock was being beaten and caressed at the same time

Paul's whole body now ached with extreme pain that burned like a fire into his flesh and yet he'd never known such sexual excitement in his entire life. And that was the predominant sensation now. Pain had turned to white hot lust.

Mistress Alicia then leaned forward so that she could suck Paul's cock. Rounding her lips and closing them around its hardness, she took his penis into her mouth, pressing against its punished wet head with her tongue. Her lips kissed and rubbed against his shaft so that it strained against her mouth. She positioned herself further forward so that she could pull more of his length into her mouth. The up-and-down movement of her head went ever faster as she sucked his cock harder and harder.

While continuing to suck Paul's cock voraciously, Alicia pulled hard on his nipple clamps. Intense pain flashed through him but he also felt extreme, all-consuming pleasure, as if his whole being had become a sexual organ that was about to explode into orgasm. He writhed in his bonds with agony and sensation, ached with pain and lust. His nerves were on fire, the heat of desire swept through his body, and blood coursed in his aching cock. Finally Paul's ever-mounting erotic rise became volcanic, and he climaxed convulsively. Arching up and writhing helplessly in his bondage, he pumped out great surging waves of cum into Alicia's hot wet mouth.

'Mmmmn, delicious,' she said afterwards, sounding for all the world like the cat that had just swallowed the cream. 'Your cum tasted even better than his did.' Whatever the hell *that* was supposed to mean.

Chapter Thirty-four

PAUL SPENT ANOTHER NIGHT in his unfamiliar bed. When he awoke and looked at the clock provided for him on the bedside table and saw what time it was the predominant sensation he felt was that of surprise. When he'd first put his head down on the pillow the evening before he'd been sure that the previous night had been some kind of fluke and that this time he'd experience great difficulty sleeping. But he had got it wrong. He'd dropped off almost instantly and enjoyed another unexpectedly long, deep and dreamless sleep. There followed another day, and several other doses of the kind of dungeon domination that had not so very long ago been the exclusive preserve of his dreams and fantasies ...

Paul stood before Mistress Alicia who was again as naked as he was, although this time with one notable exception. She didn't have a large silicone butt-plug in place while he most certainly did.

Paul marvelled anew at the sheer physical beauty of the ravishing brunette who was currently his Mistress. He marvelled at the radiant loveliness of her features, at her milk-clear complexion, her glittering blue eyes, her wonderfully full sensuous lips. Oh, those lips! And he marvelled at the magnificence of her body – her firm rounded breasts, their nipples hard; the curves of her belly and thighs; her shaven pussy, the mons as smooth as silk; the long and enticing length of her shapely legs.

'Lie down flat on your back on the bondage table,' the naked dominatrix directed. 'Then spread your arms above your head but keep your legs together.'

Paul did as he was told, his heart thudding against his chest. Mistress Alicia buckled his wrists to the two up-most corners of the bondage table and attached clover clamps to his nipples, making him wince with pain. Next she used a length of black bondage rope to bind his ankles together before securing the end of the rope tightly to the foot of the table. When she was finished Paul was left laying in Y-shaped bondage and feeling extremely aroused, his erection thick and stiff. He pushed back with his hips and felt the large butt-plug that Alicia had inserted in his anus earlier shift. He pushed forward with his chest and felt the hard bite of the clover clamps that she'd just attached to his nipples.

And all the while Paul continued to gaze in awe at Mistress Alicia. He wondered what a week or a month or a year as the dungeon slave of this most sadistic, most imaginative, most inscrutable of women would be like. It would be like it had been so far, he decided: every waking moment charged with incredible sexual excitement. When he came to think about it he wasn't surprised that he'd not dreamed during the last couple of nights. He didn't need to dream and he didn't need to fantasize while he was here in what Alicia had described as his 'new home'. He was living his dreams and fantasies – hot and horny and helpless, laying in bondage in a dark dungeon, waiting for his captor, his Mistress of Torment, to do whatever she wanted to do to him.

Paul twisted restlessly and heaved against the bonds that held his wrists and ankles so tightly. But these actions just made his clamped nipples ache even more and the large butt-plug exert an even more insistent pressure inside his anus. He could feel his erection stiffen further as well and felt it begin to throb.

Paul's hard-on began to throb even more when Alicia did what she did next: coat it with lubricant from the bottle she was now holding. Paul had become immensely turned on by this stage. And looking at Alicia's lovely face as she finished lubing his erection he could tell that she was now extremely turned on as well. Underneath her characteristically unreadable expression he sensed that she was just barely in control. Already he could see how her eyes shone and her breath quickened when she returned his gaze.

The dominatrix let go of Paul's cock and put the bottle of lubricant to one side. She ran her hands up over her erect nipples and then turned away from Paul. She climbed onto the bondage table, keeping her back to him as she straddled his thighs. Spreading the cheeks of her backside, Alicia lined herself up carefully and slowly lowered herself onto Paul's shaft, sliding it into her anus. She kept lowering herself, pausing to let her muscles relax so that she could take more of it inside her until she was fully impaled, his big erect cock deep inside her anal hole.

Alicia then started to fuck herself in the arse, using Paul as no more than a human dildo. He couldn't do a thing, not a single thing. She did it all. She set the pace and controlled the motion since Paul was immobilised by his bonds. She rose and fell gently for a while, causing a similar sliding sensation in Paul's butt-plugged anus as she continued to sodomize herself with his erect cock. Paul's breathing became ever more laboured and he moaned with Alicia's movements, which were becoming steadily faster as she ground her hips down. It made him unbelievably excited to know that there was nothing he could do to alter or affect what she was doing to him and what she was using him for.

Mistress Alicia then reached behind her with both hands and grabbed the chain attaching Paul's nipple clamps together. Continuing to energetically fuck herself in the arse, she heightened the sensation for herself and – in a very different way – for her captive by giving the chain one yank after another until Paul began to whimper with pain. But Alicia was not to be deflected. She was beginning to whimper also as she slid up and down on his shaft faster and faster, her backside quivering deliciously. Her hands tightened on Paul's nipple clamps and she cried out in ecstasy as she had her first orgasm. She climaxed again immediately afterwards, crying out on a rising note. But she wanted more, craved one more mighty wave of erotic bliss, and her movements became wilder.

And the wilder Mistress Alicia got the closer she was driving Paul to his own orgasm. He was trembling in his bonds and his skin felt so hot it was as if he was burning up with fever. He jerked at the straps holding his wrists and the bondage rope securing his ankles and he cried out as he came, shuddering with emotion. He filled Alicia's anal hole with his hot liquid which came out in spurts that kept on coming. Paul couldn't hold himself back in any way and nor could Alicia. She too went completely wild, her whole body shaking, her cries of ecstasy joining with Paul's inside the dark dungeon that she wanted him to think of as his home.

Chapter Thirty-five

OR DID SHE WANT him to think of it as his kennel? Spool forward twenty-four hours and things had changed. Boy, had they changed! Paul had experienced dog days before but never like this…

Mistress Alicia was seated, naked, on her black leather throne and Paul was on his knees before her. He was naked too – but for his puppy restraints, that is: his wrist and ankle cuffs were linked by lengths of chain through rings on a tight leather ball strap. He was on all fours and his cock was fiercely erect and throbbing. In actual fact, he had no alternative but to be on all fours, either kneeling, as he now was, or on his back. This was because his current restraints rendered any other option out of the question. Paul tried to keep his breathing steady as he waited for Mistress Alicia to make a start. But he was singularly unsuccessful. He began panting … like a dog.

'I've heard about some degenerate women using their pet dogs for self-gratification,' Alicia said, running her fingers through her shiny dark hair. 'Let's see how I get on with my little doggie.' She spread her legs wantonly apart, revealing her bald pussy in all its gaping splendour, and gestured to him to scramble forward a little and go down on her. Paul brought his lips to her sex and immediately she began to groan with pleasure. He then started licking and lapping until she was squirming in delight. And all the while he was imagining that he really *was* a dog involved in this perverted act.

After a while Mistress Alicia told Paul to stop what he was doing. 'Use your fingers now,' she ordered, leaning forward and unbuckling his wrist cuffs so that he'd be able to kneel up and comply with her instruction. Paul worked two fingers of one hand in and out of her wet pussy while massaging her clit with the other. He carried on pleasuring Alicia in this way until her body trembled to a powerful climax.

'No canine could do that,' Alicia said, her blue eyes aglow, adding briskly, 'and that's the last time you'll be able to either.' She leaned over to the small table at the side of her throne and took hold of two things from the pile of leather items on its top. She put the black leather fist mitts over Paul's hands and padlocked them into place. She constrained him still further by re-buckling his wrist cuffs, which, as with his ankle cuffs, were still attached by chains to his ball strap.

'I think you're a bad dog,' Mistress Alicia said, putting a leather puppy head harness with a muzzle over his face. 'Yes, you're a bad dog and bad dogs need to be disciplined, don't they, boy?' Paul the doggie wagged his doggie head.

'I'm going to start by giving you a hard paddling.' Alicia announced, before getting to her feet and picking up a red leather paddle from the side table. She lifted the paddle high and swung it down forcefully. It landed with a resounding Thwack! and Paul jolted forward as the stinging pain bit into his rear. This caused an echoing flash of pain in his groin when the chains pulled on his tight ball strap. But that was just the start. Alicia went on to paddle him ever more harshly and did not stop until his rear was as red as her paddle. By the time Alicia had stopped paddling Paul both his backside and his groin were in agonizing pain and he was trembling convulsively.

'Calm down doggie, everything's all right,' Alicia said, giving a good imitation of someone who actually gave a shit. 'Good boy, good boy.' She stroked Paul's neck almost tenderly before buckling a puppy collar around it and attaching a puppy dog lead with a leather hand loop to that. She then took hold of the hand loop and led him, crawling around the dungeon floor for what she called his 'walkies'.

Paul in all truth found this completely unexpected new experience of abject humiliation at the hands of his cruel new Mistress intensely erotic. She was treating him now not even as the lowliest of humans, as she had done so far, but as a dumb animal. And he loved it, loved the sheer degradation of the experience. He was acutely aware of the pain he was still suffering from that brutal paddling but he was even more aware of the aching hardness of his cock pressing against his belly.

Pain was about to take precedence again, though – and how –

because Mistress Alicia then picked up an outstandingly vicious instrument of discipline. It was a cat o' nine tails made of heavy leather and pieces of *bone*. 'This is the only bone this pooch will be getting,' she announced, waving the whip tauntingly in front of his muzzled face. Paul felt petrified, his eyes widening in terror behind the muzzle.

'You've shown me already just how much you love pussy,' Mistress Alicia continued. 'But here's the reason dogs don't like cats one little bit.' She swung the cat o' nine tails through the air with a sadistic flourish. When it landed, excruciating pain seared across Paul's backside and his body burned like fury. Alicia brought the implement down again. It was just as excruciating. She carried on thrashing him like this until the agonizing pain Paul was suffering was almost unendurable. And then, to his immense relief, she put the cat to one side.

'Roll over and lie on your back like a good doggie,' Alicia told Paul next and when he did – on all fours, of course, because of his puppy restraints – his hugely erect cock reared in the air. She took hold of two savage nipple locks and when she attached them to his nipples the pain he experienced was acute, a lightening flash of agony. At the same time, though, it sent a pulsating tremor of pleasure to his hard cock, which began to drizzle pre-cum all over his belly in a constant stream.

Alicia told Paul to remain where he was on his back and to present his anus to her. He reached his leather paws down as far as his chains would allow and held the cheeks of his backside apart. Alicia knelt down, lubricated a particularly large puppy tail butt-plug and eased it skilfully into his anal hole. She pushed the sizeable object slowly but surely deep into Paul's body, causing him to groan with pleasure-pain as he felt the muscles of his anus squeezing and releasing around it. 'Doggie obviously likes that,' Alicia commented gleefully. 'His little tail's wagging … and so's his big cock.'

The puppy tail anal plug in place, she alternated between using a small but savage flogger and the leather tip of a small riding crop to beat the head of Paul's cock until he was yelping constantly with agony beneath his muzzle. And then all of a sudden excruciating pain turned into all-consuming ecstasy as Paul became overwhelmed by a massive orgasm, sticky wetness leaping and leaping from his punished cock until he was spent. Only then did Mistress Alicia stop beating him. 'Good boy,' she said soothingly, rubbing his cum-splattered belly. 'Good doggie. Your Mistress is all finished now.'

Chapter Thirty-six

MAYBE IT WAS A delayed reaction, Paul wasn't sure, but while he'd slept like the dead the three previous nights he hardly slept a wink that night. He tossed and turned in his bed, his mind in a turmoil of doubt and confusion. Go with the flow, he tried to tell himself. The dungeon existence he was living at the moment was like every one of his masochistic dreams and fantasies rolled into one. And then some. That pet training stuff had been out of this world. What a head trip! And as for ultra-sexy, ultra-sadistic Mistress Alicia, the woman completely blew him away. She was wonderfully, magnificently cruel. In his mind she was the ultimate Mistress of Torment.

So where was the problem, Paul asked himself. The problem was that none of this was going to last. How could it? It couldn't possibly be sustained. If he let it run its course, it was very likely that he'd emerge from the experience jobless and homeless.

On the other hand, Paul reflected, he was a single man and only had himself to worry about. It wasn't as if he'd be dragging a wife and family down with him. And anyway what did he really have to lose? What was so great about the life he would be throwing away? He had few belongings and most of these were second-hand and almost worthless, including his small aged car. His rented flat was second-rate and so was his poorly-paid job. If he threw all of that away how much of a loss would it represent in the grand scheme of things? No loss at all, he answered himself; none whatsoever. All right then, go with the flow, Paul decided. What the hell!

But wait, that wouldn't work, he realised. He would very quickly be missed by his employers apart from anybody else. There would be emails sent to his home computer that would remain unanswered, phone messages likewise. Indeed that process had almost certainly already begun. There would be draft manuscripts he'd been working on not returned, deadlines not met. The shit would hit the fan in no time at all.

So he'd get the sack, right? Wrong. Palmerton's Publishing wouldn't, *couldn't* just sack him out of hand. Things didn't work like that; there was such a thing as employment legislation. His employers would conduct themselves responsibly whether they wanted to or not. They would act on the assumption that perhaps he'd been struck down suddenly by a serious illness or some such disaster. Perhaps they would involve the police. There might be a forced entry to his flat, embarrassing discoveries made, not the least of these being the contents of his Fetish wardrobe.

No, now that he'd thought it through it was clear that going with the flow wouldn't work at all. It simply wasn't a viable option, attractive though it was in many ways. Paul wished Mistress Alicia would give him an opportunity to discuss some of these issues with her. Any reasonable person would allow him to do that. But she didn't. What she did instead was to tell him exactly what to do. But not before putting him into bondage …

Paul sat bound to the vertical torture chair. His arms and wrists were strapped to its sides. Another strap circled his chest and another his waist, holding him firmly against the back of the chair. His thighs were strapped together too as were his ankles, which were pulled back tight against the lowest rung of the chair. In addition the large black dildo that was strapped to the seat of the chair was now lodged deep inside him, filling his anus. He couldn't lift himself off the implement or make it move. Now that Mistress Alicia had put him into this latest bondage Paul wondered breathlessly what sexual torment she was going to inflict on him this time.

But Mistress Alicia, who was gloriously naked again as was so frequently her wont, didn't even touch Paul. She did torment him though, torment him as never before – mentally.

'We can deal with the details over the next few days, slave,' she announced out of the blue. 'But this is what I require of you. I want you to give up your job, your car, and your flat including everything in it. I want you to do these things so that you can be completely unencumbered. Once you have achieved that you can become my twenty-four seven slave here in this dungeon. And I do mean twenty-four seven,' she added emphatically. 'I won't let you out at all, not even to get a haircut. I'll trim your hair myself. I will regularly let you have clean linen and will keep your kitchen and bathroom adequately stocked. And you in your turn will keep your quarters, including all the dungeon equipment, scrupulously clean and tidy at all times. You'll be provided with all the necessary cleaning materials and so on in order that you can do this. There are other details that, again, I can go into with you later. The essence of what you need to understand, though, is that if you agree to my proposal then here in these dungeon quarters you'll stay as my slave, twenty-four seven.'

Alicia paused for a moment so that the full import of all she'd just said could sink in. 'I'll leave you for a while to think about it,' she then said. 'When I return I want one of two answers from you. If you want what I'm offering say, "Yes, Mistress". If you don't, just say one word: "no", and I will let you go straight away – for good.' And with that parting shot she promptly left the dungeon.

Paul's first reaction to what Mistress Alicia had said – the frighteningly stark choice she'd just given him – was to panic. He could feel the blood pumping through his body, could feel it in his panic-stricken head, the veins pulsing with it. And as he panicked he struggled against his bonds. He pulled fiercely at the straps holding his arms and torso and legs but there was no give at all.

The problem was that there was no give at all in what Mistress Alicia had said to him either. And it terrified him. For a few minutes Paul lost his head entirely, struggling against his restraints like a demented being, his eyes opened wide, bulging from their sockets. The torture chair creaked as he threw himself from side to side, breathing heavily. But the chair didn't budge an inch as it was bolted as firmly to the dungeon floor as its dildo attachment was lodged firmly up his backside.

When Paul finally became quiet, sweating with fear and exertion, he remained as securely in bondage as ever. His heart was hammering and he felt a tight knot of fear in his stomach. He could feel that tight knot turn steadily, inexorably from fear to anticipation, though, leading to a corresponding ache in his groin.

It was insane, he knew, but the irredeemably dark side of his nature, the side that these days almost completely dominated his personality, caused Paul to be hugely attracted to what Mistress Alicia was now offering him on a plate.

But what exactly was she offering him? What was this great prize that could be his for the taking if he just said the word? It was to be a slave and nothing but a slave. It was to be not a person but a possession, a chattel. It was to be not a free man but a prisoner under lock and key twenty-four hours a day and tormented and tortured constantly by an outstandingly cruel dominatrix. *That* was what was being offered to him on a plate. And, God help him, he found that he wanted that, craved it.

Paul knew that he'd always craved such a life at some deep-rooted level. But for a long time that craving had existed only subliminally and in more recent times only at the level of fantasy. It was true that once it had emerged from the subterranean depths of his subconscious, with the assistance of *that* book and his own obsessive personality, it had not been just any old fantasy. It had been powerful and obsessive fantasy, constant fantasy night and day – asleep or awake, fantasy aided by regular elaborate self-bondage rituals and compulsive masturbation. It had been a whole world of fantasy. But at the end of the day it had only been fantasy. What first Mistress Nikki and then Mistress Alicia had done had been to turn Paul's dark fantasy world into reality.

And they hadn't done any of it by accident, it suddenly dawned on Paul in a moment of insight so blinding that it was like a light bulb being switched on in his brain. The whole sequence of events from the moment Mistress Nikki had first stridden so arrogantly into his flat up to the terrifying 'take it or leave it' ultimatum that Mistress Alicia had just given him had been part of a conspiracy of some sort. And the end target of that conspiracy had always been his twenty-four seven enslavement to Mistress Alicia.

In doing what they'd done with him, the two dommes – Mistress Nikki in particular – had effectively been 'grooming' Paul, he could see that now. And they'd done it so efficiently that he'd now reached the point where he knew he would find it extremely difficult to resist the insane impulse to become Mistress Alicia's twenty-four seven dungeon slave – now that he had been presented with that proposition not as a vague ideal or tantalizing possibility but as an all-or-nothing choice.

Mistress Nikki had carried out all the essential groundwork with Paul, that was clear (far less clear was Tony's role in all this).

She had done it with such skill that by the time she had handed him over to Mistress Alicia the task had been close to being complete. Mistress Nikki had already instilled in him a desire so strong to submit totally to a powerful and sadistic woman like her that right from the start he had been putty in Mistress Alicia's hands – in her *leather-gloved* hands, for it had been her in that hotel room, no doubt about it.

She had then been able to manipulate him to her own ends over a few short days, making herself the object of his by now irresistible compulsion to submit completely. Paul could see that between the two dommes he had been groomed to the point where he was now prepared to consider more seriously than he'd ever before considered anything else in his life this one-off chance to become Mistress Alicia's twenty-four seven dungeon slave.

Paul saw it with such clarity now, the way he'd been ruthlessly and single-mindedly used and manipulated by these two women. He knew how it had been done to him and why it had been done. And knowledge was power wasn't it, he said to himself resolutely. Paul knew what he had to do. It would need considerable courage, every ounce of courage he could muster. But it would only take one little word.

The heavy door to the dungeon opened and closed again, admitting Mistress Alicia. The naked dominatrix moved towards the torture chair to which Paul was bound. 'Well?' she said, her blue eyes shining. 'What's your answer?'

Paul didn't hesitate for a second. 'Yes, Mistress,' he replied, knowing without doubt that Mistress Nikki and Mistress Alicia had conspired together diabolically … to bring him to the place where he'd wanted to be all along.

It had taken a great deal of courage to do it because it was make or break, do or die, so terrifyingly uncompromising. But Paul had no doubt, when he gave that profoundly life-changing response, that he'd made the right decision. The only doubt he had was about how all of this had actually begun. It couldn't have started with him. It would be ridiculously egotistical of him to think that it had, and in any event it made no sense. So what was it that had set all this in motion in the first place, Paul wondered. How had it all begun?

Chapter Thirty-seven

FLASHBACK: IT ALL BEGAN one mild sunny Sunday afternoon in central London. Mistress Nikki had gone into the fetish market in Clapham to catch up with other scene players and check out the various stalls. Nikki enjoyed going to the monthly fetish market because it had a whole variety of stalls that sold kinky leather-wear, sadomasochistic sex toys and the like. Also, everyone at the market, whether in fetish-wear or in casual clothes, as she was on this occasion, was associated with the London fetish scene in some way or another and that made for a great atmosphere. Nikki would browse and chat and try on any outfits that particularly caught her eye. She would go round the stalls, looking at books, disciplinary instruments, kinky outfits, whatever.

On this occasion she found herself striking up a conversation with an extremely attractive woman who was shopping at one of the stalls. She was a tall brunette, about Nikki's height, and she looked to be about her own age too. She was trying on an elegant black corset made of distressed leather. The woman seemed slightly distressed herself in some ill-defined way, but was stunning to look at nonetheless. She had smooth alabaster skin, big strikingly blue eyes and an extraordinarily sensual mouth.

Nikki complimented her on how beautiful she looked in the corset. The woman thanked her for what she'd said and gave a smile that lit up her face. 'I like the look of it, too,' she said, 'and it's gorgeous leather. But unfortunately it's not comfortable on.' She took the corset off and readjusted her clothes. Her figure was beautifully proportioned, Nikki noticed, and she was graceful in her movements, like a dancer.

There was quite a bit of activity at the stall, which was an especially popular one, and it was all getting rather cramped. 'I'm gasping for a coffee,' the woman said. 'Care to join me? My name's Alicia, by the way.' Her tone was friendly and self-assured.

'And I'm Nikki. Yes I'd love to.'

The refreshment area was situated right next to the stall and they took their seats there, each holding a steaming mug of coffee that had been purchased from the counter. Alicia had insisted on paying for both.

'You're a dominatrix, aren't you, Nikki,' she said.

'So are you,' replied Nikki, a twinkle in her emerald green eyes.

'Are you sure?' Alicia smiled teasingly.

'Positive,' Nikki said. 'It takes one to know one, you know.' She added, 'Its great being a domme, isn't it.'

'Oh yes,' Alicia said, abandoning any further slender attempt at pretence. 'I love everything about it – the fantasy aspects, the disciplinary rituals, the amazing outfits, the power play … I could go on. It's all wonderful.'

'And it puts women exactly where we belong – in charge,' Nikki said with a laugh. 'Am I right or am I right?' She sipped her coffee, enjoying both its smoothness and bitterness.

'You're right,' Alicia said. 'How times have changed, haven't they. Remember the way women were taught that men were the superior sex and had to be served and obeyed?'

'I sure do,' replied Nikki. 'Thank God for Women's Liberation. Mind you, having said that, I wonder sometimes how much progress our sex has really made. It's a bit more subtle than it used to be but female subservience is still all around us in today's so-called post-feminist society.' Nikki shook her head in dismay and took another swallow of coffee.

'It certainly is and it's delusional as far as I'm concerned,' Alicia said. 'Women are, and have always been the superior sex in my view. As a Mistress I order a male to serve, honour and obey *me* – just as it should be.'

'I couldn't agree more.' Nikki said.

There was a pause in the conversation at that point as the two dommes quietly enjoyed their coffees. They found themselves settling into a companionable silence, for all the world like two old friends totally at ease in one another's company.

Nikki was the first to speak again: 'Tell me, what do you like most about being a dominatrix?' she asked. 'Apart from inflicting punishment, that is. We'll take that as a given!'

Alicia paused for thought momentarily. 'That's a tough one,' she said. 'I must say, I do love the ritual of it all.'

'Me too,' Nikki said. 'One of my favourite rituals is inspecting a slave by walking round them, assessing them, making them get into set positions: kneeling to worship my feet and the like. Do you regularly do that with your slave, or should I say 'slaves'?'

'No, it's in the singular.'

'Your 'slave' then.'

'I used to, yes.' She gave Nikki a strange distant smile.

'Used to, as in – not any more?'

'That's right,' Alicia said. 'Peter was a lovely submissive man, the perfect slave.' She could only manage a flickering half-smile this time and it didn't mask the sadness that now showed in her face.

'Was?' Nikki asked softly.

'Yes,' Alicia said. 'You see, he's dead.'

Chapter Thirty-eight

THAT HAD BEEN A conversation stopper, to say the very least. 'Look, let's get out of here,' Nikki said. She took Alicia to nearby Clapham Common and they walked slowly arm in arm together along a path lined with trees that sparkled with sunlight in the crisp, sunny weather. And as they walked Alicia started to tell Nikki all about it.

She told her that Peter had been her husband and that they'd been married for fifteen years. She said that she'd always had the dominant role in their relationship, which had developed over time to a Femdom one. However it had been a frustratingly tempered one in many ways, because of the couple's outwardly conventional lifestyle. Then things had changed radically for the better. Although his heart had never really been in it, Peter had proved himself over the years to be a naturally gifted businessman with a particular flair for new technology. He had ended up making an absolute killing by sitting on the Internet bubble and selling right before it burst. That had enabled him to give up work altogether in order to do the thing he wanted to do with all his heart and soul by that stage, which was to devote himself exclusively to worshipping Alicia.

Peter had become Alicia's full-time slave after that, serving her hand and foot in their lovely penthouse apartment overlooking Hampstead Heath. And his reward for such devoted servitude? It had been just what he craved, what they both craved: she had disciplined him constantly. These disciplinary sessions had taken place initially in their bedroom, which Alicia had got specially equipped for the purpose, and later in the superb dungeon quarters she'd subsequently had designed within part of the large apartment. This was something she'd achieved without interfering in any way with the property's splendid Georgian facade.

By mutual consent Peter had spent more and more of his time in his dungeon quarters until eventually he had been locked in there virtually all the time. It had been the cruellest of ironies that on one of the rare occasions that he'd ventured out during what had proved to be the most deeply satisfying stage of the couple's relationship he'd ended up being run over by a drunken driver. He had been killed instantly.

Alicia had been devastated by Peter's death and had suffered a lengthy period of grieving that she'd begun to fear would never end. But it's always darkest before the dawn, and she'd woken one morning to find that she actually felt glad to be alive, something she hadn't felt for a long time. There and then Alicia had decided that she'd pick herself up, dust herself off and start all over again. So, how had she gone about that? In a very small way at first: she'd come to the fetish market in Clapham where, as it had turned out, she'd met Nikki.

'What are you going to do now?' Nikki asked.

'I haven't really got a clue,' Alicia admitted.

'Let me help you,' Nikki said. And that's exactly what she did.

With Nikki's help Alicia made her first tentative steps back onto the fetish scene. Nikki introduced her to several of her friends, like Mistress Evie and Strap-on Jane, and to clients that she had also come to count as friends, Sarah, Julie and Tony included. Alicia liked them all but it was to Tony that she seemed to take a particular shine. He reminded her a great deal of Peter, she said.

After a while Nikki determined that the time was right for something more radical to help Alicia on the road to full recovery from her grief. She decided that, as long as Tony was agreeable, which he was, she'd let Alicia loose on him. 'I'll send him over to your place this evening,' she said when the two women were lunching together one day in a quiet corner of a restaurant in Covent Garden. 'Do anything to him and with him you like. And I do mean *anything*. He can take a lot of punishment, believe me.'

'But I haven't done any dommeing at all or had sex of any description with anyone for over a year,' Alicia protested.

'So?'

'I might have lost the knack,' she replied, and they both laughed.

'I think not,' Nikki said.

'I don't think I can bring myself to re-open the dungeon quite yet,' Alicia said.

'That's understandable,' Nikki responded. 'Why don't you use your bedroom. I remember you saying that it's equipped for BDSM play.'

'That's right,' Alicia said, still sounding doubtful.

'Your bedroom it is then, *Mistress* Alicia,' Nikki replied firmly.

Chapter Thirty-nine

TONY COULDN'T HELP BUT feel nervous as he took the lift to the penthouse apartment to which he'd been buzzed up just a few moments ago. Mistress Alicia opened the door, looking gorgeous. She was dressed all in soft black leather: skin-tight shorts that exposed smooth bare thighs and long legs; an equally skimpy bra that showed off her lovely breasts to great effect; and a pair of pointed shoes with sharp stiletto heels.

'Hi, Tony,' she said, trying hard not to betray the nervousness she herself was feeling. 'Follow me.' She led him along a corridor carpeted in red, his eyes transfixed by the curve of her backside and her swaying hips. As Tony followed Mistress Alicia along the corridor, his nervousness diminished with each step and his sense of sexual anticipation grew.

They continued down the corridor for about half its length until they reached Alicia's bedroom, which was large with a high ceiling. There was a big double bed, with a headboard and four posters, and a bedside table with a lamp on it. On the other side of the bed there was a black leather chair, and thick curtains hung at the windows. The wall opposite the bed was dominated by a free standing cross and there was a rack at the foot of the bed that was hung with canes, straps, whips and various other implements of correction.

Mistress Alicia switched on the bedside light and went over to shut the curtains. 'Let's get one thing clear before we start,' she said, no sign of anxiety now. 'You are not, repeat *not*, to climax unless I give you my permission. Is that understood, slave?'

'Yes, Mistress.' *Déjà vu*, Tony couldn't help thinking, remembering Mistress Nikki's regular identical instructions to him on this subject.

'Take off your clothes, get on your knees and present yourself to me properly,' Alicia said, her tone even more commanding. Tony obeyed instantly, his cock already semi-hard. As soon as he

178

was totally naked he dropped where he was on the carpet and pressed his forehead to the ground

'Lick my shoes,' Mistress Alicia demanded crisply. Tony lifted his head a little and pressed his lips against the pointed toe of the shoe she presented to him. He slid his tongue along the smooth leather, his lips caressing the sensuous feel of it, lingering over the instep and then up the sharp heel. She presented her other foot to him and he repeated the process.

Mistress Alicia then told Tony to get up from his knees and stand before her. Slipping a hand behind his neck, she pulled his face to hers and kissed him hard on the mouth. He felt the tip of her tongue probe his lips. She moved her mouth away for a fraction, and then brought it back. She kissed his open mouth again, this time pushing her tongue aggressively into his, sliding it over and over. As Alicia kissed Tony she pressed her shapely body against his and it aroused him even more than the smoothness and insistence of her tongue and the warmth of her lips against his.

Mistress Alicia then broke the clinch and led Tony over to the free standing cross. She told him to face it with his legs apart and arms outstretched. He leaned up against the slightly inclined cross, putting his wrists over his head and spreading them and also parting his legs. The apparatus was well equipped with straps and it did not take the dominatrix long to fasten his wrists, waist and ankles.

Tony tried to keep his breathing steady and waited for Mistress Alicia to begin disciplining him. He did not have long to wait. 'Aah!' he cried as the red-hot strike from her flogger landed across the middle of his backside. He gave another gasp of pain as her next stroke planted a second burning line across his rear.

Mistress Alicia continued to whip Tony hard, each searing stroke producing a sharp, fiery sting, and his backside rapidly reddened. He moaned and gasped at the pain and his flesh quivered constantly as she increased the momentum of his beating. The increasing vigour, accuracy and regularity of the carefully aimed blows made him writhe in every direction in spite of the tightness of his bonds. His moans grew louder and in time with the swooping impact of the whip with which she was disciplining him so beautifully.

179

Yes, beautifully. It hurt, certainly, and very badly, a red heat that seemed to be burning into his skin, sinking deeper and deeper. But he could also feel its heat spreading to his shaft which had become steely hard. Mistress Alicia kept on whipping Tony and every strike tingled deliciously through his genitals. His backside was now red all over and he was panting and shivering with acute pain.

A less experienced dominatrix might have paused at this point, but not Alicia. Nikki had been right; it was like she'd never been away. She kept on beating Tony until his pain turned to sizzling hot lust. His nerves were on fire. He was consumed by desire and a swelling sensation of pure carnality flowed through his body. Blood was flushing into his pulsating cock. He willed himself desperately not to climax … And she stopped.

Mistress Alicia unfastened Tony's restraints, turned him round to face her, and refastened him to the cross. As she did so she looked into his submissive blue eyes and saw the bright shine of desire there. Her own eyes shone too and sheer animal lust made her lips look even fuller.

She took hold of a small flogger and whipped Tony's genitals with it in a dozen quick bursts, causing the veins in his testicles to fill until they appeared ready to burst. His hard shaft and bulbous cockhead turned a dark purple under the harsh whipping. Tony bucked and thrashed against his tight bonds as the pain burned hotly. Alicia whipped him again in the same manner but even more harshly this time. The stinging pain was that much more intense, forcing an excruciating cry of agony from him.

And so it went on. Mistress Alicia whipped Tony's aching cock over and over again, causing his flesh to quiver and burn as sharp spasms of pain sang through him. Then she stopped and the pain gradually subsided to a hard, insistent throbbing that was intense pain but was also intense pleasure.

Alicia put the flogger to one side and took hold of Tony's punished shaft at the base, her fingers wrapped around it tightly. She began to masturbate him, running her hand up and down, stroking the smooth hardness of his cock. The more she masturbated him the faster she went, her hands going up and down in the pre-cum wetness that began to cover it until, again, Tony felt on the verge of climaxing. But he knew he must not. He closed his eyes tight shut and willed himself not to climax, willed himself with every fibre of his being. She stopped.

'Let's take a moment, slave,' Mistress Alicia said and put her fingers, sticky with Tony's pre-cum, to his lips.

'Taste good?' she asked.

'Yes, Mistress.'

'Let me see if I agree,' Alicia said before getting onto her knees, dipping her head and letting her tongue lick the ridge around the glans of his penis. She took the glans into her mouth then, closing her lips round it, tasting the beads of fluid seeping from its slit. She licked these onto her tongue and pulled back, a silvery thread of pre-cum stretching from cock to tongue. My God, Tony thought, that had been *so* close. He had been certain he was going to climax that time.

Mistress Alicia stood up then and released Tony from the cross. 'Get on to all fours,' she told him, looking him directly in the eyes again. It was a hot, ravenous look that she gave him and it nearly took his breath away.

As Tony got onto his hands and knees Alicia buckled a strap-on dildo over her tight leather shorts. She lubricated it and as she started to push inside the tight opening of his anus Tony could feel the painful negotiations of muscles. He cried out as he felt the dildo penetrating him, stretching him as she held him by the hips and pushed in deeply. It was very painful but it made him shudder with desire.

As Mistress Alicia moved inside him, her breath hot against his neck, the strokes of her strap-on were at first slow and powerful and then fast and thrusting. Her leather-covered breasts brushed Tony's shoulders as she moved in and out. The thrill of being penetrated with such skill was edged deliciously with the pain that Tony felt inside his anus and yet again he almost climaxed despite his best endeavours. And yet again, with an empathy born of years of experience as a dominatrix, Alicia stopped just before it was too late. She withdrew the dildo and unbuckled the strap-on harness.

'Get onto the bed,' she ordered, her voice husky. Her whole body seemed to be crying out for sex; but she would make it wait, she told herself. Mistress Alicia picked up four lengths of red bondage rope. She carefully tied Tony to the four posts of the bed flat on his back in a spread-eagled position, his erect cock sticking up like a flagpole.

Alicia then stripped naked, breathing hard with lust. She knew that she could not wait much longer as she felt her blood boil and a frenzied excitement building within her. Tony thought she looked quite magnificent in her passion. Her face was utterly radiant, her breasts were prominent and full, the nipples hard, and her skin was as smooth as satin. This included the skin around her dripping sex since, Tony had noticed when she'd removed her tight leather shorts, she did not have any pubic hair at all. His own body was almost hairless; hers was *completely* hairless.

Mistress Alicia turned away from Tony's gaze and, keeping her back to him, straddled his upturned face. Tony watched excitedly as the shiny lips of her vulva opened up to him. She sat over his mouth and he found that she was completely soaking wet. Tony began to lick Alicia's pussy and she moaned out her pleasure. He continued as he had begun, his tongue on her clitoris insistent as she quivered with passion.

Alicia then lent forward and took Tony's hot shaft into her mouth, fastening onto it hungrily and rolling her tongue up and down its length as he flicked his over her clit. They sixty-nined each other like this in a state of ever mounting passion. Desire sang through them as they sucked and licked deliriously.

It was pure sex, pure enjoyment, and it was not long before Alicia climaxed. Her orgasm was long and violent, its spasms and contractions seeming to go on for ever. It was a huge little death and she took Tony's pulsing shaft from her mouth so as to cry out her ecstasy.

Tony knew he really couldn't hold out any longer this time. Every nerve in his body told him that he was going to climax. 'Permission to come, please, Mistress,' he managed to plead indistinctly from beneath her quivering wet thighs.

'Yes, yes, yes,' Alicia cried out, as much in response to her continuing orgasm as to Tony's desperate, muffled plea. Then she engulfed his raging cock in her mouth once more. Tony groaned painfully and pulsed and pushed and bucked against her teeth. Finally, and with massive relief, he ejaculated, spurting out thick gobs of pearly cream into her mouth. And it tasted delicious, Alicia found, *de-lic-ious*. She swallowed down every last drop as her own climax continued to rage, shaking and scorching her to ecstasy.

When her orgasm had finally, steadily faded Alicia pulled away from Tony. Her climax had been brilliant, ecstatic, glorious, and it had left her weak and trembling. She did not know how long she had been with Tony, had lost all sense of time, but she noticed that moonlight was now creeping through a gap in the curtains.

'Thank you, Mistress,' Tony said.

'It's me that should be thanking you,' Alicia said, putting a hand softly to his love juice-soaked face. After the last miserable, celibate year that she'd endured this had been a wonderful new beginning for her.

But it had been more than a beginning, much more, she realised afterwards when she thought about it. Because here was the amazing thing: she found that she'd taken a lot more than a mere shine to Tony. She really liked the man. I mean, *really* liked him.

Alicia felt that she could face bringing her dungeon back into use now. Indeed she would like nothing better than to bring it back into use – as long as it was occupied by the right slave. Her ideal scenario would be to have Tony imprisoned there pretty much twenty-four seven, just like Peter had been in the best, the golden years of their precious time together.

Tony could never replace Peter in her affections, of course. No man could ever do that, she was sure. But Tony was pretty darned special in his own right. He'd make a great dungeon slave.

But *whoa there, hold your horses*, Alicia cautioned herself in alarm. What was she thinking? Had she taken complete leave of her senses? Surely what she was envisaging was entirely out of the question, a thoroughly mad and outlandish idea. Or maybe it wasn't. Maybe she was actually onto something here. Alicia just didn't know. She'd have to talk to Nikki about it, she decided, see what she thought.

Chapter Forty

NIKKI DIDN'T THINK ALICIA had taken complete leave of her senses. She didn't think her idea was entirely out of the question, didn't consider it mad and outlandish at all. She thought it was great. In theory. In practice she was as sure as she could be that Tony wouldn't go for it. Over the three years that she'd been both his dominatrix and his friend Nikki had got to know Tony well and she felt that she had a good understanding of what made him tick.

She advised Alicia that, as she read the situation, Tony was a man who was basically happy with the balance in his life and would not be willing to consider the highly restricted – let's face it, the virtually *hermetically sealed* – alternative being suggested. Nikki said she'd broach the subject with him, though. She did and she was proved correct. Thanks but no thanks was essentially what Tony said, even though he said it in the politest, most respectful way possible.

But as things turned out, Tony came up trumps anyway. It happened shortly after he arrived for one of his afternoon appointments with Nikki. He only just managed to get to her on time that grey, drizzly weekday afternoon and couldn't wait to explain exactly why that had been. He told her all about the wholly unexpected encounter he'd had earlier with his old friend and doppelganger, Paul. 'It would be great to be able to help him, Mistress,' Tony said at the end of his account of their meeting. 'Any ideas?'

'I'll give the matter some thought,' the dominatrix replied non-committally, although more than the germ of an idea was already formulating in her mind. Was there a possible opportunity here to kill two birds with one stone, she asked herself. Yes there most definitely was, she decided after she'd made her personal – her *extremely* personal – assessment of Paul, which she did the very next day, having obtained his address from Tony.

Nikki realised from the start that the implementation of her plan would require both boldness and subterfuge. It would also require Alicia's agreement if it was to get beyond first base. For all she knew, Alicia might think that *Nikki* was the one who'd taken complete leave of her senses. If so Nikki would then have to immediately move to the backstop strategy she had in mind. This was to give Paul a free disciplinary session in her dungeon, accompanied by Tony who *would* be paying, before steering him firmly in the direction of one of her other domme friends, probably Mistress Evie. Evie usually had a slave in tow, sometimes male and sometimes female, but currently she did not. Paul would appeal very much to Evie, Nikki was almost certain of it.

But it wasn't necessary to take this alternative course because Alicia didn't give Nikki's proposal the cold shoulder. Nothing ventured, nothing gained was the gist of her cautiously enthusiastic response when Nikki put her idea to her immediately after her visit to Paul. That was all the go-ahead Nikki needed and she then lost no time in developing her highly ambitious plan, which was to groom an unwitting Paul to be Alicia's *willing* twenty-four seven dungeon slave.

Right from its inception Nikki realised that her plan had one major weak link. And that was Tony. She did not intend to divulge her proposals to him because they might easily all come to nought and in any event he might not approve. After all, he'd already courteously but firmly turned down the suggestion that he himself be Alicia's dungeon slave.

The trouble was that Tony already knew too much. He knew Alicia and what she was looking for and he knew Paul and what was lacking in his life. It wouldn't take much for him to put two and two together and work out, at least in rough terms, what Nikki was up to. Some comment to Paul from Tony, inadvertent or otherwise, could easily screw everything up.

Nikki decided that she needed to silence Tony as fast as possible. She achieved this in two swiftly executed stages. Both of these took place in Nikki's dungeon, the first the day after her visit to Paul and the second the day that followed that.

After those two occasions disciplining Paul and Tony together and the strict instructions she'd given them both about not communicating with one another, the job had been done, the weak link effectively fixed.

Nikki was then able to see her plan through its subsequent stages all the way to her handover of Paul to Alicia, first temporarily in that anonymous hotel room for a 'trial run' and finally in her luxurious penthouse apartment and its magnificent dungeon quarters. The rest was beyond Nikki's control. It was all up to Alicia.

Chapter Forty-one

TIME PASSED. AND AS one day of Paul's strange dungeon existence merged into another and the days turned into weeks, which turned into months, there came a time when he stopped wondering how it had all started. It didn't matter how it had begun, he told himself. He was just more thankful than he could possibly say that it had and that he was here now where he felt he truly belonged – as the twenty-four seven dungeon slave of Mistress Alicia, a woman with whom he had become completely besotted. Her name throbbed in his blood all the time. Paul couldn't get her out of his mind. She meant everything to him.

He felt safe under her control too, safe in her dungeon. The outside world slowly but surely lost any sense of coherence for him. Being inside Mistress Alicia's dungeon, controlled and disciplined by her, was all that mattered to him.

Paul assumed that he hadn't seen the last of Mistress Nikki, though. And he was right. He hoped he and Tony might be allowed to see each other again too. And they were. Sort of …

Paul was looking out from the wall-mounted cross to which he was tightly strapped in a spread-eagled position. His head and face were encased in a black leather hood and he was gagged with a black ball gag. Otherwise he was completely naked, his shaft rigidly erect.

He was gazing over at the equally naked Tony, who was on his knees in the cage and was wearing a red rubber mask with open eyes, nose holes and mouth. His shaft too was rock hard.

Paul shifted his gaze from Tony to look at Alicia and Nikki. The two Mistresses were standing together in the middle of the dungeon and both looked stunningly beautiful.

Alicia was wearing a very short, tight black leather dress and high-heeled shoes of the same colour. Nikki's outfit, black leather as well, consisted of a halter-top and tiny skin-tight shorts that revealed the cheeks of her well-shaped backside and outlined the lips of her sex. In addition she was wearing knee-length boots with very high heels.

Alicia turned to Nikki. 'Let's make a start, shall we, my dear,' she said and the two women strode towards the cage. They opened it and led Tony crawling over to the cross to which Paul was strapped. Paul's erection was now jutting out in front of Tony's face.

'Suck him,' Mistress Nikki demanded. 'Suck him hard.' And Tony obediently complied, sucking violently on Paul's stiff cock. As he did this Mistress Alicia picked up a candleholder from the dungeon floor. This contained half a dozen red candles, which she lit.

While Tony carried on fellating Paul as if his very life depended on it, his lips fastened tight on his cock, Alicia drizzled hot wax on his back. Tony trembled with pain in reaction and his shaft began to trickle a rivulet of pre-cum onto the dungeon floor.

Meanwhile Mistress Nikki had put a strap-on over her shorts. She lubricated the dildo before positioning herself behind Tony and thrusting it into his tight anal hole. She immediately began vigorously sodomizing him, pushing and pushing and pushing.

As Nikki buggered Tony in this robust manner, Alicia continued to pour hot molten wax on his back and he continued sucking forcefully at Paul's cock. Then, on a word from Alicia who could sense that Paul was now perilously close to ejaculating, they all stopped.

Mistress Nikki withdrew the strap-on from Tony's stretched anus and led him over to the vertical torture chair that had the large dildo attachment. She helped him to lift himself onto the dildo, his erect cock squirting out a throb of pre-cum as he pushed himself down on it. She went on to strap him into the chair at the neck, wrists, thighs and ankles.

'Lift up your face and open your mouth wide, slave,' Mistress Nikki then ordered Tony and she put her lips against the mouth hole of his rubber hood. Her tongue met his and she sucked it into her mouth for a moment before pulling back and spitting down his throat. Tony gasped and gulped on her saliva and then, upon a further order from his Mistress, he opened his mouth wide again. Nikki let another gob of spittle fall into his throat and he gulped on it, drinking her again.

At this point Alicia appeared at Nikki's side with a box of large sterilized needles. 'I think it is time, don't you?' she said and Nikki nodded her agreement. 'You can go first if you'd like,' Alicia added and Nikki smiled a smile to her friend that said: oh yes, she'd like that very much.

'I want you to scream for me now, slave,' Mistress Nikki told Tony just before inserting a large needle through one of his nipples. And he did scream, tipping back his rubber-covered head and letting out an agonized cry. When she inserted a second large needle through Tony's other nipple he let out another ear-splitting scream and simultaneously erupted into orgasm, sending a great long spray of ejaculate into the air that then splattered down onto the ground.

Mistress Nikki carefully removed the needles from Tony's nipples. She undid the straps that had bound him to the torture chair, and helped him to lift himself carefully off the large rod that had been buried in his rear. 'On your knees and lick up your cum from the dungeon floor,' Nikki demanded then and the whimpering, rubber-hooded slave obeyed instantly.

'Your turn now,' Mistress Alicia said, her blue eyes blazing, as she made her way over to the cross to which Paul was strapped. He tensed himself for what he knew was coming but at the same time was shaking his leather-hooded head in denial, absolutely terrified. Paul twisted in his bonds, tugging in panic at the straps that held him. The strangled noises that came through his ball gag were loud in his ears and he could feel the sweat of his panic drenching his naked body.

As Mistress Alicia drove the first large needle through one of his nipples Paul nearly fainted with the excruciating pain he experienced. When she drove the second one through his other nipple, he was in an agony so extreme that it suddenly spilled over into a fierce climax. And as it unleashed its full orgasmic fury, his cum spurting out in a hot liquid burst, Paul did what he'd so nearly done a moment before – he fainted dead away.

When he eventually came round and became aware of his dungeon surroundings once more, Mistress Nikki and Tony were nowhere to be seen. Mistress Alicia was there though, and that was all that really mattered to Paul. He averted his gaze and winced in pain as the dominatrix gently removed the large needles from his chest.

Chapter Forty-two

IT IS A FACT of life that after a time the most abnormal of existences becomes normal to the person living it. That was certainly the case with Paul even if the abnormal existence he was now living had come about as a kind of self-fulfilling prophesy. His craving to explore the very darkest parts of his own psyche had taken Paul on a journey that had led him to Mistress Alicia's dungeon – and to the sort of existence about which he had once constantly, obsessively, dreamed and fantasized and which at some level he now felt had always been his destiny to achieve.

That amazing journey had led him, via Mistress Nikki – a woman to whom he knew he would always feel immensely grateful – to becoming the twenty-four seven dungeon slave of Mistress Alicia. And she was stricter than any dominatrix he'd dreamed or fantasized about in the past, stricter even than Mistress Nikki; *incredibly* strict. Evidence the fact that, after a brief period early on when she'd allowed him out to 'put his affairs in order' as she'd expressed it, she never let him out of his dungeon quarters again – not even once – in almost a year. Then one night she did.

It all happened so quickly – too quickly for Paul to be able to think too much about it. An already leather-coated Mistress Alicia handed Paul a leather outfit of his own to wear: a jacket, skin-tight jeans and a pair of short boots. She said: 'I am going to take you to a small, select fetish party – just three Mistresses indulging ourselves with a handful of slaves.' She added, 'There will be one or two people there that you already know.' Paul immediately thought of Mistress Nikki and Tony. As it turned out he was wrong on both counts. Nikki was on holiday at the time and Tony, for whatever reason, hadn't been invited to the party.

Paul was initially very nervous, could feel his heart start to race six to the dozen with anxiety. He was not at all sure how he'd respond to being in the outside world again after such a long time locked up in the dungeon. But his concerns proved to be academic. Immediately Mistress Alicia had got him into her car, a silver-grey Bentley with darkened windows, she put a blindfold over his eyes. She only removed this – gagging him instead, using a black ball gag – after they had not only arrived at the premises where the party was taking place but had descended a staircase and were in the very *room* in which it was being held.

The first thing Paul noticed when Mistress Alicia removed his blindfold was that the large, dimly-lit room they were in looked very familiar. This was because it was windowless and contained many and various pieces of dungeon equipment and instruments of correction. It was very similar to Mistress Alicia's dungeon although it was even bigger. It was big enough in fact to hold a party in: a fetish party.

The room had been well set up for such a party too. A succession of beautiful black and white bondage photographs were being projected onto one wall to particularly good effect. They added to the darkly erotic ambience already provided by the room's dungeon equipment and implements of discipline ... and by its occupants, Paul included, since Mistress Alicia had made him strip naked as soon as she'd removed his blindfold and gagged him with the ball gag.

Alicia herself, her leather coat also now removed, was looking incredibly beautiful in a tight black leather halter-top, a miniscule see-through skirt of dark mesh beneath which she was naked, and high heeled boots.

The hostess of the party – a woman even more scantily clad than Alicia as she was topless and wearing only a tiny leather g-string and stiletto-heeled boots – was a dark-haired beauty introduced to Paul as Mistress Katrina. Alicia explained that Katrina was an old friend of hers who had been living in Italy for the previous three years with her house-slave James.

She and he had just returned to the big house Katrina owned in London and it was in the converted basement of that house that they were now standing. Mistress Alicia told Paul that she had used its design as the basis for the creation of her own somewhat smaller dungeon, living quarters for a slave *et al*.

'I liked it that you copied my design, Alicia,' Katrina said with a smile. 'They say that imitation is the sincerest form of flattery.

You even used the same company to do the work as I did, if I recall correctly.'

'That's right,' Alicia said. 'They were a great choice as well – extremely efficient and one hundred per cent discreet.'

As the two women continued their animated conversation Paul studied Mistress Katrina more closely. The dark-haired dominatrix had striking coal-black eyes, *sinful* eyes. She had a short nose and a sleek chin and high small breasts with erect nipples. The tiny leather g-string she was wearing was incredibly tight, the lips of her shaven pussy protruding from its sides, and her boots had stiletto heels that were exceptionally tapered and sharp.

When Paul finally dragged his gaze away from Mistress Katrina he caught sight of two familiar figures as they emerged from a dark corner of the dungeon to come and join them. It was none other than Sarah and Julie, who had on identically minimal outfits: leather collars and wrist and ankle cuffs, all of red leather. Sarah wandered up to Paul, giving him a mischievous grin. 'What's the matter, Paul,' she said, bringing a finger to his ball gag. 'Cat got your tongue?'

The group was then joined by a good-looking man, bearing a tray of drinks. He was introduced to Paul as James, Katrina's house-slave. James had a shock of auburn hair and a nicely toned body and was naked apart from a red leather collar. His nipples had been clamped and a red leather ball stretcher encased his scrotum. His cock, like Paul's, was partly engorged.

Mistress Alicia had a drink and chatted with Mistress Katrina and the rest of the assembled group for a while, with the ball-gagged Paul standing by their side feeling a little like a spare part. Then, taking Paul by the arm, Alicia announced to the others: 'It's time for my slave's first beating of the evening – on one of the crosses, I think.'

As Mistress Alicia led Paul towards the nearest St Andrews cross she gave a friendly wave and mouthed hello to two beautiful naked women, both of oriental appearance, who had just arrived in the dungeon. They were the last of the guests to have been invited to the party, she told Paul. He recognized one of the women straight away. It was Mistress Evie – and she recognized him too, gracing him with a nod of recognition, her eyes smiling. Her young companion had cropped black hair and a trim figure.

'That's Isabel, Mistress Evie's latest slave,' Alicia said.

Mistress Alicia then turned her attentions entirely to Paul's discipline. She started by attaching chained clamps to his nipples and scrotum and adding weights to both, making him groan with pain beneath his ball gag. Having then strapped him face-forward to the St Andrews cross, she chose the implement with which she wished to beat him first: a heavy leather flogger. Alicia raised the flogger and brought it down hard across the cheeks of his backside, imprinting a pattern of red lines on his flesh. She brought the flogger down a second time, the leather snapping hard on his backside and leaving more angry imprints. The dominatrix continued to thrash his aching rear ferociously until the pain burned into his flesh like fire.

Mistress Alicia then released Paul from the cross, although she chose to leave his weighted nipple clamps in place as well as those attached to his scrotum. She led him crawling over to a whipping bench and secured him to it face down with his wrists buckled to its side. His rear was upraised and legs spread so that his anus, his weighted balls, and his cock, which was now fully erect, were entirely exposed. He found this deeply – deliciously – humiliating.

Mistress Katrina, her small breasts jiggling enticingly, strode over to Mistress Alicia, bringing Sarah and Julie with her but not James whom she'd just put in one of the dungeon's metal cages. She and Alicia then both used black and red braided leather floggers to whip Paul's backside viciously. One after the other they brought these cruel implements down with swift arcing movements. The noise from the stinging blows filled the dungeon, the sound of hard leather on soft flesh echoing louder than Paul's sharp exhalations of breath.

The burning pain he was suffering was eased to a degree when Sarah, with the two dommes' permission, began to gently stroke his shoulders and back with her small delicate hands. Alicia and Katrina didn't stop beating his rear though. Also Julie soon replaced Sarah and used a spiked stimulator to inflict on Paul the most agonizing of contrasts to her lover's tender fingers. 'As I believe you already know,' Alicia murmured into Paul's ear, 'Julie's a switch. She likes to give as well as receive.'

Alicia and Katrina continued beating him with the braided leather floggers, each of their strokes serving to deepen the red

194

flush across his backside, making him breathe harder and faster. And still Julie continued torturing his shoulders and back with the spiked stimulator … When it became evident to Alicia that the pain Paul was suffering was becoming too much for him, she stopped disciplining him and asked Katrina and Julie to do likewise. Paul sighed with great relief beneath his gag.

Next Mistress Alicia freed Paul from the whipping bench and told him to get on his knees again. She then led him crawling over to the metal cage that was already occupied by James who was also kneeling. James's nipples remained clamped and his red leather ball stretcher was still in place. He was now gagged with a red ball gag as well and his arms had been tied behind his back with bondage rope, which was also red.

Alicia left in place Paul's ball gag and weighted nipple clamps but removed the weighted clamps attached to his scrotum. Unlike James, Paul's hands were free and as Alicia walked away from the cage, she turned and said, 'Paul, wank yourself and also masturbate James, but make sure of two things: first, that you do not look at James and, secondly, that you are careful to ensure that neither of you climaxes.'

Paul moved his right hand to his hard cock and started gently pulling it. He also reached his left hand over to James and took hold of his equally stiff member. Wrapping his fingers around James's cock tightly, he eased his hand along its length. He slowly masturbated James and himself, both his hands stroking and pulling in a slow synchronised rhythm. And, though he was very careful not to take either of them over the edge, both their cocks were soon oozing with pre-cum.

With his two hands continuing to work up that slow masturbatory rhythm, Paul watched from behind the bars of the cage what was going on elsewhere in the large dungeon. He watched as Mistress Alicia strode over to Mistress Katrina, Sarah and Julie to observe what they were doing. This is what she saw, what Paul saw too:

Sarah was lying on the dungeon floor and Mistress Katrina and Julie were clipping her ankle cuffs to either end of a metal spreader bar that hung by a chain from the ceiling. They winched up the chain and then, once she was hanging upside-down with outstretched arms and her fingers just brushing the dungeon floor, locked it into place.

Next Mistress Katrina picked up a riding crop and savagely thrashed Sarah's backside with that, while Julie stood in front of the slave and licked her pussy, her darting tongue moving quickly over the lips of her sex. Then she began to masturbate Sarah. Her fingers plunged down into her wet pussy, really working it. She twisted three of them deeper inside her sex and drove them in still harder as Katrina continued to cruelly berate Sarah's rear with the riding crop. They carried on like this until Sarah climaxed, her upside-down body shuddering uncontrollably within its bonds.

Mistress Katrina then carefully cranked down the chain attached to the spreader bar and released Sarah's ankles. She repositioned the bar to six feet from the ground and gestured for Sarah and Julie to stand back to back beneath it and raise their arms. She clipped their wrist cuffs to either end of the spreader bar, got them to spread their legs, and secured their ankle cuffs to a wooden hobble bar. She attached surgical clamps to their nipples and chained metal clamps to their labia. Katrina added metal weights to both of these, and then left the two slaves in this agonizing spread-eagled bondage as she strode across the dungeon toward the cage that currently housed Paul and James.

Leaving Paul to masturbate in the cage on his own, Mistress Katrina led James away, still with his arms tied behind his back and his gag, nipple clamps and leather ball stretcher in place. The dominatrix took him over to an upright torture chair. Having removed the bondage rope from his wrists she strapped him into the torture chair so that his wrists were buckled to its side, his legs held apart and genitals exposed. She added metal weights to both his nipple clamps and ball stretcher. Katrina lit a candle and used it to drizzle hot wax onto his erect cock and to singe the body hairs above his pubis. The ball gag could not entirely muffle his maniacal screams of agony.

Still slowly pushing his fist up and down on himself, Paul looked over at Mistress Alicia again. He saw that she was now watching Katrina's current activities with interest; saw her nodding and smiling in obvious approval at her friend's extreme sadism.

Then he watched as Alicia strode over to the large revolving bondage wheel to which the nude Mistress Evie had strapped the equally naked Isabel, who was now blindfolded and gagged. Evie had also attached a mass of red pegs to the slave's breasts and labia.

Alicia helped Evie to turn the wheel a half circle so that Isabel was upside-down, and to then lock it into place. She caressed Evie and gave her a wet lascivious kiss. She then moved her hand towards the woman's sex just as Evie inserted a red dildo down into Isabel's vagina. As Mistress Evie worked the dildo in and out of her slave's pegged pussy, Alicia masturbated her fellow dominatrix until she climaxed convulsively. Isabel soon did likewise, breathing heavily into her gag as she mounted to an orgasm so powerful that she, like Sarah so recently before her, trembled upside-down and without control in her bondage as the muscular spasms shuddered through her.

Mistress Alicia next returned to the cage and freed Paul from it. She told him to stand up and led him by his erect cock over to some steel manacles that were fixed at shoulder and ankle level to one of the dungeon walls. Alicia locked him into these with his back to the wall and his arms and legs outstretched. She removed the clamps attached to his nipples but still left him gagged.

After a brief conference with Mistress Katrina, she released Sarah from the spreader bar and hobble bar that she shared with Julie but left Julie exactly where she was, still spread-eagled to the two bars. She removed the nipple and pussy clamps and weights from both slaves.

Mistress Alicia blindfolded Sarah, told her to get on to her hands and knees and led her crawling over to where Paul was shackled with his back to the wall, his pulsing erection sticking out in front of him. Alicia positioned Sarah so close to Paul that his shaft was brushing her lips. At the same time, Mistress Katrina freed James from the torture chair and removed his gag, weights, nipple clamps and ball stretcher. She led him over on all fours to kneel up directly behind Sarah, his erection touching her shapely backside.

Mistress Katrina then strode over to where Julie had been left attached in a spread-eagled position by her wrist and ankle cuffs to the two bars. She kissed her violently on the mouth and then looked in Mistress Alicia's direction. Alicia gave a nod to Katrina who immediately began finger-fucking Julie.

Alicia next instructed Sarah to suck Paul's cock and James to fuck her from behind. At the same time as Sarah opened her lips and took Paul's hard shaft deep into her mouth, James placed his hands on her thighs and thrust himself into the tight slick warmth of her sex.

As Sarah sucked Paul and James fucked her, Mistress Alicia began caning James's backside. James responded to each harsh strike with a gasp of breath that was both pain and pleasure. Julie watched this display very intently while being masturbated by Mistress Katrina with increasingly feverish energy.

The momentum intensified as Mistress Alicia's caning increased in tempo and severity. The harder she caned James, the more his cries became moans of erotic pleasure. And the more forcefully he fucked Sarah, the more violently she in turn sucked Paul's stiff cock, and the harder Mistress Katrina masturbated Julie, her fingers now like ramming rods.

Harder and harder they all went at it until … 'Climax now, slaves,' Alicia snapped out, her eyes blazing. 'Come like you've never come before.' And that's what all four of them did as if as one. They climaxed frenziedly in paroxysms of delight, shaking all over with lust and shame and pain. They lost themselves completely in the ecstasy of the moment, lost themselves completely in their submission to the Mistress of Torment, the magnificent Mistress Alicia.

Chapter Forty-three

ALICIA LEFT IT UNTIL the fetish party had ended before she at long last removed Paul's ball gag. She also left it until then before she dropped her bombshell. There was only one other person in the dungeon now apart from Mistress Alicia and Paul and that was Mistress Katrina's house-slave, James. He was clearing up after the event and was currently out of earshot. 'What did you think of the fetish party?' Alicia asked Paul.

'It was wonderful, Mistress,' Paul enthused. 'Thank you so much for bringing me.'

'Do you like this great big dungeon?' she asked.

'Yes, Mistress,' he replied. 'It's fabulous.'

'Oh, you think it's fabulous, do you,' she said, a knowing smile playing around her lips. 'Well, I'm glad you like it so much because you're going to be locked in it for … a time – with Katrina as your Mistress.'

With that Alicia swept away, leaving Paul open-mouthed. He heard a key scrape as she locked the door behind her. Paul hadn't for one moment expected anything like this to happen and his sudden change of circumstances sent him into a flat panic. His face went white and his heart began beating so hard that it hurt. He could feel beads of sweat forming on his skin.

James, who was as naked as Paul, wandered over to join him, and Paul did his best to recover some composure. 'Welcome aboard,' James said, a friendly smile lighting his face.

'You know about me staying?' Paul asked.

'Of course,' James said. 'It was all pre-arranged. I've been kicked out of my rooms down here so that you can use them while you're with us.'

'Sorry about that.'

'No problem,' James replied amiably. 'My temporary quarters upstairs are more than adequate and, to be honest, I'm looking forward to the change. By the way,' he added, 'Mistress Katrina

199

has told me she wants us both on our knees when she comes back into the dungeon.'

'Now there's a surprise,' Paul said, attempting a jokey response, but his lips trembled and there was a nervous break in his voice as he spoke.

'Are you OK?' James asked with a look of concern.

'To be honest, no I'm not,' Paul replied. 'I'm frightened stiff, really shit scared.'

'Don't worry,' said James, touching his arm. 'I'll look out for you while you're here, trust me. Now, hurry and kneel down. I just heard the key in the lock. Mistress must be coming.'

Katrina entered the dungeon, strode over to the two kneeling men and stood regally above them. She was looking resplendent in the stunning outfit she had changed into since seeing off her guests. The tips of her small firm breasts were barely covered by a miniscule leather bra. Her short leather skirt was molded over the tops of her thighs, completely exposing her well-shaped legs. The high, black shoes she was wearing had four thin straps that crisscrossed over the foot.

In one hand Mistress Katrina was holding a pack of playing cards. She started to shuffle the cards, gazing down at Paul and James as she did so. 'Get to your feet, the pair of you,' she said once she'd finished shuffling the pack. 'We're going to play a little game of cards I've devised.'

When the two naked men were standing she held the pack out to Paul in the palm of her hand. 'Cut,' she said, her black eyes narrowing slightly, slyly.

When Paul did as she had instructed, he pulled the nine of hearts. She noted the look of confusion that crossed his face, James's too. 'But I'm getting ahead of myself,' she said. 'You'll want me to explain the rules of the game to you both, won't you, slaves.'

'Yes, Mistress,' they both replied.

'The rules are as follows,' she said, her ink-black eyes going from one to the other of them. 'You two slaves cut at the beginning of each round. Paul has just cut, so it will be you next, James. The winner of the round will be the one who has the highest card, the loser the lowest.

'Any picture card – a Queen, the Ace of Spades, whatever –

will count as a ten. If it's a draw you both cut again. The loser in each round has to be punished, but *not* by me. In this game, it is the winner that has to cane the loser. He must do this as hard as he can and as many times as the value of the winning card. The overall loser in this competition is the one who gives up first for whatever reason that may be.' Katrina's lip curled into a sadistic smile 'Understood, slaves?'

'Understood, Mistress,' James said.

'Understood, Mistress,' echoed Paul, looking distinctly uncomfortable, not to say downright distressed. The prospect of inflicting physical pain on James, or on anyone else for that matter, held no appeal for him whatsoever. It occurred to Paul that if it had been Mistress Katrina's intention, in dreaming up this cruel contest, to hit an out-and-out masochist like him where it really hurt – and not at all in a nice way – then she had already succeeded with a vengeance.

Katrina held out the cards to James. He chose one and turned it over to show to his Mistress. 'Four,' she said. 'Bad luck, slave. You will recall that Paul had a nine.'

Paul and James both handed her their cards, and she shuffled all the cards together into a pack ready for the next round. Then she picked up a rattan cane and handed it to Paul who was shaking nervously.

Mistress Katrina said, 'All right, James, bend forward and reach towards your toes.' She then turned to Paul. 'Cane him as hard as you can.'

Paul held the cane as still as he was able to, but even so it trembled in his hand. His heart was beating like a drum and his mind was racing. Apart from that shaking hand, he did not move for ages as he tried to muster his courage. Then he brought the cane up in a wide arc and swiped it down onto James's backside as hard as he could. James could not stop himself from letting out a cry at the hot slash of pain.

'Silence, slave!' Mistress Katrina barked. 'I don't want to hear anything at all from you during this round. Do you understand?'

He nodded that he did, his face still wincing with agony.

One down, eight more to go. The second harsh strike did not result in any cry from the obedient James but his upper lip curled back grotesquely with the searing pain. Paul continued to rain down the blows as hard as he had been instructed to do, and each one landed ferociously stinging and sharp, until the ninth was etched across the slave's punished behind.

As the winner of that opening round, Paul was the first to be offered the deck of cards by Mistress Katrina for the next round.

'Cut,' she said.

Paul cut the deck and held up a Queen. James drew a six.

'Oh dear, I'm sorry to say that you've been unlucky again, James,' Mistress Katrina said. 'Assume the position.'

James bent forward once more. But Paul did not make a move.

'Paul,' Mistress Katrina snapped, noticing his reluctance to do what was expected of him. 'Get a fucking move on – you know what you have to do.'

Paul took a deep breath, swallowed hard and raised the cane once more. This so much went against his character. He felt heavy, daunted, crazed, as if he was under some kind of hideous dark spell. But he did as he was told. He caned James, and caned him again. And again, and again and again. It was obvious by the tenth strike that James was in tremendous pain. He gasped with the agony of trying to bear it. And then succumbed. Heaving sobs began to jerk his body and tears streamed down his cheeks.

'Perhaps my slave will get lucky this time,' Mistress Katrina said with apparent sincerity. Paul drew first and got a five. That wasn't much to beat. It looked as if James's luck might indeed be turning.

James did his cut, lifting his card out so the other two could see it, holding up the four of spades. *Oh fuck!* Paul cried out inside his head in anguished desperation. A four again, like James's first cut. *Oh fuck, oh fuck, oh fuck, oh fuck!*

James was still tearful, but then again Paul's own eyes were blurred with tears as he raised the cane once more. He felt a kind of overwhelming despair, as if he were drowning. Inflicting pain was not for him, not for him at all. But he did it yet again, belabouring James's backside with furious blows as he shuddered and wailed from the intolerable pain.

One thing must be said, though – deeply masochistic as James clearly was, he also had a truly formidable erection. Meanwhile Paul had nothing approaching a hard-on. He felt nothing but mental anguish and misery as he looked at James's lacerated backside, seeing all the searing lines etched into his punished cheeks, lines that *he* had put there.

It was time for the next round. For a long while Paul just stood and stared at the cards that Mistress Katrina held before him.

'Stop messing about,' she said irritably. 'Cut.'

He put his hand out quickly and picked a card. Oh no, it was a Queen again. Perhaps, Paul hoped against hope, James might also pick a picture card and they would have to cut again. All was not lost.

Alas, James picked the four of clubs. A four again, for Christ's sake!

Something snapped in Paul when he saw that card. There are actions a person will take sometimes by obeying a sudden overpowering impulse, actions they take without stopping for even a second to think. This was one such moment for Paul. He threw both his card and the cane onto the dungeon floor.

Nobody said a word. There was a long silence punctuated only by Paul's heavy breathing. Eventually he spoke, his voice thick with emotion. 'I give up, Mistress,' he said. 'I've lost. James is the winner.'

James emitted an involuntary groan of relief that the savage caning Paul had been forced to inflict on him had finally come to an end.

'But you don't know the penalty for losing, Paul,' Mistress Katrina said, her black eyes shining. 'Are you quite sure you want to give up?'

'I'm certain, Mistress,' Paul replied, standing before her, naked and trembling and utterly distraught. 'I just can't bear to inflict any more pain on James.'

'Have it your own way,' Katrina said with a shrug. 'Act in haste and repent at leisure, as the saying goes. Do you know what would have happened if you'd won this game?'

'No, Mistress.'

'You would have spent only one short night under my roof before being returned to Mistress Alicia. You'd have liked that, wouldn't you?'

'Yes, Mistress.'

'Shall I tell you what is going to happen to you as a result of losing this game or would you prefer that it remain a mystery?'

'Please tell me, Mistress,' Paul said, his lips trembling.

'Sure, I'll tell you,' Katrina responded, the flicker of a devious smile on her face. 'You'll be spending a lot longer than one night with me as your Mistress. You'll want to know for how long, of course,' she added, unable to keep the gloating tone out of her voice as she deliberately protracted his agony a little further.

'Yes, Mistress.'

'For two whole months, that's how long. Oh and Paul, I ought to tell you something else. Want to know what it is?'

'Yes, Mistress.'

'I cheat at cards.'

And for poor benighted Paul, that was the unkindest cut of all.

Chapter Forty-four

SPOOL FORWARD TWENTY-FOUR hours, a period of the most anxious trepidation for Paul as he tried without any discernible success to adjust himself to his new circumstances. A couple of months isn't too long, he kept telling himself unconvincingly. It sure *felt* as if it was going to be a long time though – an awfully long time. And here he was with James again in the dungeon, both of them naked and on their knees together once more.

The two men looked up at Mistress Katrina as she strode towards them, her body completely naked on this occasion but for the high black leather boots with spiky heels that she was wearing. 'Do I have your attention, slaves?' she said. There was an unpleasantly raspy edge to her voice that Paul hadn't noticed when he'd been introduced to her at the start of the fetish party, but which he'd noticed more and more during the infernal card game that had followed it.

'Yes, Mistress,' he and James replied together.

'Would you two slaves like to play a game?' she asked.

Oh shit, Paul thought, biting his lower lip. Here we go again. 'Yes, Mistress,' he said and so did James. Well, what were they *supposed* to say?

'What a coincidence that you should give that reply,' Katrina said. 'Shall I explain exactly why it's a coincidence?'

'Yes, Mistress,' they replied, speaking as one again.

'It's because this game happens to be called 'Yes, Mistress',' she said. 'Would you like to hear what the rules are?'

'Yes, Mistress,' came the chorused reply.

'Whenever I ask one of you a question,' she explained, 'you have to answer "Yes, Mistress", no matter what I've asked you. If that isn't your reply you'll have to suffer something you really and truly won't like. Do you agree to those rules?'

'Yes, Mistress,' the two slaves replied, exchanging nervous glances.

'Then you must be fucking mad,' she said derisively. 'Talk about leaving yourselves hostages to fortune – or my capricious whim! Is that what you've done, slaves?'

'Yes, Mistress,' they both had to agree.

'Let's start with our guest,' Mistress Katrina said. 'Stand up, Paul.'

'Yes, Mistress.'

'Good answer!'

She led him over to a St Andrews cross and strapped him to it in a spread-eagled position, facing the wall.

'Would you like me to flog you?' she asked, picking up a heavy leather flogger.

'Yes, Mistress,' came the expected reply as he tried to look back at her from over his shoulder. Before he even had a chance to turn frontward again she brought the whip down on his backside really hard, causing pain to sweep through him. The searing jolt subsided into more pain with the next strike and the one after that and the others that followed with increasing frequency.

'Would you like me to whip you harder?' Katrina asked.

'Yes, Mistress,' he replied, still grimacing with pain from her initial efforts.

'Then who am I, a humble dominatrix, to deny you your wish?' said Katrina, her tone witheringly sarcastic. She whipped him harder still, the harsh pain burning into him. His backside ached so much, the smarting pain of each impact blazing through his body.

'Do you feel the need to be paddled, by any chance?' Katrina asked, setting the flogger to one side and picking up a red leather paddle.

'Yes, Mistress.'

'Your word is my command,' she said with an unpleasant laugh, raising her arm and swinging the paddle down hard on his taut rear. Then she paddled him again, an even sharper strike that made him cry out with pain. She raised her arm again and brought the paddle down even more forcefully and swiftly to make contact with his backside once more. She beat him over and over again ever more vehemently until his rear was as red as the paddle and his agonized cries were echoing round the dungeon.

Mistress Katrina finally stopped paddling Paul, unbuckled his restraints, turned him round on the cross so that he was facing her and strapped him into position again. 'Did you enjoy being whipped and paddled?' she asked, her black eyes gleaming.

'Yes, Mistress.'

'A satisfied customer. Oh good,' she said with her now familiar sarcasm. 'We do aim to please. I'm using the royal we, of course. Is our aim good, do you think, Paul?'

'Yes, Mistress.'

'I wonder if you'll like what's in store for you next,' she said with sadistic relish. 'Stick out your chest and poke out your tongue.' Paul didn't like the sound of this *at all*. She bent on to one knee, foraged in a box and brought out three metal clamps. She attached one to each of Paul's nipples and one to the end of his tongue, sending tremors of intense pain through his body. 'You like?' she asked cheerfully.

'Yeth, Mithtreth,' was the best he could do by way of a reply. His eyes were misting with agony.

'You theem to have developed a rather charming lithp,' Mistress Katrina said, following her mimicry with a cruel laugh. 'How delightful! Do you think your lisp is delightful, slave?'

'Yeth, Mithtreth.'

'You've been monopolising my attention, Paul,' she said, suddenly changing tack. 'Shame on you. Mustn't forget my house-slave, James.' She left Paul where he was, acute pain still shooting through his body, his nerves teased raw.

Mistress Katrina turned her attentions to James. 'Our guest has been making me horny,' she told him, and from where Paul was kneeling he could see that she was indeed soaked. Dribbles of pussy juice were smeared down her thighs. She pressed two fingers directly into her shaven sex, sliding between the tumescent labia. 'Taste me,' she said, bringing her soaking fingers to James's lips. He kissed the moisture from them, sucking hard at her fingers and lapping his tongue over them sensuously.

'Do you like the taste of my pussy, slave?' she said, removing her fingers from his mouth, grasping hold of his mop of auburn hair, and looking him in the eye.

'Yes, Mistress,' James replied.

'Good,' she said. 'Extremely wet, aren't I?'

'Yes, Mistress.'

'Perhaps I'll give you some more of my wetness to sample a little later. But I have other things on my mind at present that will require you to be in bondage.'

Mistress Katrina told James to get to his feet. She manacled his arms to the leather wrist cuff attachments at either end of a metal spreader bar hanging by a chain from the dungeon ceiling.

She then returned to Paul in order to remove the clamps attached to his nipples and tongue. Everything seemed to scream inside him when she did this. His tongue felt excruciatingly sore and his chest was marked with red around the nipples, which ached with intense pain.

Mistress Katrina next unbuckled his restraints and released him from the St Andrews cross. 'Would it be fair to say that you didn't enjoy inflicting pain on James yesterday one iota?' she asked.

'Yes, Mistress,' he replied with undeniable honesty.

'Would you like to inflict pain on him now?'

Initially, Paul gave no response. Confused thoughts were spinning around in his head like a carousel.

'Answer me,' Katrina rasped. 'Would you like to inflict pain on James now?'

'Yes, Mistress,' he said, flinching.

'Paul, really! You must learn to be more consistent,' she said, shaking her head in a mockery of disbelief. Oh, the hilarity. Oh, how hugely amusing she found herself to be.

She handed him a single-tailed flogger and told him to use it on James's backside. 'Before you start, I think you'll need a bit of guidance from me,' she said, picking up an identical flogger. 'You must beat him as hard as I'm beating you.'

Mistress Katrina stood behind Paul and brought her whip down on his rear once and very hard. Paul repeated the process on James's backside, leaving an angry line across his rear. Mistress Katrina whipped Paul harder still the next time and he did the same to James, watching in dismay as a second searing line etched itself into his backside. Katrina beat Paul's rear even harder the third time and Paul beat James just as hard. He hated doing it but, really, what was he to do? Katrina beat Paul until every muscle in his aching rear felt bruised and, God forgive him, he did the same to James.

'Very good, Paul,' Mistress Katrina said, at long last, retrieving his flogger from him. 'Now get onto your knees.'

The dominatrix then left Paul where he was and detached James from the spreader bar. She laid out a large black plastic sheet on the floor of the dungeon, telling James to lie flat on his back on it. She lit three white candles that were held in a metal candle holder.

She drizzled copious amounts of hot wax onto his naked body. He didn't scream exactly. The sound he made was more a kind of constant, desperate gibbering and his body shook without control.

'Did you like that?' she asked her slave.

'Yyyes, Mmmistress,' James replied in a stammer, still shivering with pain.

'Would you like another treat?' she said. 'Oh, and speak more distinctly this time.'

'Yes, Mistress,' he replied, trying to compose himself.

'Would you like me to piss into your mouth?'

'Yes, Mistress,' James replied in a flat voice. But Paul had a horrible feeling that this was what he actually *did* want. Well, rather him than me, Paul thought. He hated the idea of water sports, loathed it.

'Then, James, open wide,' Mistress Katrina said before squatting over his face and sending a golden stream of urine into his open mouth.

'Do you think Paul would like me to do that to him, too?' she asked.

'Yeaghsss, Mighsstresss,' James gurgled and gargled and spluttered. Paul saw a look of shame come across his eyes. And well he might look ashamed, Paul thought bitterly. Thank you James, he said to himself, thanks a whole fucking bunch. So, you'll look out for me while I'm here, will you? That's what James had promised with such apparent sincerity only the day before. Trust me, he'd said and yet here he was already sending him right down the river, and it was a river of piss.

'Crawl over and lie next to James,' Mistress Katrina told Paul and he did so with a horrible sense of inevitability about what was about to befall him. He lay there listening to his heart race as he waited for some kind of golden shower. But Mistress Katrina surprised him. She did not proceed to urinate on him, as he'd been certain she would. Instead she picked up one of the three lighted candles that she had used to torment James earlier and poured molten wax over his body. Paul shivered with pain and his head shook jerkily as the intensity of his shivering increased.

Mistress Katrina laughed softly, delighting in his extreme discomfort. 'Open your mouth,' she said next. Here it comes, he thought, wait for it. But he was wrong again. Katrina inserted the unlit end of the candle into Paul's mouth. 'Do you like that?' she asked.

'Yesh, Mishtresh,' was the best he could manage this time, and he really meant it. He'd rather have a melting candle drizzling into his mouth than Katrina's urine, any day of the week.

'That lisp of yours seems to have developed into a real speech impediment,' Mistress Katrina said. She was sarcasm personified once more. 'Perhaps this will help.' She removed the candle, blew it out and threw it to the corner of the dungeon.

'Better?'

'Yes, Mistress.'

'Are you enjoying yourself?' she asked. Her black eyes were suddenly fixed on him with hypnotic intensity.

'Yes, Mistress.'

'Having a really great time with me, are you?' she went on, holding that stare.

'Yes, Mistress.'

'Having such a great time with me that you would like me to be your permanent Mistress, would you, rather than Mistress Alicia? Is that what you're telling me?' And as she said this she positioned herself astride his prone form.

Enough was enough. This was where the game would have to come to an end as far as Paul was concerned and the devil with the consequences. There was no way he was going to be disloyal to his beloved Mistress Alicia. But he was undeniably frightened and his reply was stammering: 'Nu … Nu … No, Mistress … '

'… is the wrong answer,' Katrina said triumphantly, unleashing a great stream of piss over his body. She did not urinate in his mouth, though, so he was grateful for small mercies.

There were precious few such mercies during the course of the rest of his stay with Mistress Katrina, who continued to piss on him from a great height, metaphorically speaking. She just did not let up on Paul at all, pushing his limits excessively all the while. Maybe she thought it would be good for him, make him a better slave, he didn't know; but it really got him down after a while. She was forever trying out bizarre and ultra-sadistic games on him, invariably ensuring that he was the sad and sorry loser. No sooner had she finished making him miserable with one of her cruel games than she seemed to want to start another.

All in all, it was a rough time for Paul, very rough indeed, a *testing* time. *I'm doing this for Mistress Alicia*, he got into the habit of repeating to himself over and over like a kind of prayer. If he could just get through this hellish stay with Katrina without screwing up, how proud of him Mistress Alicia would be, he told himself. But Katrina remained frighteningly determined to make it as difficult for him as she possibly could.

When he'd first been introduced to Mistress Katrina at the start of the fetish party he'd found her undeniably alluring. Well before the end of his secondment to her, though, he had come to think of her as the queen-sized bitch of all time. He thought Katrina had a heart that was as black and cold as her eyes.

And what did he think of James? Could he trust him, like James had asked him to? Had James looked out for him, as he'd said he would? Had he hell! He'd just been taking the piss – something of a speciality of his as it transpired, literally speaking.

Chapter Forty-five

PAUL HAD COME OUT the worst from all – *every single one* – of the innumerable cruel games to which Mistress Katrina had subjected him and James since Paul's initial incarceration in her dungeon. It was therefore unsurprising that he'd grown to loathe the perpetrator of those sadistic games. As for James, Paul felt that he had reneged on his promise to look out for him during his stay, and he couldn't help but feel bitter about it. Then James said something that made Paul think again. It started with a simple apology.

'I'm sorry,' James said. He and Paul were on their own in the dungeon. The two men were both naked and were standing face to face, Mistress Katrina having earlier clipped their wrist cuffs to either end of the same metal spreader bar that hung from the ceiling by two chains.

'Sorry for what?' Paul asked, giving James a quick, sharp look.

'For causing Mistress to piss on you that time, for starters,' James said. 'Personally I enjoy water sports but you clearly don't at all. You obviously hated the experience. I said I'd look out for you during your stay, didn't I. Well, I certainly didn't that time and I haven't during any of Mistress's other games for that matter. I made you a pretty empty promise as things have turned out and I'm truly sorry for that.'

'Apology accepted,' Paul mumbled without much conviction.

'I couldn't help it, you know,' James said quickly. 'I still can't, for that matter.'

'How do you mean?' Paul bridled. 'That makes no sense.'

'Maybe it'll make sense if I tell you this,' James said. 'Before I came into the dungeon to join you that second day, Mistress told me she expected me to win all the games she was going to play with us during the rest of your stay, no matter what it took. Let me ask you this, Paul – What would you have done if Mistress Alicia had said the same thing to you?'

Paul thought for a moment. 'Exactly the same as you,' he said. 'I have to admit it.' And with that all the festering resentment he had felt towards James disappeared like dew in the morning sun.

There was silence between the two men for a while, which Paul was the first to break. 'Tell me a bit about yourself, James,' he said. 'How'd you first get into all this?'

'The BDSM, you mean?'

'Yeah.'

'Well, I'm bisexual ...'

'So am I,' Paul interrupted, entirely at ease for some time now with that aspect of his sexuality.

'In fact, if anything, I used to be more attracted to guys than girls – or so I thought anyway.'

Paul had once been like that too. 'Fair enough,' he said. 'But what's that got to do with BDSM?'

'It all began in the woods,' James replied. 'Would you like to hear about what happened to me there?'

'Sure,' Paul said, intrigued.

James began to tell his story: 'I used to love going into the woods when I was a young man. I'd always been something of a loner and the woods were somewhere I could be on my own...'

The woods were a place where James could be perfectly alone, a place where he wouldn't encounter another living soul. But he needed to venture deep into those dark woods to find the solitude he sought: through the depthless ranks of trees where all was quiet except for the occasional shuffle of fallen leaves; then deeper still, through a part of the woods that seemed preternaturally silent, inert, devoid of life. A curtain of trees surrounded him, loomed over him. They pressed in from every side before miraculously opening out to that lovely secluded spot – a sun-dappled clearing with a pebbled stream and a seductively secretive atmosphere. It was the ideal place to have a wank.

James was sexually confused back then, though not perhaps for the most obvious reason. He knew he was attracted to his own sex as much as, maybe even more than, members of the opposite sex. That wasn't the problem. He didn't feel uncomfortable with being bisexual, but he did with some of the darker desires he had begun to have – because he'd started to fantasize frequently about being tied up and beaten. He had no idea where these thoughts were coming from. He hadn't been abused as a child or anything like that, had never been subjected to any form of corporal punishment at all. So, he found these fantasies mystifying and disturbing. But he also found them powerfully erotic, and masturbated constantly to the mental images he was conjuring up from … well… who knows where?

James was a chronic masturbator in those days, taking every conceivable opportunity he could find to pleasure himself. He liked nothing better on a fine sunny day than to go off on his own to the woods at the edge of the town in which he lived. He would wear as little as he could get away with. That was usually a T-shirt, tight jeans with no underwear, and trainers. Getting as well off the beaten track as possible, he would venture into the very heart of the woods where all was quiet but for the murmurings and stirrings of nature, the occasional creaking of a bough. Then he'd arrive at his favourite spot: that clearing by the edge of a pebbled brook.

Just before he got there he would remove his clothes and leave them by a fallen log, always the same one. He would then make his randy way to the clearing, his hard cock throbbing in his hand. Once there, enveloped again in blissful seclusion, he would wank himself senseless.

Afterwards, he would wash off in the stream, dry himself in the sunshine, get back into his clothes and set off home. The thrilling recollection of what he had just been doing combined with the rough feel of his tight denim jeans on his cock meant that by the time he got home he was ready to jerk himself off again. And that's invariably exactly what he did.

Then one day everything changed. James had gone off into the woods alone once more, full of the horny joys of spring. The air was lazy and mild, and speckled sunlight filtered through the branches overhead. There were clumps of wild flowers rising through the carpet of leaves and the trees were in bud. The sap was rising in James as well and he was looking forward no end to indulging in a major bout of masturbation, his penis becoming increasingly stimulated in anticipation by the tight denim of his jeans.

As soon as he got to the fallen log, he stripped off and had already started rubbing his stiff shaft as he made his way to the clearing. But when nearly there, he heard a dry crack of wood and the careless rustle of undergrowth coming from where he was headed. Then he heard something else, something that made his heart pound: the sound of voices.

James stopped for a moment, then crept gingerly forward and peeked with great caution through a canopy of leaves into the clearing. What he saw when he did that really got his erection pulsing, and with very good reason. Because there before his eyes were half a dozen young men of about his age, all naked, standing in a circle and masturbating.

James was thoroughly enjoying the sight of those six wankers and was wanking away himself as he watched them, when all of a sudden … 'Well now, someone's obviously enjoying the show', said a voice from behind James, jarring him out of his lustful reverie.

He turned round to see just about the best-looking young man he'd ever set eyes on, a real Adonis. Blond-haired with vivid blue eyes and high cheekbones, he too was naked. And he was displaying an enormous erection, his penis as thick and strong as his body was athletic. He put a friendly arm around James's shoulder and an even friendlier hand on James's hard cock, gesturing for him to reciprocate.

'Let's watch together for a bit,' he said, his blue eyes sparkling, and that's what the two of them did as they continued masturbating one another.

'I'm the ringleader of that little wanking club,' he announced after a while. 'Would you like to join?'

'I sure would,' James replied eagerly.

'I feel I ought to warn you, though,' the ringleader said, 'there's an initiation ceremony you have to go through to join. You may not enjoy that. On the other hand,' he added with a salacious grin, 'you may enjoy it a lot.'

He led James into the clearing and interrupted his masturbating friends, who all gathered around James, clutching their erections – and several of them clutching at his.

'We've got a potential member of the club here,' said the ringleader. 'Come on guys, you know what to do.'

At this instruction, they hurried over to their discarded clothes and removed the leather belts from their jeans. They used these to tie James's wrists together in front of him before stretching his arms up and tying his bound wrists to the overhanging branch of an oak tree. They also belted his ankles together.

At a signal from the ringleader each took it in turns to whip James's backside with a leather belt, their lashes sharp and stinging. James found this increasingly painful but also immensely exciting as was obvious by his rock-hard cock and the rivulet of pre-cum trailing from its head.

But the fierce red pain burning across James's backside started to become unbearable after a while. They stopped beating him then, much to his relief, and untied his wrists from the branch of the tree as well as untying his ankles. James thought that was the end of the initiation ceremony, but no. Because they then re-tied the belt around his wrists, this time behind his back.

'Have you ever sucked cock?' the ringleader asked.

'No,' James replied truthfully.

'That's the last time you'll ever be able to say that,' he laughed. 'Kneel down and suck every one of the guys' cocks in turn, until in each case I tell you to move on to the next one. If one of them climaxes while you're sucking him, you must swallow his cum – understand?'

James nodded his head yes, and went on to suck all six cocks. One of the young men – the sixth – did indeed ejaculate in his mouth and he swallowed down all of the creamy cum that spilled from his shaft.

'Good boy,' said the ringleader. 'Now for the last part of the initiation ceremony.' On saying that, he pushed James roughly to the ground, where he lay on his back. The mud underneath him felt tepid and soft against his naked skin.

'Let's baptize him with boy juice,' the ringleader said to his companions and they all masturbated feverishly until one after the other of them squirted their hot seed over James's torso and face. Even the young guy who'd already come in James's mouth managed another impressive load. The ringleader then wanked himself with one hand and James with the other until they both spurted out thick gobs of pearly cum onto his stomach.

James's wrists were untied then and they all just picked up

their clothes and disappeared into the thick woods without a word, leaving him on his back in the dirt, his nostrils suffused with the odour of moss and mud and cum.

Chapter Forty-six

'HOW I LONGED TO see the ringleader and the others again after they'd initiated me so sadistically into their wanking club,' James continued. 'The problem was that I didn't know a single one of those guys and therefore didn't have any means of making contact with them. I'd no way of knowing when, if ever, they'd turn up in the woods again. I'd never seen them before that time, after all. Would I ever see them again? All I could do was go there as often as I was able to, in my usual horny state, and just hope for the best. Apart from anything else they'd really fuelled my innate masochism, so I was ever hopeful. But nothing, no sign of them at all, ever again.

'And that, Paul, is what happened to me in the woods,' James said, concluding his account on an anti-climax. 'My life moved on after that. I stopped going into the woods on my own in due course and started to get a lot more interested in the opposite sex. I also got even more interested in BDSM. My ever-deeper craving to be beaten and humiliated led me to extreme S&M sex clubs and even more extreme fetish parties. I met Mistress Katrina at one of these and, well, you can guess the rest.'

Paul had started to become aroused during James's account but the mention of the hated Katrina's name immediately had the opposite effect on him. And talk of the devil …

At that moment as if on cue, Mistress Katrina re-entered the dungeon, looking every inch the cruel dominatrix she indisputably was. She was all in black, wearing a leather cap with its peak pushed down over her forehead and a leather dress that was both extremely tight and extremely short. She completed the ensemble with thigh length boots with very high heels.

Katrina was carrying a long black leather hold-all and didn't say a word as she placed its contents on a dark table that stood against one of the dungeon walls. On the table there already stood a jug of water, with two glasses by its side.

She set up a row of six disciplinary items, placing a card in front of each showing a number. Item one, the card indicated, was a leather spanking mitt, item two a paddle, three a heavy leather flogger, four a cranberry-red fibreglass cane, five a tawse and six a cat o' nine tails. She flanked the items with a dice and small tumbler to go with it at one end of the table and at the other end the jug of water, which she repositioned there along with the two glasses by its side.

'We're going to play a game,' Mistress Katrina finally said. What a surprise, Paul thought sarcastically, and I wonder who'll end up the fall guy this time just by way of a change? He might as well face it, he couldn't win here. The dice was totally weighed against him – in all probability quite literally, knowing Mistress Katrina.

'Here's the deal this time,' Katrina said. 'I'll roll the dice. Whatever number comes up will correspond with the number in front of the instrument of discipline I'm going to use, and which, let me add, I will use in whatever way I like and for as long as it pleases me. I shall then move on to the next slave. If my second roll of the dice results in the number of a disciplinary instrument I have already used, the slave misses his turn to be disciplined, and gets a nice refreshing glass of water instead. I will then move on to the next numbered instrument of correction, and so on. The first slave to beg for mercy is the loser and will have to pay the price of his defeat. Understood, slaves?'

'Understood, Mistress,' came the joint reply, neither slave meeting the other's eye.

'You go first, Paul,' Mistress Katrina said, rolling the dice for the first time. 'A one. That's appropriate enough. It means the spanking mitt. Right, let's get you where I want you.' She unclipped his wrist cuffs from the spreader bar he shared with his fellow slave, leaving James to witness the proceedings from where he was. She led Paul over to a whipping bench and told him to bend over it.

Mistress Katrina put the leather mitt over her right hand and paused for a moment before beginning her spanking. Then: Smack! The sharp snap of sound echoed through the dungeon, an explosion of pure pain that made his backside burn. Paul had no time to recover as she brought the mitt down again. He tensed and jerked forward as it slapped down harshly on his naked rear.

Another harsh spank with the mitt landed flat on his backside. It brought another explosion of hot pain followed by a gasp that he could not hold back. Her next blow landed even more furiously on the reddened cheeks of his backside, forcing him hard against the leather surface of the whipping bench. The cheeks of Paul's backside smarted with a fire that made him squirm with pain as the full effect of the spanking spread through his body.

Mistress Katrina removed the spanking mitt. 'That'll do to start with,' she said, her tone brusque. 'Stay where you are, Paul, while I roll the dice again.'

'Yes, Mistress,' he said. Yes sure, he'd stay where he was, he thought. He reckoned he knew full well the way this game was going to go. There really was no point in moving.

There was a rattle and a roll of the dice. 'Oh, shame,' said Katrina unconvincingly. 'It's a one again.' She poured out a glass of water from the jug and held it to James's lips until he'd drunk it all. She then picked up disciplinary instrument number two, the paddle, and turned her attention to Paul again.

'I'm going to beat your backside with the paddle,' Katrina said. 'I want you to count off each strike and thank me for it. Understood, slave?'

'Yes, Mistress.'

Katrina raised her arm up and brought it down hard.

Thwack!

'One, thank you, Mistress,' he panted.

Thwack!

'Two, thank you, Mistress,' he groaned.

Thwack!

'Three, thank you, Mistress.'

Thwack!

'Four, thank you, Mistress.' … And on and on, six times more.

Katrina repeated the process with the dice. 'Well, who would believe it!' she exclaimed. 'It's a one again. Now, what are the chances of that happening?' Yes, Paul thought sourly, who would believe it? He certainly didn't. What *were* the chances of that happening? About nil. He was in the process of being royally stitched up here, and there was absolutely nothing he could do about it, as usual.

Mistress Katrina gave James another glass of water, holding the glass to his lips again, and then moved back to Paul, picking up the heavy leather flogger from the table as she went. She raised the whip, swung it through the air, landing a heavy blow on his backside. He squealed and cowered as she laid several more blows to his rear, marking his skin redder still with the thongs of the whip. On and on she beat his backside with savage blows, each of which was a flash of pure pain that made him cry out more and more as the full effect of the whipping spread through his body. Each time the heavy leather flogger landed it brought another jolt of agonizing pain and another cry from him.

As the merciless whipping continued, Paul tried desperately – despairingly – to withstand the ferocious pain. Katrina continued to thrash his backside viciously and by the time she finally decided to stop it was covered with numerous ugly welts.

Mistress Katrina gave another roll of the dice and Paul remained bent over the whipping bench, awaiting the inevitable with bitterness in his heart towards his relentless tormentor. This time it was a three. Paul had just about had a belly-full of this cruel game, of *all* Mistress Katrina's cruel games. James had just about had a belly-full too, literally. By the time he had struggled down yet another proffered glass of water, his stomach was thoroughly bloated.

'Now I'm going to cane you, Paul, and I'm going to do it with my 'special cane'' Mistress Katrina announced next, showing him the thin length of red fibreglass. Paul readied himself for the savage caning he knew he was about to receive, tensing his body and gritting his teeth. The sharp stinging pain swept through him as the cane came down. He barely had time to draw breath before her second strike landed. Again, the razor sharp pain swept through him as the cane landed on his rear. He could feel the heat burning on the cheeks of his backside, the skin raised and imprinted with the pattern of the cane as well as the welts from his earlier flogging.

On and on she caned his rear with the vicious fibreglass implement until he closed his eyes, feeling that he was unable to endure the severity of his punishment any longer. But he had to, because still she went on. His backside ached, the sharp pain of each impact merging with the ones that had preceded it and seeping through his body. He tried not to think of anything, tried not to see himself being so brutally chastised by Katrina, tried not to imagine her gloating black eyes focused on his backside reddening further with every savage strike from the fibreglass cane.

Mistress Katrina stopped briefly and stroked the cane over Paul's backside, before recommencing the beating. Three vicious swipes in swift succession left Paul whimpering in agony. Katrina examined, with sadistic satisfaction, the painful-looking lines that now covered his backside. But this was not enough for her.

'I want your stripes to be the same shade of red as my cane,' she said and lifted it high above her head. She began to rain blow after furious blow on his backside until he was racked with coruscating agony. He let out a terrible piercing scream before desperately pleading for mercy.

'You lose, Paul,' Mistress Katrina said, her black eyes glinting with cruelty. 'It's time for you to pay the penalty. Lie down on your back on the floor between James's spread legs.' Paul did as he had been told, his severely punished rear smarting horribly against the dungeon floor. He looked up at James, who remained where he had been all along – suspended from the metal spreader bar. Paul could see the intense anxiety in his eyes.

'Piss on him, James,' Mistress Katrina ordered, her eyes like black ice.

There was a long silence in which you could have heard a pin drop.

'I said, piss on him,' Katrina said, breaking that silence with the rasping reiteration of her command. 'Do it right this minute.'

And James did exactly that, did exactly what Paul would have done if Mistress Alicia had demanded the same of him. It was a salutary thought and one that Paul held in his mind until his hideous golden shower was over. And when at last it was, he lay on the dungeon floor, his urine-soaked body shaking uncontrollably. He was desperate for the nightmare of his stay with Mistress Katrina to come to an end.

It wasn't the woman's extreme sadism that he minded. Mistress Alicia herself was extremely sadistic, there could be no denying that, and it was not a problem. Paul, it had turned out, was extremely masochistic. But he had felt cherished when he'd been under her direct control. He felt anything but that under Mistress Katrina's 'rain' of terror. He survived, though, falling back on his constant mantra: *I'm doing this for Mistress Alicia, I'm doing this for Mistress Alicia, I'm doing this for Mistress Alicia* ...He prayed with ever more desperation for the time that he would be returned to her, for the time he would be returned to his beloved Mistress Alicia. And finally that time arrived.

Chapter Forty-seven

PAUL WAS RETURNED TO Mistress Alicia one night by Katrina. In a repeat performance but in reverse of his manner of delivery to Katrina's home two months before, Paul was kept blindfolded right up to the point that Katrina's large dark-windowed Daimler arrived at Alicia's apartment block. Having delivered him to Mistress Alicia, Katrina left swiftly and without ceremony. It was the most cursory of handovers imaginable and had obviously been pre-arranged that way by the two dommes.

As soon as Katrina had left the apartment, Mistress Alicia, who was looking magnificent in a skin-tight black leather cat suit, focussed her attention on Paul. 'Strip naked and then get onto your knees before me, slave,' she ordered imperiously, seating herself on her sumptuous leather couch.

Paul obeyed hurriedly, shaking with excitement. He was thrilled beyond measure to see Mistress Alicia again and do her immediate bidding. This was the moment for which he'd been waiting for such a long time. He felt a tattoo of pulses build in his chest as he knelt naked before her.

'Is there anything you'd like to say to me, slave?' Alicia asked, her voice emotionless.

'I'd like to thank you for having me back, Mistress,' Paul replied through trembling lips. He wanted to say so much more, wanted to say all the words he had rehearsed for days now, weeks. He wanted to tell Mistress Alicia how much he worshipped and adored her, how desperately he had missed her, that he would do anything for her. He wanted to tell her that he would walk through a million blizzards for her if that was what she wanted him to do. But none of the words came out; they all stuck in his throat. He curled a hand to his mouth and, he couldn't help it, started to sob.

'Stand up,' Mistress Alicia said and when he got to his feet he did also. She put her arms around him then, the first time she'd ever done such a thing. It made him feel so privileged, so

224

cherished, so *loved*. He buried his head in her shoulders and cried his eyes out. It was such a colossal relief to be back with her, and so wonderful to be in her arms for the very first time like this. Her hair smelt so clean and felt so soft, soft enough to hide himself in for ever and never come out.

Mistress Alicia lifted his face then and planted her lips on his. The kiss she gave him was long and very passionate. Paul delighted in the demanding feel of Mistress Alicia's hot wet lips and frantic tongue as she gorged herself on his mouth.

And it didn't stop there. It is true that Paul had to return to his dungeon quarters, where he was locked in as before. But Mistress Alicia's attitude towards him seemed to have subtly shifted, and for the good. Could it be happening, he wondered. Had his awful time with Katrina been some kind of test that had been set for him by Mistress Alicia and which he had passed? More than that, was Alicia actually in love with him now as he was with her? Could that actually be so? Probably not, he conceded sadly. That really would be too much to hope for. But she certainly had very passionate feelings towards him that she seemed to have bottled up in his two month absence and could now release with their full force.

The next few weeks were memorable indeed, crammed as they were with steamy sex as Mistress Alicia fucked Paul constantly in the dungeon. She fucked him with a large butt plug while sucking his cock and manipulating his balls with a vibrating massager. She fucked him with a long black rippled dildo while pulling hard on his cock. She energetically finger-fucked him in the anus while masturbating him with a vacuum pump. On one occasion she tied him on his back to the horizontal torture chair and fucked him frenziedly with a strap-on dildo while raining blow after vicious blow onto his chest and crotch with a cat o' nine tails. Then Alicia did something else. She brought the leather body bag into use ...

Mistress Alicia, who was as naked as was Paul, zipped and tied him into place in the body bag, leaving his genitals exposed. She blindfolded him with a soft leather blindfold but otherwise left his face free so that she could sit on it whenever she felt so inclined. Alicia then strapped a leather cock ring tightly around the base of his penis. When she did this Paul's cock, which had been semi-hard, stiffened fully and let out a silvery squirt of pre-cum. 'Careful, slave,' she warned. 'You are not to climax unless I give you permission.'

Mistress Alicia then knelt on the dungeon floor and took hold of Paul's shaft. She encircled it and started to masturbate him, her hand coming and going in short rhythmic strokes. She played with the head of his cock, moving her palm around the top of his slit, spreading the trickling pre-cum all over his cockhead until it shone.

Alicia then knelt forward, stretched her lips and wrapped them around that glistening bulb. She sucked on it hard while stroking his pulsing shaft until Paul was sure he was going to climax imminently despite his best efforts. Thankfully she stopped blowing him then and, while he concentrated hard on retreating from the brink, she changed positions and swung her thighs over his blindfolded face. She squatted down slowly until she could feel his breath on her inner thighs.

Mistress Alicia touched her pussy then, her fingers instantly wet with her juices. She arched her back, pushing the mouth of her vagina down towards Paul's waiting lips. He licked her pussy, which was now so soaking wet that it was drenched. His mouth moved with increasing force and with small and then bigger flicks of the tongue. Paul kissed the lips of Alicia's sex with his own burning lips, slid his tongue into that inviting cavity, and pushed his face upwards, burying it in her humid wetness. His tongue played inside her sex, and her body trembled with pleasure as she felt the first tremors of an orgasm start to flow. Her groin began to spasm then and her whole body started to shake as she ground down onto his face.

The naked dominatrix squeezed her eyes tightly shut when she crested to first one shuddering orgasm, followed by another and another. Then, her heart still racing from her most recent climax, she opened her eyes. She could see clearly but Paul, of course, remained blindfolded, unable to discern even the tiniest glimmer of light.

Mistress Alicia shifted her position once more. She was back on her knees, sucking Paul's cock again, this time with slow, regular movements. She swirled her tongue around the head of his

226

cock, flicked it around his cum-slit, and moved it up and down the shaft, tasting every part of it all the way down to the leather cock ring tightly gripping its base. It was the four-star blow job of all time and Paul felt as if he was in S&M paradise there, zipped and tied and blindfolded within the leather body bag. He felt totally controlled and malleable and utterly consumed by desire for Alicia, his Mistress of Torment.

Alicia kept on languorously blowing Paul, driving him wild with desire. Her tongue came and went, licking and lingering as she felt Paul's pleasure rising more and more. She took his cock deep in her throat and then pulled it out again with infinite slowness, accentuating the pressure of her lips, really taking her time. She stopped when she felt his pleasure was once again in danger of erupting and for a few seconds she slowed down even more, keeping only the end of his cock on her tongue, before plunging it deep in her throat again, savouring every inch of his aching, throbbing shaft.

Paul was perilously near the breaking point of ecstasy now. But he wouldn't climax unless she gave him permission, he wouldn't. *But Jesus* … She lifted her head for a moment. 'You have my permission to come,' she said before engulfing his cock with her mouth once more. Suddenly her head began furiously pumping. Paul began to shudder in spasms as he arched up and strained against the body bag. He climaxed violently, spilling his creamy load into her mouth. His orgasm kept on coming in great bursting spurts, producing endless loads of thick white cum that she kept on sucking until every last drop had drained out of his spent cock.

Mistress Alicia held this veritable mouthful on her tongue without swallowing it. She turned and kissed Paul and opened his mouth so that she could return all of his jism. She unfurled her tongue to release the mass of creamy liquid and he swallowed all of it down.

Next Alicia removed Paul's blindfold. Her blue eyes locked into his. 'Anything to say, slave?' she asked.

'Only that I worship you, Mistress,' he said, continuing to gaze besottedly into her eyes.

'I know you do,' she replied, her face an enigmatic mask, her eyes unreadable.

Chapter Forty-eight

MISTRESS ALICIA RELEASED HIM from the body bag then and walked out of the dungeon, locking the door behind her. Paul was left alone with his thoughts, which were nothing less than euphoric. He didn't think he had ever known such blissful happiness. Eventually he came down from his endorphin high, though, and doubts began to creep into his mind. He started to get this awful pain clutching at his chest as he asked himself what he would do if Mistress Alicia ever tired of him, decided to let him go – not temporarily, he could live with that again if he really had to, but *permanently*. His heart beat wildly and his stomach turned and he felt faint as he imagined it.

He felt much the same way at first the next time Mistress Alicia told him that she was going to let him out of the dungeon again. Actually his initial thought when she told him this wasn't that she was going to get rid of him for good but that he was in for another miserable secondment to Mistress Katrina. Alicia was stark naked when she informed him she was going to let him out, though. So Paul decided on immediate reflection that he might have got that wrong. Her next announcement made it clear that he had.

'I don't want to sleep alone tonight,' she said. Mistress Alicia then led Paul out of the dungeon, halfway down the corridor and into her bedroom, which he could see was impressively equipped for BDSM play. There was a rack of disciplinary implements at the foot of the four poster bed and a free standing cross next to the wall opposite it. But Mistress Alicia did not take hold of any disciplinary implement and it was not to the cross that she led Paul but to the bed. 'Lie on your back,' she told him.

Paul lay on top of the bedspread looking up at the high ceiling, his heart beating quickly as he waited for whatever Mistress Alicia was going to do. His sexual excitement was intense, his hard cock standing up from his naked body in readiness. Alicia then joined

Paul on the bed and, with her back to him, straddled his face. She guided his mouth to her sex and he started licking, his tongue moving with a steady rhythm over her pussy lips and tumescent clit.

Mistress Alicia enjoyed the persistent licking on her sex and leaned forward to reciprocate, sliding her mouth down Paul's hard cock. He felt the warmth of her mouth, the sinuous press of her tongue as she started to suck at him and he continued to lick at her. She was as wet as anything now as his tongue carried on spinning pleasure on her sex and she kept on moving her lips up and down over his shaft. Paul ejaculated a squirt of pre-cum and Alicia swallowed the delicious taste of it before withdrawing her mouth slowly from his thickened, pulsing cock.

The dominatrix then changed position, turning to face Paul and straddling his thighs with her own. But she didn't let him push his cock inside her sex ... not yet. Alicia had never let any man push his cock into her sex in all her life apart from her husband and she'd sworn to herself long ago that she never would. But she was going to let Paul, and for one reason only – she now felt about him the same way she had about Peter, something she had not dared for a single moment to allow herself to hope for at the start of this whole extraordinary affair.

When Mistress Alicia had first begun to have these feelings towards Paul she felt she had to put them to the test; she just *had* to. That had been what his two month secondment to Mistress Katrina had been all about. It had been the longest two months of Alicia's life. But it had been worth it, because when he'd been returned to her she'd known without a shadow of a doubt that it was true. She was as much in love with him as she had ever been with Peter.

So Mistress Alicia was going to do it. She was going to let Paul enter her sex with that beautiful hard cock of his – but not before tormenting him, not before making him wait. The head of his shaft touched the mouth of her sex and was held there, poised, but when Paul tried to press himself up into the hot warmth – all slippery and wet and waiting for him – she gripped his wrist hard and he went still. Alicia, his Mistress of Torment, looked down at him, feeling the anticipation of his body and in her own, every nerve electric. Her naked breasts heaved with quickened breathing that was echoed by his own. It was time. She sank down onto Paul, his cock forced deep and high, drawing a guttural moan from him. And from her too.

Mistress Alicia's muscles flexed around Paul's stiff cock, rocking him, her pussy tight and wet, for it was dripping liquid. And it made wet sounds too – *wonderfully* wet sounds – as it worked up and down over Paul's erection.

Paul carried on moaning with Mistress Alicia's movements and ran his hands over her thighs and her breasts as she rose and fell on him. She shuddered hard and cried out loudly, pushing her pussy against his groin as her orgasm rolled through her in mighty waves. Feeling and hearing Alicia come made Paul want to come too, urgently. He started to thrust his hips upwards fast, plunging into the wetness of her pussy until the sensation was heavy, intense, unrestrained. He climaxed then convulsively, filling her sex with hot spurts of cum.

Mistress Alicia and Paul pulled apart then and lay on the bed together panting for a long while. Finally Alicia lent on one elbow, looked down at Paul and spoke: 'You know that you are not really my captive,' she said, the expression on her lovely face as unreadable to him then as it had ever been. 'You can leave any time you like.'

'But I don't like, Mistress,' Paul replied, his stomach turning in alarm. 'I don't like at all.'

'You say that now.' Alicia said. 'But it won't always be so. One day you'll grow tired of your dungeon existence here, tired of being my slave, tired of me.'

Paul shook his head vehemently. 'That isn't ever going to happen, Mistress. That day won't ever come. All I want is to be a good slave to you. If I left you my life would be completely empty. Nothing would be any good without you as my Mistress. You might tire of me one day, God forbid. I dread it. But I could never tire of you. You are everything to me now and always will be.'

And it was all true, every single word of it. Paul was well aware that his dungeon home with Mistress Alicia was not exactly a high security prison, that in real terms his imprisonment was entirely voluntary. But he also knew that if he were to try to walk away from Alicia at any time – today, tomorrow, next month, next year, next decade – it wouldn't work. He was irrevocably changed now, his past nothing but a blank surface. He had already forgotten the man he'd once been; had forgotten what he'd thought about before his thoughts had become utterly absorbed by Mistress Alicia.

'You really mean what you say, don't you,' Alicia said, a tone of genuine wonder colouring her voice. 'You really mean it.'

'Absolutely, Mistress.'

'Would you like to go all the way then?' she asked.

'Mistress?' Paul looked back at her in confusion.

'Would you like to be my slave for life?' she clarified, fixing her piercing blue eyes on his. 'You know – till death do us part.'

Paul felt something like a tsunami haul through him. 'Yes, Mistress,' he replied in exaltation. 'I'd like that more than anything else in the world.'

'Then it shall be so,' the dominatrix pronounced, 'as of this very moment.'

Paul thought his heart was going to burst with happiness when he heard her speak those words. His sense of elation knew no bounds. He was now the slave *for life* of the only woman in the world for him: Alicia, his Mistress of Torment. What a wonderful outcome … And what a truly amazing story his had been.

He didn't know the whole of that story himself, of course, didn't even know how it had all begun. But that didn't matter to Paul because he knew the most important thing for him. He knew that he had been the prey in all of this, the kill … and that were he to have his time all over again, he wouldn't hesitate for a moment before offering his throat.

About the Author

Alex Jordaine is the author of various works of Femdom erotica, both novels and short story collections, and is regarded as one of the foremost writers of the genre. Alex is a regular contributor to Europe's leading fetish magazine, *Secret*, and his work has also been anthologised in several collections of BDSM, gay, lesbian, and general themed erotica. He and his long-term partner, Mistress G, have been involved in the UK fetish scene for a number of years and are also nudists.

More great books from $\boxed{\text{X}}$cite...

Slave to The Machine
A fantasy for grown-ups who still like to play, by
Aishling Morgan
9781906373689 £7.99

The True Confessions of a London Spank Daddy
Memoir by Peter Jones
9781906373320 £7.99

Girl Fun One
Lesbian anthology edited by Miranda Forbes
9781906373672 £7.99

Sex and Satisfaction Two
Erotic stories edited by Miranda Forbes
9781906373726 £7.99

Ultimate Curves
Erotic short stories edited by Miranda Forbes
9781906373788 £7.99

Naughty! The Xcite Guide to Sexy Fun
How To book exploring edgy, kinky sex
9781906373863 £9.99

For more information and great offers
please visit
www.xcitebooks.com